MARK ANDERSEN

MERLIN'S KNOT

BOOK 1 OF MERLIN'S THREAD

PENGER
PRESS

Houston, Texas

Cover design, interior book design, and eBook design
by Blue Harvest Creative
www.blueharvestcreative.com

Merlin cover model: Marion Z. Skydancer
Courtesy of Dragon's Chyld Studio

MERLIN'S KNOT

Published by
Penger Press

Library of Congress Control Number:
2016935022

ISBN-13: 978-0692657621
ISBN-10: 0692657622

Visit the author at:
www.markandersentales.com

 Visit the author's website by scanning the QR code.

MERLIN'S
KNOT

CHAPTER 1

"I AM MERLIN. You must help me."

The filthy old man blocked my way to the parking lot.

Oh, great. A wino looking for applejack. Like I needed a hassle. No way. Not after spending another luckless day looking for a job. At least I hadn't sunk that low. I wasn't begging for booze. Not yet.

I ducked my head and shifted to go around him—dismiss him—just wanting to get home. But when I raised my eyes to scan the lot for my car, somehow he blocked my way again. I pulled up short, sucking in a stale and musty aroma. Fishy smelling, not booze. *He needs money to get booze.*

I didn't want any part of him. His scraggly, white beard snarled around clumps of dirt and filth. And those eyebrows! Thick and long in a dusty mix of white and gray. *How ancient could this guy be?* At a wrinkle a year, a hundred at least. I lifted my briefcase, putting it between us, following an ancient instinct for a defensive shield.

"Did you not hear?" he said. "I have need of your help."

I glanced back toward the revolving door into the west Houston career center. A sporadic flow of people exited the building before it closed for the night. But of course, all of them looked another way, any other way. *Why can't this dirty old bum pick someone else?*

The rotating door slid to a stop, flashing our image. Odd. The reflection showed us almost the same height, but when I turned back, his head was tilted up at me. *Must be the angle.*

If I tried to slip around him again, I knew I'd look foolish. I had to engage with him, tell him to go away. I couldn't give him money. I didn't have any to spare. That would be enough, surely. And since it was true, I could be sincere. Truly sorry, don't you know?

I looked into the old man's face. My words froze in the steady gaze of the most arresting eyes I'd ever encountered. His protruding eyebrows framed gray irises, keeping me focused on his right pupil. That black spot expanded, drew me inward, became the only thing in my world. Bright flashes streaked by me, like being in the sky with a meteor shower. Then a few of them resolved into thick bands. They had substance—different colors of yarn flowing past me from every direction. As I watched, they multiplied again and again until they surrounded me, entangled me, lost me in complex interweaving strings of color.

"Humph. To this was I led."

His words broke the spell. The world reappeared.

I caught my breath. "Sorry, old man. I don't have any cash on me, really." It sounded whiny and not at all the forceful dismissal I'd intended.

"Cax?" He spoke with a lilting, foreign quality I couldn't place.

"No money. Laid off, you see."

He stared at me like I spoke another language.

I shook my head and enunciated, "I'm out of work."

"Ah, good," he said. "I have a work for you."

I almost laughed. A crazy old man in a filthy choir robe had just offered me work. Twelve years in Houston, and the first time I met a bum not panhandling on a street corner, he offered me a job. A religious nut? That would explain the long robe. He probably found it in some church trash bin, and now he'd taken up the calling.

I looked closer—maybe at one time it'd had a fur trim. Some society matron's donation to a shelter? If so, years without care had turned it filthy and ragged. Dull ribbons held the arms and sleeves together. The way it hung on him, I couldn't imagine any meat on his bones. I wondered how many months—years—he'd gone without a decent meal. His stringy, white hair hung past his collar, and that long beard looked like a pair of angry mice had fought over filthy scraps in it. If I'd had any gumption, I would've turned and walked away. Maybe if he'd smelled of booze I would have.

The old man watched me while I examined his clothing. Just when the time came to tell him to go away, my gaze returned to his arresting eyes.

"Appearance is illusion," he said.

For a moment— just a moment—I saw a tall, powerful man attired in a white robe lined with ermine. Then the frail old man drooped and reached for me.

I winced. I tried to avoid touching him, but he gripped my arm and leaned onto me. I couldn't just let him fall. I guided him to a concrete bench and eased him down. He didn't answer when I spoke—so far as I could tell, he'd checked out of the world.

I should've left him. He was no worse off than when he first confronted me. At least I'd gotten him to a seat. But I didn't leave him. Maybe I recognized how little distance separated his state from mine. Or maybe I just didn't have anything better to do.

I sat at the other end of the bench and stared at the building. I'd spent hours in there these past months. Career center, right. A place to stick the castoffs after the merger. Keep them busy so they won't come back with an axe or a machete and start hacking at the new bosses. Look for a job, where? With the whole petroleum industry in another down cycle, everyone buried their heads in spreadsheets—hoping, praying for high prices again.

The old man squeezed my arm. "I thank you. It may be that you are indeed the one."

"What one? What are you talking about?" Despite my revulsion, for some reason I couldn't shake him.

"You must help me. I know not the ways."

"Alzheimer's? I can't help you with that. There's places you can go, I'm sure." Actually, I wasn't sure. Hadn't they turned the homeless crazies out onto the streets? Was he one of them?

"What words you speak! Such is the burden I bear, this heathen language."

"Ah, you must be French. But you don't sound French. Melvyn, are you French?"

The old man watched me. He was waiting for something, but I couldn't tell what.

"Frenchie? Parlay vu's Frenchie?"

No reaction.

This got me nowhere. I had to try another tack. "Look, old man. Just tell me what you want. Then I'll tell you that I can't help, and we can both go about our ways." I smiled and nodded, hoping he would do the same and I could leave feeling OK about myself.

"I seek for Arthur."

"You're looking for a friend. Well, I'm afraid I don't know anyone named Arthur. Certainly not one of your…um…social group. Sorry."

I smiled.

I nodded.

I lifted my briefcase and stood to leave.

Before I could take a step toward my car, the wizened old man appeared in my way again.

"No. You are the one. You must help."

I almost shouted. "I am the one *what*?" His persistence exasperated me. I calmed myself. "You're crazy, old man." I reached deep inside myself to sound firm. "Time for you to move out of my way. I don't want you to get hurt." Pushing him out of the way—even with my limp muscles—could break his frail bones.

He muttered something I couldn't understand and stared at his hands as he waved them in front of his chest. He filtered the air through his fingers, studying the space between them. I had a fleeting hope that he'd gotten lost in his battered and confused mind and I could just slip away.

His hands flew to mine, and his eyes captured my gaze before I could protest. His words drilled into me, almost commanding me. "You must attend me. His thread joins to yours. You are the one. You must lead me to Arthur."

I tried to pull away, but his hands held me, and his gray eyes held me tighter.

I sighed. "I told you—Mervin, isn't it? I don't know any Arthur."

His dirty eyebrows rose, and a darkness passed across his eyes—or maybe I just saw a reflection of clouds obscuring the sun. For an instant the hair on the back of my neck prickled.

I shook myself. What a ridiculous situation. I needed an easy way out of this. Maybe humoring him. "Is this Arthur around here?"

"Yes, I followed the thread. He is here." His voice sounded frail again, but he spoke with certainty.

I looked around. Not a one of my fellow career-hunters in sight. Even the reception desk sat empty, so the building must be locked. Everyone cleared out at five.

I shrugged. "I don't see him."

The old man spat on the ground beside me. "Addle-brained oaf. He resides in this town."

Addled? Me, addled? Now that's funny.

Humor him, I reminded myself. *And don't laugh, either.*

"You lost your friend somewhere in Houston? Where? Where did you last see him?"

"That matters not."

"Of course it matters," *you silly old fool.* "Where was he?"

"I last saw him in Britain."

"Pfthh. England?" I stifled a laugh, despite my resolve to humor him.

His eyebrows knotted as he spat out the word. "England. Yes, so you call it. But he is here, now."

"And you came here from England, looking for him?"

"Britain."

"OK. Great Britain. What do I care? Just who is this Arthur? Does he have a last name?"

"You would know him as Arthur Pendragon. He was High King of the Britons."

Now I knew he was nutso. I don't pay much attention to international news, and history was never my strong suit, but I knew that couldn't be right. Elizabeth had been queen, like, forever—and her husband? Not Arthur, for sure. Nor the king before—her father, I thought. I couldn't remember his name, but for sure—well, pretty sure—it wasn't Arthur.

"He is not couth to you? Ken you not Arthur, the High King?"

I didn't know whether to laugh or run. *Did this dirty old bum just call* me *uncouth?*

Wait, does he think I'm Ken? *That could explain a lot.*

"Look, my name is Alfred, not Ken. Go find him. Find Ken."

The old man shook his hands in front of his chest, like he was trying to fling something sticky off his fingers. Seemed as good a time as any to leave. I shrugged, but before I could turn around, one of the names he'd said bubbled to the top of my mind.

"Pendragon? I know that name."

Crap. I could kick myself for saying that out loud. I just wanted to get away.

The old man's gaze became intense, unavoidable.

Pendragon did mean something to me. Something to do with my computer. Or software. I felt my mind racing around, trying to find Pendragon filed away somewhere. Software. Yes, somehow that name had to do with software. But what? Games? I didn't have a game called Pendragon, and I wasn't into the swords and sorcery dragon stuff. But my mind kept returning to the games.

I liked simulation games, with little simulated people whose lives I could control. Set up their little town, watch it grow, then change the weather and fight to keep the town from dying. And of course, the conquer-the-world games. Start with a tribe, build a civilization from nothing. Then subjugate the neighbors.

Wait—Pendragon, of course! A company. They made the one about the Saxons invading England. Yes.

The old man collapsed into my arms.

"Hey. Are you OK?" I said. "Oh, shit. What's wrong with you?"

I looked around again—not a soul in sight. I couldn't just leave him. Where, then? An emergency room. That would do it. He needed an ER. Then I could slip away.

I put his arm over my shoulder to get him to my car. I thought I'd gotten used to his smell, but the stench of sweat and grime and—now that I leaned into him—the more than faint aroma of stale fish almost made me drop him. I must have looked ridiculous, with a tottering old man on one side and my briefcase careening on the other as we stumbled to my car.

Skin and bones. Couldn't weigh more than ninety pounds. I leaned him against the car while I unlocked it. I spread an old picnic blanket across the back seat to protect the upholstery. He roused a bit as I laid him in.

"*Slat an draoichta.*"

"What?"

His eyelids fluttered. "My staff. I need it. There."

Without opening his eyes again, he pointed toward a tall hedge by the entrance to the parking lot. I found a branch, my height, with a knobby knot at the top, propped against a bush. I gripped the smooth section. An image of gnarled hands swinging the staff in battle popped into my head as I returned to the car. The vision disappeared when I passed the stick to the old man. He hugged it hard to his chest. I had to force-tilt it onto the floorboard to close the back door.

As I pulled out of the parking lot, movement in the rearview mirror pulled my eyes to him again. He sat up and murmured to himself.

"Are you all right?" I asked.

He continued to mutter.

"You gave me a bit of a scare there."

He took a deep breath, then murmured a chant.

"I'm taking you to an emergency room. To have you looked at."

I pulled into the street. His chanting ceased. I glanced in the mirror again. He clutched the back of my seat, his head whipping from side to side—from the towering buildings on one side of the street to the middle school on the other.

"Such a wonder," he said. "Such a time is this."

"I'm sorry, what was that?"

His gaze hardened into steel again. "Do we go to these soft wares?"

"I'm taking you to a doctor."

He shook his head. "I do not need to bleed."

"What? Are you bleeding?" I turned to scan him for blood. "Did you hit your head?"

"No *docteurs*. I must find Arthur."

"You need a doctor."

"No."

I felt the certainty of his answer through my whole body. At the next intersection, my hands turned the wheel toward home.

CHAPTER
2

HOW DID I *get myself into this?*

I brought the old man—Melvin or whoever—into my apartment. He wanted to find out about the Pendragon company as soon as we arrived, but the trip up one flight of stairs exhausted him. He needed food, and, well, now he'd become a guest in my house. It surprised me to find that meant something to me.

My first visitor here. A homeless bum. What did that say about my life?

I still didn't know why I'd brought him home rather than leaving him at an ER. I knew that was the best thing for me, and probably the best for him, too. But every time I'd thought about turning toward the hospital, my hands kept the car pointed homeward.

Anyway, the filthy old guy couldn't sit on my rented furniture. I didn't want to have to pay for the stains when I turned it back in.

I found an old pair of sweats and an old pullover shirt and took him into the bathroom. The faucets fascinated him, and when he felt hot water coming out of the bathtub tap, he whooped. At first I feared he'd burned himself, but his every action asserted delight. He pushed me out. I tried to take his old rags, but he wouldn't give them up, even when I promised to wash them. He threatened me with that long stick of his.

I should've left it in the bushes.

I put two cups of soup into the microwave. While it heated, I wandered to the breakfast bar. As usual since my layoff, I sought advice from the picture of my wife. Sorry, ex-wife.

"How'd I let this old man wheedle his way into my apartment?" I stared at her photo.

A studio pose. The only image Janet left behind. A perfect pose, you know, as good as the images that come in the frames you buy at Target. I regretted that the pretty picture lacked her soul, her personality. I'd always thought she was girl-next-door cute; at least this photo captured that look. I'd been lucky to have her, being something of a nerd. No one described me as handsome or overly tall, at just under 5'11". People who worked on the same floor as me for years didn't know me when we were introduced. My eyes caught interest, at least from those few people who paid enough attention to me to notice them.

Janet had started calling my light-brown hair *mousy dishwater blond* just before the end. That should've been a warning. She swooped out of my life the same way she swooped in. Suddenly and unexpectedly. It was a good ride while it lasted. With her, I had fun. We had friends.

Janet took both in the divorce.

I needed her guidance, all the more since the layoff. But her photo never gave the advice that I used to hear so often. And tonight, as usual, the picture remained silent. No suggestions about my unwanted houseguest.

I heard a few minutes of sloshing from the bathroom, then water draining. A short time later, the transformation came out. His hair stuck to his head, but he'd untangled it, and it looked like he'd combed his long beard. I couldn't help noticing his cleaner, whiter eyebrows. The sweat suit hung on him several sizes too wide, but at least it made him look like he belonged in the twenty-first century. Except for the six-foot-long stick he carried everywhere.

He sniffed over the bowls and made a face. "What gruel is this?"

What a disagreeable old man. "Chicken and stars soup. It's all I had. Just sit down and eat."

"Humph."

He held the spoon overhanded and began shoveling the soup into his mouth. *Real kingly table manners*, I thought. *Were you the court jester?* I laughed to myself.

He paused after a few bites. "Let us talk of these soft wares."

I shook my head. "Eat."

"I eat. Have you no herbs? This gruel is but salted water."

Aargh. "What do you want from me? Do you just need someone to bitch at? Is that why you picked me?"

He slurped another spoonful into his mouth.

"I chose you not. I followed Arthur's thread—here it forms a node with yours. Your threads plait together. I cannot sort yours from his and others that lead onward. I would choose another, could I."

"I wish you would."

He spooned more stars past his beard and mustache and didn't respond to me.

"What's with these threads? Do you see them on me?" I brushed at my shirt, looking for loose threads to clear off. He probably did see things on me. He seemed to be from a different world than the one I knew.

"Truly, you are a fool, boy."

Boy? I'm not easy to anger, but this mean old man seemed determined to push me. Before I could collect my thoughts to tell him off, he spoke again.

"You know of the Fates, yes? That is in your sagas, your mythologia?"

What a roller coaster ride I took talking with him.

"Of course." I shook my head in bewilderment.

"Clotho, Lachesis and Atropos. Spinners of the fabric of life."

He might as well have named Dopey, Doc and Rumpelstiltskin. *Did I know any psychiatrists?* The career center would have some names.

I humored him. "Can you see them spin? Is it their threads that you see? Or do you talk to them?"

He sighed. "No, I do not see these sisters of Fate. Should I see them, I would call them by older names, much older names that you could not comprehend."

I can't comprehend anything you say.

"The threads," he said. "That is another matter. My life and Arthur's interwove in a complex pattern. The first thread formed before me. His father and mother joined others to me. More developed over his life. Our lives became entwined.

"They all severed. All save one final thread. I follow that thread now, but neither Arthur created it nor did I. Indeed, three sisters made it, but they were not the Fates. Forsooth, they set my fate, and Arthur's, when they cast that thread into the Aether. And that thread led to you."

"Oh. Now everything is crystal clear."

He dismissed me with a flick of one eyebrow. "If you will not understand, ask not." He slurped the last of his soup.

"Sure. Threads. Tying you to your buddy, Arthur the king. Got it."

He began to mutter again, but I couldn't understand a word. I dropped the empty bowls in the sink. I hoped he'd move on pretty soon. I didn't have much food in the apartment and had no money in the bank.

His mutterings ended with a loud sigh. He focused on me again. "Pendragon. We must find this company of Pendragon."

In for a penny, in for a pound, I guess. I led him to the second bedroom, the one I'd set up as an office. Janet left me the computer. She got a new one when she got a new life.

While the computer booted up, I dug through boxes in the closet. It didn't take long to find *Invasion: Britannia vs Angleterre*. When I first got the game, I didn't understand that the British and English started out as two different peoples. We'd call the English Saxons. The British, well, they were ones who lived there before. I didn't care about the details. The two peoples warred, and that made it a game.

The package sported a Pendragon Games label.

The old man tapped the box. "This is of Arthur. I know this."

"The game?"

"No. This is his sigil." He touched the package again, pointing to the company logo. A white dragon on a golden shield.

"His coat of arms?"

"That is a Frankish name for it." He rubbed the container. "This is of Arthur."

The desktop appeared, and I clicked the game icon. The opening graphics rock—a realistic rendering of swordsmen battling on a greensward. If you let it go long enough, one of them stabs the other, then turns to fight another warrior, and the sequence repeats.

The graphics bored him. "How does this find Arthur?"

"Huh?" I'd started a game by setting out the first sortie—playing the Saxons, as usual. I couldn't win as the Britons.

"Where is Arthur? I see no thread to him here."

"No, this is a game. See, I'm controlling these Saxon warriors here. We landed in an unoccupied area. But pretty soon, some of the Brits will wander in, or I'll go find them. Then we start fighting."

"You should not wish to fight. It is dirty and dangerous. Even for the victors."

"Not on the computer. It's clean. And if you start losing, one click and the game restarts."

"You are truly a fool to play at war."

"Yeah, right. As if you know."

The old man glared at me for a long time, his pupils the size of pinheads, eyebrows forming a flattened V. I looked back to the computer screen. I don't need an old bum's approval.

He put his hand on my shoulder. "No. You are right. This is your time. It is not for me to judge your pleasures."

"Judge away. See if I care."

"By your leave, I have interest in Arthur. How does this help me to find him?"

Yes, please leave. I didn't say it, though.

I shrugged. I'd never thought about the people who make the games. Probably someone liked the era of the Saxon invasions into England, and in their research found the Pendragon coat of arms. Voila! A name and a symbol. Morton didn't believe that explanation.

"No, this is where the threads must lead. To you, thence to Arthur, through this soft ware. Where do you get these soft wares?"

"Software. One word. When I bought this, I ordered it online. They mailed me a CD. Nowadays, it's just a download."

"I do not understand these words."

"I didn't buy it from Arthur. Look. The company, Pendragon, sells it to others. They sold it to me. See?"

"You bought from a traveling peddler?"

I shook my head. "You don't buy things from the people who make them. Even the people I bought this from wouldn't know the people who made it."

"So this software helps not." Frowning, he rotated his staff, the knot at its top forming a small circle in the air between us.

"Here, let's look at the About screen. Sometimes the developers put their names there."

The opening screen linked to the About information. Sure enough, it had a rolling marquee of names.

"There, watch for Arthur's name," I said.

"I cannot."

"What?"

"The letters are too small, and they form strange shapes."

"You need glasses?"

"I am not thirsty."

"No," I laughed, despite myself. "Eyeglasses. Do you need eyeglasses?"

"I have heard this term. What does it mean?"

"You don't know what eyeglasses are? They help you see."

"I see well."

"You can't read."

"I can read. I cannot read strange, small letters."

Illiterate, but unwilling to admit it.

I restarted the About screen, examining the scrolling text. No Arthur, and Pendragon appeared only as the company name. Morton made me watch again, and yet again. When I mentioned the help screens—oh, what a fool me—he coerced me to read them. Aloud. He didn't understand most of what I read him, so it took hours to explain. Yet, I sat there and did it. Either I was a spineless fool, fated to jump through every hoop the old bum put in front of me, or I helped him because he brought a sense of purpose to my evening.

Only after I made up the sofa for him and went to bed did it occur to me that I hadn't said anything about software before he first asked about it.

CHAPTER

3

IN THE MORNING, I woke determined to make him leave. I felt almost giddy when I found the couch undisturbed, the living room empty and, after a quick look around, reassurance that he'd stolen nothing. I started whistling some stupid ditty from a commercial.

I still had cereal and milk. Not much else to eat, but I'd have to get by until the next unemployment check. The deposit always went in Friday at midnight. I'd have money tomorrow.

I flipped the TV on to the local news station. The apartment came with basic cable, so I had that luxury.

The patio door slid open.

The old man came in.

"I am rested," he said.

Aw, crap! What's he doing on the balcony?

"I thought you'd left."

Either he didn't recognize the disappointment in my voice, or he chose to ignore it.

"I beheld the morning awakening from your parapet. A mist lay about all the night, but it lifted. What do you eat?"

"Look, old man. I've done more for you than I should. You've got to go. Have some cereal and scram." I'd skip breakfast tomorrow, if it would get this bum out of my hair.

"You have another computer in this room?" he said as I poured the cereal.

"No, that's a TV."

His eyebrows raised in an unspoken query.

"Surely you know what a TV is? No? Television."

"Ah, this is the apparatus known as a telly?" He touched the screen and its black housing.

"Yeah, in England I think they call it that."

"What does it?"

"It receives pictures. Programs."

He didn't seem to follow.

"It's for entertainment. Or news. Right now, it's news." I put two bowls on the table.

"This is something new? Britain has had telly for some years."

"No, *news*." I shook my head in awe at his stupidity. "They tell us what happened today. Listen."

The local anchor reported a brutal murder outside Brenham. The station didn't go into specifics, but it must have been pretty bad for a murder seventy miles away to make the Houston news. A new bill in Austin to join the Atlantic Alliance had been voted out of committee. The pretty woman reading the story paused half a second, then smiled and bounced to a reporter at an elementary school.

I had to explain why the children wore witch and ghost costumes, and why a young girl would wear colored hair and a leather dress while singing into the camera. He questioned me at great length about Halloween. He seemed pleased that it occurred tomorrow.

I turned the TV off and screwed up my resolve. "Look, old man. Now you've got to go. Find your friend Arthur Pendragon. I can't help you any more. I've got to go find a job."

"I gave you a work. You must help me."

I laughed. It felt good. "You gave me a work. Great. How much does it pay? Do you see that empty bowl in front of you? That was the last food I had, except a couple cans of beans. Go away old man."

"It is your fate to help me."

"Your threads again, eh?" I smiled my best condescension at him. "Sorry, old man. I don't believe in fate. Have you heard of free will?"

He shrugged. "The argument is old. Fate or free will. It appears a dichotomy, but it need not be. Let us say that you are fated to choose to help me."

"I choose not to help. Find another patsy, old man."

He moved his hands again, like sign language for the deaf, but it didn't seem to satisfy him this time. He stared at me, eyebrows shadowing his eyes.

"Go away."

He sighed. "May I keep these clothing?"

"Knock yourself out." He frowned and tilted his head. I said, "Yeah, keep 'em."

OK. If it only cost me some sweats and the last of my food to get him out of my place, I'd be in good shape.

"I thank you for your kindness." He retrieved his robe and staff from the patio and walked to the door. "I will see you again."

THE PREVIOUS UNEMPLOYMENT check had gone to cover the rent, so I was short. Another day, another check, and I could fill my belly. But the end of my allotted time on the dole loomed imminent. The President in Austin had clamped down with another austerity budget, and the national legislature followed his lead and cut benefits again. Didn't they realize people like me needed help in the down cycle of the oil industry? They sure took from me during the up cycle.

I needed to redouble my job-hunting efforts. I decided to bounce some ideas off my counselor. I hadn't seen him in a while, so I stopped by the front desk at the career center to get his office location du jour.

The young lady at the reception desk acted oh-so-interested in helping me, just like all the other center staffers. A problem arose: she didn't know me from Adam.

"You said your counselor was Tom who?"

"Tom. I don't know his last name. Bald guy. Oh, he's from San Antonio."

"And when did you last see him?"

"I don't know. A couple of weeks."

"Sir," she said, "I've been here for almost a month, and I don't know any counselors named Tom."

"Well, maybe it's been more than a couple of weeks."

"That's OK, sir. The Center Manager will give you a new counselor. What's your name?"

"Alfred Marlborough." I handed her my name tag.

How absurd. My counselor had moved on and no one told me. He probably got a better job. Lord knows, he hadn't helped me when we last met. Could that have happened more than a month ago?

The new counselor they assigned me wasn't any better. She couldn't even find my file. She gave me the standard pep talk I'd heard a dozen times here at the castoff-center. You know the drill: look at this disaster as an opportunity to start a new life.

I paid attention to what's-her-name's pep talk because that's what they expected me to do. I nodded in all the right places and got the regular pablum answers to my questions. Then, I retreated to an empty cubicle. What a waste. No wonder I hadn't been to my counselor in weeks.

The telephone was supposed to be my friend. The link to my network. Right. What network? I didn't have a job, my wife had divorced me, and I was running out of unemployment insurance. Well, Janet left me before the company did. So it goes.

I studied the list of companies to make a run at. I stared at the phone. But to pick it up, I had to be ready to sell myself. I was an engineer, not a salesman. I could run a reservoir simulation and I could even explain the results to management. They sold the ideas.

Not that any of them could find oil in a crankcase.

I scanned the list of names to call. I picked up the phone and started dialing. Halfway through, I realized I didn't know what to say. I put down the phone and stared at it some more.

The desk held my notebook and the phone and lots of empty space. It didn't get any worse than this. Except when I actually talked with someone who informed me in oh-so-polite terms that they had no openings. We're in a down part of the cycle, don't you know?

Hire, wash, rinse, spin, fire. That cycle.

I stared at a blank piece of paper for several minutes. I hashed out a script. I lifted the phone. It connected, and after three rings, the phone mail system picked up.

I hung up the phone and looked down the list.

I didn't belong here. This wasn't supposed to be my life. I knew that. But I couldn't see a way forward. All I saw were blank pages.

Almost lunch time. Well, almost eleven. Close enough. I'd have to go home and open one of the cans of beans. Maybe I had a hot dog left in the freezer. I didn't think the dollar ten in my pocket would buy much of a lunch.

AS MY APARTMENT door closed behind me, I sensed something amiss. The curtains to the patio door billowed, and I smelled smoke. Some of the kitchen cabinet doors stood open.

"Who's there? I'm calling the police on my cell. You better hop that railing and run before they get here." I didn't want to move too far away from the front door, so I didn't go to the phone in the kitchen. I hoped the burglar wouldn't look in and discover I couldn't afford a cell phone.

I heard a quiet *ting* on the patio.

"Hello, police? Someone broke into my apartment, and I think they're still here."

The patio curtain flew back, and Marvin stuck his head into the room. "Humph. Why do you speak to an empty room?"

I felt relief. Then anger.

I said, "What are you doing here? I told you to go away!"

"You said you had no more food. I brought food." He beckoned me onto the patio.

"What?" His non sequitur confounded my anger. How did he do that, over and over again?

"I obtained food. It shall be ready anon."

I looked over his shoulder and saw smoke rising from my barbecue grill. It was filled with glowing embers—he'd made a wood fire in it.

"What are you doing? That's for briquettes."

The old man stared at me for a moment, then turned back to his cooking. He unrolled a pack that turned out to be his tattered robe, and reached into a pocket in the inside lining. He removed a small pouch, opened it, and sniffed. I saw something that looked like dried herbs. He pinched a bit off and dropped it into the pot.

"What's in there?" It smelled pretty good. Like a hearty stew.

"I found things to eat. Greens. Meat. More filling than your gruel."

I watched as he stirred the pot, and I began to wonder how he could buy food.

"Where did you get this?"

"I walked by the stream."

"Buffalo Bayou? What food did you find at the bayou?"

"Snake. The rodent I heard someone call squirrel: a creature pleasing in its girth. Greens I knew to be good to eat. There are many plants here I ken not."

"Plants you can not?" He was trying to confuse me, again. I shook my head. "I'm not eating snake. Or squirrel, for that matter."

"Free will you have. Bring two bowls. It is ready to eat."

It did smell pretty good. Could it be worse than canned beans? Maybe I'd watch him eat first.

He waved his hand over the pot, and as he pulled the aroma to his nose his bushy eyebrows rose and fell twice. While he ladled stew into the bowls, I filled two glasses with water and set out spoons.

As I thought about it, I realized this was some kind of hobo stew. Part of a great tradition of found food among the rural homeless. Maybe that's where Martin came from.

He slurped a spoonful of broth and sighed. "Indeed. Better than your gruel. Did you find work this day?"

"No."

"I have work for you. I can pay you for it."

"Oh?" I sipped the stew. It had a wildness to it that tasted good.

He reached into his pocket and took out a green wad. He stretched out his hand and dropped the paper into mine.

"This is your money, yes? This compensates your time?"

I unwadded a filthy twenty. "What's this white stuff all over it?"

"Likely it is birdshit."

I dropped the bill on the table.

"I found it in the nest of a large black bird. A crow, I believe you call it. They pick things up."

"You found a twenty dollar bill in a bird's nest? Just sitting there?"

"Yes."

"Were you climbing a tree? Aren't you a little old for that?"

"Older than you know." He smiled.

Wow. The first time I'd seen the old man smile. It made me feel almost charitable toward him. "OK, I'll bite. How'd you know you'd find money up the tree?" Maybe not so charitable after all. "Did a little bird tell you?"

"Of course not. A crow is large. I did not know people still spoke with birds."

I dropped the spoon, unsure I wanted to finish the stew. "You're crazy, old man."

"Ah, so that was sarcasm. I remember sarcasm. Mordred became adept at it. In fact, I first learnt the Greekish word from him. It makes an appropriate sound when spoken. *Sarcasm.* It starts with a rolling pleasantness in the mouth, and then its harsh ending unveils its nastiness."

I shook my head at his continued craziness.

He frowned. "Finish your food, It shall cause you no harm."

We ate the stew in silence. Afterward, I picked up the bill using a paper towel. The birdshit washed off, so I laid the twenty on another towel to dry. The old man watched me at the sink.

"You have no wife," he said.

I shrugged. "I had one."

"Ah, she died."

"No, divorced."

"Most curious. You have no close friends."

It wasn't a question. "How's that any of your business?"

"My business is finding Arthur. His thread comes to you. But your threads, they confound me."

"You make no sense, old man."

"Few strong threads bind to you. You have no close friends and no family. Some threads about you seem twinned."

"Twined?" I didn't know whether his accent or his words confused me more.

"Indeed, they also are twined, wrapped about one another in a curious way. But I said that the threads are twinned, doubled."

Before I could respond, the old man gripped his staff and hobbled into the living room. He stopped in the middle, tilting his face to the ceiling and then back down. He gestured for me to sit on the couch in front of him.

"I have given you payment. You will help me now."

I looked up into his intense staring eyes. "Twenty dollars wouldn't have bought an hour of my attention a few months ago. But now, I guess you've bought some of my time. I'll give you the afternoon."

"And the evening?"

The absurdity struck me. I had a new boss, at least for a day. I laughed. "Sure, why not?"

"Good. Now, you shall see something of importance in the life of Arthur. Sit and learn."

I stretched my arms on the back of the sofa. I hoped he could tell a good story; he did have an arresting way about him. The old man closed his eyes again and turned his face back to the ceiling. He raised his staff.

CHAPTER
4

A woman on a wooden parapet about fifty feet away gazes into the distance. I must be on its twin, because I'm level with her. She's gorgeous, looks to be in her late teens. Her hair cascades down her back in layers; it's a deep honey color. Her smooth skin glows tan from the sun, but today there is no sun. The clouds form a low roiling mass frozen in the sky.

The woman stares. I wonder what she's intent upon, but I cannot turn my head. I see her face in profile. She has a strong nose, not sharp or oversized, but it could never be described as pert. I look closer and see a hint of freckles beneath her tan. I'm surprised at how sharp they appear at this distance.

Her gown is simple, a dun color. She's dressed to work. Colored ribbons…no…thick colored strands of yarn lace through the cuffs, pulling the material tight around her forearm. The material looks moderately heavy, in deference to the slight chill in the air and the lack of sun. An occasional draft of cool air ruffles her lovely hair and sings in my ears.

About ten feet below us, a low stone wall connects her tower to mine and continues on the other side of her parapet. I see a lightly fortified gate in the wall. It guards a path cut up the hillside. A man posted above the closed gate stares in the same direction as the young woman.

She runs a hand through her hair—it looks like a gesture of concern for someone or something. She turns to me, and I look into her light green eyes. I think she will acknowledge me, perhaps wave. But her expression doesn't change at all as her eyes fix on me for only a moment, then move back to her vigil of the distance.

The lush grassland behind her rises in rolling hills covered with several stands of trees. Thoughts of small game come to me. Rabbits and squirrels. I think the fields and woods must teem with animals. The broken stalks in the fields tell me farmers just completed the harvest. I taste the pollens of autumn and a deeper, tangier flavor I can't place.

The woman looks my way again. This time her eyes focus on me for more than just a moment. She thinks, wonders about something. Something that relates to me. I see her sigh, then turn back to the distance.

I turn in the direction she has been looking. A cloud of dust hangs on the other side of the first hill, some distance away.

I glance back at the woman. She's staring at me with intent and purpose now. I think she's trying to send me a message, but I cannot think what it could be.

Without warning, I fall from the tower, hurtling toward the stone wall below. I shriek, knowing my body will be dashed and broken when I hit the rocks. Instead, the wall recedes. I glide along halfway down to it. My shriek becomes a cry, a call. I slide over the closed gate. I feel a rhythmic pulling on my back, on my shoulders.

Wings! Omigod, I'm a bird!

I beat my wings, rising toward the woman on the tower. She watches my approach. I see no surprise in her eyes, only expectation. I veer just before reaching her tower. My chest contracts and I hear another shriek.

I fly in the direction she had been looking. The ground falls away beneath me. I soar upward with the rhythm of my wings and sense my body undulating up and down with each beat. The wind thrills through my feathers. My muscles sing with the pleasure of flying. I glide again, and my fingers feather to tend left or right. I want to shout with joy, but I have no control over my body. I seem to be along for the ride.

What a ride it is. My body cuts through the air with little resistance, yet that air has enough substance to hold me aloft. Below, I see the drying stalks of the wheat harvest rustling in the breeze and realize I can also smell grasses drying. Despite the great distance to the ground, I perceive the movement of individual leaves.

I approach the trees on the first hill and beat my wings again to rise over them. I hear flapping and see a rapid movement below. A small bird dives from an upper branch deep into the trees. I watch it disappear with some regret but continue on my way.

I wonder if the young woman is making me do her bidding somehow. She is lovely, and had she asked, I would have done most anything for her. I don't know what she wanted when she looked at me with such intensity, yet I feel I'm doing something for her anyway.

The first hill disappears behind me, and another hill rises between me and whatever is raising the dust. I see a few men below me. Some run toward the next hillock; many of them carry spears. A man stands alone, leaning on a heavy sword with tip planted in the ground. His broad chest expands and contracts. Cocking my head, I hear air huffing out with each of his exhalations. I'm amazed at the clarity of my senses. I must be some kind of hunting bird.

Other men stand or sit, all gasping after heavy exertion. Still others lie prone; a few women gather around one figure on the ground. I see blood and taste it in the air—the tang that I sensed earlier.

I recognize rather than see one man's eyes on me. He's hidden in the deep shadow of a copse of trees at the top of the next hill. Even with the bird's clear sight, I cannot make him out. But I know him for my master. My path does not go near the trees he stands within.

Master? I realize that some of my sensations come from the bird, because I don't feel this man is my master.

I fly high enough to see over the hillock; the dust rising from the other side comes from a fight spread across a harvested field. Many men lie on the ground, and I taste death here. Four men reach the crest of the hill just as I pass above, moving toward the battle as I do. They raise a shout and run downhill. One man, bigger and taller than the others, leads the way. His leather armor does not slow him. The others, also strong men and not so well-armed, struggle to stay with him. Near the bottom of the hill, they split up, rushing each to a cluster of men fighting.

Beating my wings, I rise higher and circle the field. I estimate about forty people in combat.

The big man wears a leather helm, his dark brown hair stringing down his back. Sweat has braided and clumped it together. He runs with grace, the heavy sword carried in his right hand balancing in his gait. His head stays up, scanning ahead, but he's surefooted on the broken field.

Ahead of him, three men—one wielding a long knife and two others swinging short clubs—harass one man with his back to a tree. He wastes no moves, parrying each man in turn with efficient strokes. They thrust and swing as they can, wild and untutored. He must defend against assault from three directions. Offense is not an option. Although he holds them off with his sword and a small shield, they attack without respite. Sooner or later, one of them will get in a quick or lucky strike.

The three attackers do not see the big man coming down the slope. At the last instant he shouts, creating confusion as he barrels into them. He slices the club arm of one man while slamming his elbow into the face of the second. The knife-man swings at him, but it is an unschooled swing, and the man at the tree strikes with his sword, making a gash in the man's gut. The other two men scramble up and run away, leaving their clubs and the fallen one behind.

The newcomer and the man at the tree hug, then speak together for a moment, clutching one another's forearms in a four-handed grasp. The big man appraises the battleground and turns back to his friend, nodding his head and laughing with his full belly. The arrival of the four warriors turned a near-even fight into a rout. The other side runs away. Some few are pursued, but most are allowed to flee.

The taste of blood in the air overwhelms me. I fly away from the battle to find an undisturbed field. I swoop low, following movement. It's only a field mouse, but I have it in my talons, squeezing against its strug-

gles. I bend down and rip into its neck, and it goes limp in my grasp. My brain floods with a satisfying smell of fresh blood; I fly toward a lone tree to enjoy my meal.

CHAPTER

5

MY WINGS WOULDN'T beat. I opened my eyes, expecting the ground to rush at me. Instead, I saw the ceiling of my apartment. I lay on the floor, legs tangled around the coffee table. The old man stood beside me, leaning on his staff.

"What the hell?"

I was confused by whatever had just happened. What I'd seen, where I'd been.

It left a tingle of excitement. Flying. Flying just above the ground, with nothing holding me up but my own power. My own wings. I had never experienced such a thrill.

I didn't know what he'd done, but he'd done it without telling me what would happen. He'd screwed with my mind without giving me a choice. He had played with my senses, and had left the taste of blood in my mouth.

I didn't know whether to be pissed or thank him. Pissed won out.

"Who do you think you are? You hijacked my mind."

He ignored my anger. Now, he acted like the frail old man I'd carried to my car. But I could tell by his grip on the staff that he still had strength.

"Oh, no you don't. I'm not falling for that weak old man line again. I think you should leave." I pointed to the door, but in my awkward position with feet still caught among the coffee table legs, I rolled onto my face. The pratfall didn't help my mood.

"I am sorry, boy," he panted. "I do not…understand…I…could not stop…the memory."

He even sounded sorry. Not for hijacking my mind; he was sorry he didn't stop when he'd planned to.

I rolled to my feet. "I don't care. Just go." Now I could point at the door.

The old man slumped onto the couch, pulling the staff into his lap. He looked up at me, bushy white brows drooping over deep wrinkles around his eyes. "I had to. Show you." His words came out in quiet bursts between quivering breaths. "Guinevere. She became. A lovely queen."

The girl. She did seem a queen. I remembered. She could command me in anything.

But not him. "Now. Go. I mean it. Get out of my apartment."

"You must…understand," he said. "What I ask of you…is not…a normal task."

Then it hit me. *The stew. He put something in the stew.*

Both my body and mind spun in circles. From the door to the old man to the patio door. Images of stew, crazy herbs, psychedelic flashes of insanity.

"Mushrooms," I said. "Am I going to have flashbacks? It was mushrooms, wasn't it?"

I rushed outside to smell the remaining pot of stew, fearing what was in it. I stood in the patio door.

His head tilted to one side. "No mushrooms."

"Oh, man. Drug tests." I paced from the patio to the sofa and back. "Some wacky herb is gonna show up in a drug test. Probably hallucinogenic. Nobody hires without a drug test. I'll never get a job now. Crap. Crap. Crap."

He leaned on the staff again, ignoring my outburst. "I know not of this drug test. Herbs flavor the stew."

"Yeah, I bet you don't know about drug tests. Rummy wino. Listen to me. They can test for traces of drugs days and weeks after you take them. I'm screwed." I paced again, despair outpacing anger. "Yep. Screwed."

"It is unimportant. This test of drug."

"I'm totally screwed." I saw myself losing job after job because of a drug test.

"Boy!" He thumped his staff. "It is unimportant."

I dropped onto the couch. What did it matter? I'd had no luck finding a job anyway. I'd have to take a couple of weeks off the job search, and then hit it again after my body had time to clean up. Maybe find something part-time in between to earn a few bucks.

I looked up at the old man, resigned to my new fate. But not to him. "Quit calling me *boy*. I'm almost forty-five."

"Tell me the last you saw."

I bet that taste of blood came from biting my tongue. During the hallucination that he caused.

"I'm not a kid. Don't treat me like one."

"Look at me. What did you see?"

I sighed. I needed his twenty bucks even more now.

"In the vision? The queen. Beautiful girl. Then a battle, two men hugging. Then I flew away." *And ate a mouse.* But he didn't need to know about the blood that I could still almost taste. Or the exhilaration it had stirred in me.

"You saw the battle end, and the vision stopped?" His eyes opened wide, pulling me into him.

I must have nodded, because he did also—a slow, deliberate nod

"I tried to stop," he said, "before you flew over the hill to the battle. I could not. Fighting is a nasty, bloody thing. It was not my intent that you should experience it. My apologies. I have never before lost control of a vision."

I shook my head and waved as though it were nothing. But it was something. It was exciting. Better than playing on the computer, because those men fought while I watched from above. And the mouse tasted like victory.

"The fortress—what you would know as a castle—was Arthur's first, and the woman was Guinevere, his queen."

"Guinevere. Lovely name for a queen. Never heard it before today."

"Odd. And you know naught of Arthur?"

"Was he one of those men, in the battle?"

"Yes. He it was led the charge down the hill."

"And the other man? At the tree?"

"He was Cai."

"What was the battle? It didn't seem like much of a fight."

"He had not yet become Arthur, the High King. The bridal dowry included a small holding. A neighbor, a petty tyrant, sent a raiding party to test his strength. His victory impressed the man. Later, that king had the honor to bend his knee to Arthur. A choice to submit or die."

"Cool." Like the computer game come alive. The game had realistic CGI, but this vision...I was there. "Can I do that again?" With my blood already tainted, I might as well have another psychedelic vision.

He studied me with furrowed eyebrows, and then shook his head. "It served its purpose. This day we must seek for Arthur."

Arthur. Back to him again. "Old man, I don't know where to look."

"In Britain today are books with lists of people. A way to contact them. Have you not the same?"

"Phone books? Well, yeah, for local. But the box didn't have an address. I don't know what state to check, much less what city."

"This city."

I shook my head. *The geezer's a fool. Why would the company be in Houston? But...easier to prove him wrong than argue.* "OK. You're the boss."

If I had a smart phone or internet connection I could search the web, but I couldn't afford them. I opened the business white pages that came with the apartment and flipped to the Ps. I almost shat my pants when I saw a listing for Pendragon Games. *Son of a bitch. Up in The Woodlands.*

My landline still worked, at least until the next month's bill came due. The woman who answered at Pendragon didn't know anyone called Arthur. And no Mr. Pendragon worked there. Just a name, she said. I relayed this to the old man. Sorry, I tried. No Arthur there. Hoping we were done now.

"Arthur is there," he said. "I will go to him."

When I started to protest, his eyes tightened. *Oh, hell. Such a stubborn old man.*

I didn't see how we could get in the door, and with my hand over the telephone, I told him so. The lady seemed pretty uninterested in us.

"This game you play. I am familiar with that time. I will speak with the person who created this game."

"Are you kidding me? You're a historian?"

"Say what I have told you."

Ah. Play the big lie. I didn't think it would do us any good, but I relayed it to the receptionist. Somehow, it was the right lie, because she opened up to me. Mr. Brice and Ms. Tascosa would love to meet with us, and she suggested we come by at three. I gave her my name and asked for directions. I didn't know the north suburbs of Houston well. She gave me directions to the west side of The Woodlands.

Milton wouldn't talk to me the whole way up there. His eyes remained in constant motion, though, like he absorbed every sight along the highway. I tried to get him to tell me how he planned to get past Brice and Ms. Tascosa to find Arthur, but he ignored me. I gave up and drove, listening to classic rock music on the radio.

The local news came on, and the big story remained the murder out by Brenham. The guy'd been dead a couple of days before they found his body. A DPS detective named Martell told the reporter that they'd tied it to another murder perpetrated a week ago in Tomball, but wouldn't tell the reporter why or how they'd made the connection. In international news, during a stop in Mexico City, the new Kaiser encouraged Mexico to fight California for the Baja region. The station went to commercials and then back to music without a traffic report. Too early in the afternoon.

Traffic crawled on I-10 and got even worse on I-45. All lanes slowed to a crawl, and at one point we all stopped. Except for one a-hole in a Porsche who zoomed up the breakdown lane. The big pickup right in front of me with he-man double back tires slipped over and blocked both our lane and the breakdown lane. I saw the Porsche driver stopped beside me hitting his steering wheel and cursing. I cheered the pickup driver and imagined how satisfying it would be to take a buck knife to the Porsche's tires while encouraging horns honked all around me. I didn't do it, but I made him crawl along awhile before he pulled in ahead of me.

A few miles later, traffic eased. We made it to The Woodlands without having to come to another complete stop on the highway. Woodlands Parkway led us back to the west. I didn't realize the suburb covered so much land. I began to think it would have been easier for us to go up through Tomball and back east to the Pendragon office, but I found the street we needed.

The Woodlands is a planned upscale suburb, except for the old part the city planners would rather people miss. Once, I took a wrong turn and drove through the blue-collar part on my way to a job interview. It's not a ghetto or anything, but the homes are a whole lot smaller, and the landscaping is…well, for the most part, it isn't.

The showy part of town, the part we drove through, comprises lots of office buildings and some high tech businesses. The planners made the companies hide their buildings behind trees and bushes, so the commuters don't have to see that people do work out there.

Pendragon had a discreet sign with the logo, or coat of arms, visible from the street. I took the next left and pulled into a parking lot. Their office stood ahead, just another low-rise red-brick building, like most of the others around. I drove past a wide pebbled-concrete walkway that led to a tinted glass entryway. I caught a glimpse of the receptionist behind a big wooden desk in the foyer. One car occupied a visitor parking slot.

The old man still wouldn't talk to me. He retrieved his staff from the back seat and strode toward the front door. He showed no concern that the sweatpants and pullover shirt he wore weren't business-meeting attire.

We passed a small pool bracketed by stone benches. Milton switched the staff to his other hand to push the glass door, but it slid open with his approach. He halted, clutching his staff against his chest. I laughed.

"What, you've never seen an automatic door before?"

He stepped back. The door closed again. He approached, and when the door slid aside, he walked through, glancing to both sides. It looked like he was trying to find the people who'd opened the door for him.

I kept chuckling until I reached the desk with a big sign that said *Shirley*. A plastic jack-o-lantern filled with candy in black and orange wrappers sat on the desk. Shirley operated a telephone that had at least thirty buttons on it. Her finger hovered in the air, asking us to wait just a moment. The wait didn't seem to please the old man.

She was a middle-aged woman with her hair in a Texas bouffant. A tan scarf draped around her neck set off her pale blue suit. While talking on the phone, she studied us with her brown eyes. Her high cheekbones sported a slight rouge highlight.

She hit a button and looked at us. "Afternoon. How can I help you gentlemen?"

The old man seemed flustered. Shirley had a deep West Texas accent. I expect what he heard sounded more like, "Af'noon. How c'n Ah he'p you genna-m'n."

"We have a three o'clock to see Mr. Brice and Ms. Tascosa."

"Oh, you must be Mr. Marlborough. Ms. Tascosa got so excited when she heard y'all were coming. Not many people've studied Britain before the Saxons came. She'll talk your ear off, if you let her. And Mr. Brice will try to join y'all later."

"It's my friend here who's the historian. I just love to play the game." I glanced at the old man. He still had no idea what she was saying. "Introduce yourself to the lady."

He bowed to Shirley. "I am Merlin, my lady."

"Well, Mr. Merlin. We're real glad you're here. Y'all aren't from around here, are you?"

I waited a moment, but Merlin, or Milton, or whoever he was today, didn't respond.

"No," I said, "Mr. Merlin is visiting from the old country. Me, I'm an immigrant from Maryland."

She enunciated for the old man. "Mr. Merlin, welcome to Pendragon Games." Then she turned back to me. "Could I see some ID?"

"Certainly." I pulled out my wallet and handed her my Texas driver's license.

"Mr. Merlin?"

The old man just stared at her.

"Do you have ID?" she asked. "A passport?"

"What is eye-dee?"

"A picture. With your name." I turned back to Shirley. "He's a bit confused sometimes. Is my ID enough?"

"I'll just call Ms. Tascosa and let her know y'all are here. If you gentlemen will have a seat over there." She pointed to a leather-covered sofa near one of the windows. A display of polished agate in brilliant colors rested on the table in front of the sofa.

I sat, but Merlin remained standing, leaning on his staff, facing the window. He stared at the bushes outside. I could see that something had him stewing.

"She did not ken my name," he said.

"Should she?" I'd figured out that *ken* meant recognize.

"I know not. I feel Arthur here. There is something else. Forsooth, his thread has been changed. I have not seen its like before. Its color has changed, or some other thread has been woven in with it. And yours is entangled as well."

"I suggest you keep your threads to yourself."

If he started in that way with Ms. Tascosa, we'd be lucky to get out of here without a police escort.

He began his hand gestures again, the staff leaning on his shoulder. This time, it looked like he was sorting through the threads he'd been describing, untangling them. His concentration didn't waver when a woman stepped into the lobby from the office area. She glanced at us and did an about-face, returning through the door. As the door clicked, Merlin cocked his head to one side and then looked over his shoulder. No one was there but Shirley, pushing buttons on the phone again. Merlin grasped the staff in his left hand and swept it across the space that contained the imaginary threads. With his right hand, he plucked one and pulled it toward his face. He studied the air in his empty hand.

"Excuse me, gentlemen," Shirley called to us. "Ms. Tascosa just rang and said she wouldn't be able to see y'all this afternoon. I'm so sorry y'all had to drive up here and not get to see her. She hasn't been feeling well lately, I'm afraid."

I translated to Merlin.

"We shall wait for Mr. Brice," he said.

None of my arguments would convince him otherwise. He turned to face the lobby, still clutching an imaginary thread.

I returned to Shirley and explained my predicament.

"Mr. Brice hasn't returned to the office, and Ms. Tascosa doesn't think he'll make it back. Really, sir, it's pointless to wait."

I laughed. "It's pointless to try to convince Mr. Merlin of what he doesn't want to hear."

She returned a delightful laugh, and we continued chatting between her duties with the telephone. I'm not much of a flirt, but she seemed open. I looked around for an excuse to keep talking with her.

After she connected another call, I asked, "May I have a kiss?"

She blushed, then pushed the bowl of Hershey's candies across the desk.

"You have the most unusual eyes," she said.

I ducked my head, embarrassed as usual.

"I get that all the time." *How I wish they were normal.* "One is mostly green with a hint of blue, and the other greenish-blue. Used to drive my wife—ex-wife—crazy. She wanted to get shirts that complemented my eyes, but that was tough. Coordinate with one and the other looks even odder."

"I can see how that'd be hard."

Her smile was sweet. Cute. She looked about my age, after all. Maybe she liked my eyes. Maybe I was being sensitive.

"The eyes. Runs in the family. My grandfather had it. He told me his mother and her brother both had it, too. Not everyone got it. Skipped some generations, like my mom, but as far back as anyone knew, someone in the family always had it."

"I've got the Cherokee cheeks." She gestured at one cheek. "I'm only a skillionth part Indian, but the cheeks are still there."

"It gives you distinction."

"That's what Lenny says. Lenny's my husband. He's the one started calling 'em Cherokee cheeks."

Damn. Married. Wouldn't you know it? I chatted with her a bit more, but when the phone rang again, I smiled and turned back to Merlin.

He wasn't in the lobby. Crap. I knew he hadn't gone into the main part of the building. I would've seen him go there.

Wait. Why should I care where he went? I'd earned my pay. I could leave him here. Just get in the car and go. He'd never be able to find me again, not forty miles from my apartment. Someone else's concern. Maybe he'd latch onto Mr. Brice. I could get back to my own problems. Find something to do until his drug wore off.

The door slid open, and I stepped into a warm October day. Days like this remind you how nice fall can be in Houston. Mostly cloudy, but a bit of sun just now, with a slight breeze carrying a clean, woodsy smell. The summer heat broke in mid-September, and now the temperatures remained in the upper 70s and lower 80s. And today was fine, just fine.

"Boy," the old man said. "Come here."

Maybe not so fine.

Merlin waited in the company garden. He looked out of place in this—professionally designed and properly sterile—businesslike spot of greenery. Several big goldfish swam around in the small pool bracketed by curved stone benches. Water gurgled down a rockfall on the opposite side.

"Hunh-uh. I've decided to leave. Your Arthur is here, you said. You don't need me, old man."

Merlin ignored my comment. He studied the fish. When the sun shone his wild eyebrows looked pure white, not the dirty gray-white they'd seemed this morning at my apartment.

"Stay. I shall give you another lesson."

"Lesson? What lesson?" I eyed him with suspicion.

"A vision, you called it earlier. When you flew as a hawk."

"Oh. Sure. That's a different matter." That wasn't a lesson. I enjoyed that. And since whatever drugs he used had already tainted me, I might as well enjoy another show.

"You did not control the hawk. You saw a memory from long ago. This time, you will control your actions. Are you ready?"

"Man, the hawk one was great. If it gets better, then sign me up."

He looked at me, waiting.

"I said, let's do it."

"I trained the boy who became Arthur thusly. He first experienced a fish. So shall you." He nodded toward the pond.

A fish? That didn't sound very exciting. Oh, well. Play along with his fish, and maybe he'll give me a tiger. Yeah.

"Give me the drugs. I'm ready." I held out my hand.

"You need nothing. Sit."

I dropped onto the stone bench. Merlin waved the top end of his staff and the world shifted.

CHAPTER

6

Blue. Everything's tinted blue. I hear an odd echoing sound, like rain falling on a tin roof—somewhere near, but not overhead. In the distance, something greenish ripples back and forth. I move toward it, curious. But I'm not walking. My body wiggles from side to side, and I feel a fluttering in parts of my body that I didn't know I had.

I'm a fish! Wow. He did it! I'm swimming. I'm slicing through the water like I belong in it. What a trip! I didn't think it would be cool, but this is neat.

As I get closer, the green thing comes into focus. It's a frond waving in the pond's slight ripples. I nudge it with my nose. Or the front of my face, whatever. The frond floats away, then drifts back toward me. It flavors the water, a fresh taste like prickly pear tea.

A fuzzy spot of gold in the blue distance gets bigger and morphs into another fish. I watch it move its fins, and I think about moving mine the same way. I must be doing something wrong, because I twist sideways in the water. But it doesn't matter. This is fun. The other fish comes up and nuzzles me with its mouth. It tickles like a gentle kiss.

I try to shrug my shoulders, but I swim backward instead. The other fish darts away.

A flash of light catches my eye, and I gaze at a shimmering reflection way above me. The surface of the water. A sunbeam streams through, and rainbow colors ripple around it.

The surface is far away. I had no idea the pond was so deep.

Deep. Ohmigod. How long have I been down here? I can't breathe. I'm running out of air.

I've got to swim to the surface. Huh oh, I'm rolling over backward. What's wrong with my muscles? They're not working right. Why can't I swim now? I could swim so well before. What happened?

Mustn't panic. Stay calm.

I've got to get to the surface. I'm going to die.

No, calm! Stay calm. Concentrate on surface.

Yes! Yes! I'm moving up. I can feel my body undulate, pushing through the water. But I'm not fast enough. I have to get to the surface.

I'm not going to make it. I can't hold my breath much longer. How many minutes have I been down here?

Surface. Oh, dear lord, thank you. I've hit the surface.

Why can't I breathe? I feel even worse.

I'll make another quick dash. I hope I've got the strength left. I'll leap high into the air.

Damn, I still can't get a breath. I know I broke out of the water that time. What's wrong with me?

Oh crap, I'm an idiot.

Fish use gills.

I sink back into the blue, letting myself calm down. I feel movement behind my cheeks. Above my shoulders? My mouth sucks in water, and I feel it rushing through the gills.

I gulp and spew water out my mouth. I'm thinking too hard about the process. Just breathe...or gill. I don't know what to call it.

The rhythm returns. I'm OK.

I want to explore. The edge of the pond is limestone. My eyesight isn't the greatest, but I can sure smell something different as I approach it. I don't have a vocabulary for this. It doesn't smell like dirt. I remember some intro chem-

istry, and calcium carbonate isn't supposed to smell, but there's a presence of it in the water that I taste when I'm close. Wow. Fish are different.

The pond forms a distorted oval. I follow its boundary, passing by another fish. It ignores me, intent on something on the pond bed.

I find the waterfall. It gets louder as I approach. Hmm. I didn't realize fish hear. And the water tastes more full as I get closer. Aeration? Must be. The taste sensation seems to come more from my gills than my mouth. My body also informs me that the water flows faster here.

I swim on and finish the circuit around the pond. I make the loop again, passing between two fish traveling in the opposite direction.

Hmm. I've swum around and investigated the plants, the waterfall, the other fish. Not much else to do.

I rise, controlling my movement this time. I see a tall shape standing beside the pond. That must be the old man. I break the surface and mouth his name, then drop back down. When nothing happens, I rise to repeat the silent call, wanting to get back to my body.

CHAPTER

7

I CAME BACK to myself, sitting on the bench gazing at the pond. Merlin was staring at a fish at the surface of the water.

"Cool."

Merlin's head jerked toward me. "You are back?"

"Didn't you end the vision?"

He rubbed his chin through the beard. "No. I did not."

I tried not to flinch when he put his hand on my head. He said, "Most unusual. Arthur never did that. Perhaps…the eyes?"

My different-colored eyes generated no—well, rare—admiration from people, so I assumed he meant some veiled insult. "Stuff it."

"You remind me of a different boy. He had eyes like yours."

"Arthur?"

He shook his head. "No, another. A fool."

I shrugged. He was an annoying old man, with unfathomable stories. I had more interest in these trips he sent me on. Was he a Svengali or some holdover hippy from the sixties?

"What'd you do? How'd you make me hallucinate? Drugs? Or was it hypnosis?"

He closed his eyes and sighed, shaking his head. "This will I answer, though never shall you understand the truth. I give you these experiences as a payment for your help. Your…mind…that is the word you understand. Your mind I transferred to the fish."

"You swapped my mind for the fish?" *Yuck!* A shiver rolled from the base of my neck out both arms.

"Not a swap. The fish stayed. You joined its essence."

He paused, cocking his head to the side, listening. Whatever he heard, he seemed to dismiss it. For my part, I decided yet again that he was crazy.

"Both minds together. Yours is the higher mind, but the other knows its body. The fish knows how to move, swim, how to breathe. You must let the fish do such things. Unless it senses danger, a fish does as you will it. And so, a fish is a good first animal to join. Fish and some birds, they have few desires, making it easy to control such a one. Do you understand?"

I nodded. He spoke with intensity. This seemed to be a crucial element to his dementia. I waited for him to continue.

"Predators are difficult. They struggle for control and must be trained with care to share the mind. Mice are easier than rats, but most mammals are difficult. Cats are impossible, but on occasion I have traveled with a dog after establishing a trust."

"What about other people?"

His eyes whipped toward me, narrowing. "It is not done."

I wanted to hear more, but a man around thirty years old wearing a purple turtleneck stepped out of the office door. He walked with a jaunty, cocky stride, his black hair held back with a generous coating of gel. A happy sparkle jumped from his green eyes.

Salesman, I thought. *And probably a good one.*

"Hiya. I'm Billy Brice. Shirley said I'd find y'all out here. Y'all like the old Brit history? Way cool. Call me Billy."

He had a soft twang. Texan, but he had the sound of someone who'd spent some time in America. He spoke just a bit too fast for a true Texan.

I took his hand and introduced myself, grinning in response to his wide smile. He had a firm grip, and I could tell that he worked to be the kind of man everyone likes on the first meeting. Judging by his cologne, he also wanted to make an instant impression on the ladies. I stepped away to make room, but Merlin stayed back, both hands gripping his staff.

"You are not Arthur," he said. "I seek for Arthur."

"Y'all are lookin' for Arthur, huh? Would that be Arthur Pendragon?"

Merlin's reaction startled me. He swept me aside with one hand and stabbed his staff on the ground beside Billy's foot. He jammed his face to within a few inches of Billy's.

"Where is he?"

Billy staggered backward, losing his smile for a moment. It came back as he put his hands out in front of the old man. "Whoa, hold your horses, pal." He patted the air between them. "Intense, dude."

He smiled again and held out his hand. "I'm Billy. Whadda they call you?"

"I am Merlin." This accent he could understand. He took Billy's hand. "Tell me where Arthur can be found."

The handshake didn't stop. At first, Billy appeared to be testing Merlin's grip. The muscles on the young man's arm tensed, then tightened. Meanwhile, Merlin exhibited no effort. It looked like he had no more than a firm grip on Billy's hand.

Billy pulled away first, rubbing his right hand.

"Whoa, Merlin, my man. You're a tough old cuss, ain'cha?" He shook his head. "OK, so lemme tell you about this guy Arthur. He lived a long time ago. Like, dark ages, centuries back. He was some obscure British king who fought against the Saxons. You know about our big seller, right? Our game? Well, he was a king way back then, when our game takes place. But we don't use his name in the game. We let a player be the king honcho." Billy flexed his fingers one by one, then all of them together.

The old man leaned forward. "You said you knew Arthur Pendragon. Where is he?"

Billy backed up again. "Look, Mr. Merlin. I know bupkis about those old sword-slingin' cowboys. My partner named the company. She really groks all that stuff, and she wanted to call it Pendragon. What do I care? It's got a good sound to it. Makes the D&D crowd look us over, ya see?"

"You know nothing of Arthur?" Merlin glared at the young man.

"Nada. I sorta tune out when Amber—she's my partner, Amber Tascosa—yeah, when she talks about ancient history I just zone, ya know? But Amber wanted to research everthin' written about that king. We brought in some world-famous history geeks from over at U of H to do some research for the company. They found diddly squat. History professors at one of the biggest U's in the nation of Texas, and they came up empty-handed. You'd think a king would be a big shot and somebody would write his stuff down. Amber told them all kinds a crap about him, stuff she thought they could check. They never said she was wrong, but they couldn't confirm any of her tales. We asked profs in America, and even over there in England."

He chuckled. "I pretty much decided that she'd made it all up. Parta her grand delusion, ya know? You're the first person I've ever met that's heard a the man."

Merlin plucked at his invisible threads again. Billy raised an eyebrow at me; I shrugged. I had no idea what he was doing, either. Billy rolled his eyes and smiled. *Yeah*, I thought. *The old man's crazy, all right.*

Merlin said, "You say that these men who profess history knew nothing of Arthur? Did they know of the monk Geoffrey of Monmouth? Indeed, he wrote a history of Arthur. It was read by many."

"Mon myth? I remember that the profs looked into Brit mythology. That monk couldn't a written a best seller, or for sure they'd a found it. She paid 'em enough. Maybe Amber's read the book, but she never mentioned it to me."

"I must meet Amber."

Billy shook his head, smiling with false sympathy. "She's not takin' visitors this afternoon. She's feelin' poorly."

Merlin seemed to float toward Billy. The young man's green eyes opened wide, looking like the proverbial deer caught in the headlights. I thought he'd back away again, but instead he froze in place. The old man stopped when his eyebrows brushed Billy's forehead. He leaned his staff forward, placing the knobby top part beside Billy's ear.

Merlin repeated, "I must meet Amber. Now."

"I...I don't think so. She's been kinda tired, and she said she couldn't, so..."

"She shall see me. Go. Tell her Merlin is here."

"I, uh, yeah." Billy shook his head. "I guess so. I guess maybe I should tell her. Lemme go check."

Billy backed up, almost stepping in the pond, and then scuttled away. He looked back over his shoulder several times as he hurried into the building. He wasn't smiling any more.

"Good luck," I said. "Shirley told us that the lady was tired and wouldn't see us. No wiggle room."

Merlin pulled his staff upright. After a moment, he said, "She shall see me."

He leaned on the staff. No, not just on it, into it. It appeared that all his strength had disappeared and he drew everything he had from the staff. For a moment, I thought the knotted wood on its top reflected light from somewhere.

He wouldn't respond to anything I said, so I sat down to watch the fish. I couldn't tell which one I'd been. They all looked the same to me. Oh, bull. I hadn't been any of them. The old man used some kind of mind trick on me. All the while, he told me what to feel. That must be it.

But it was fun, whatever he did. I couldn't be mad at him about it.

The sun broke through the clouds just before it dropped behind the trees. I looked at my watch—almost five o'clock. *Great, we're going to get caught in Friday rush-hour traffic.*

Billy called from the door. "Mr. Merlin? She'll see ya now, I guess. Uh, you too, Al."

"Alfred," I called back, but he'd already gone inside.

I waved at Shirley as we passed through the lobby. She gathered her stuff to go home. "Y'all have a good talk," she said. "But don't keep 'er too long. Amber needs to get herself home and get some rest."

Billy waited, holding the door to the main part of the building. He looked at Merlin, then into the building and back at me. He didn't seem to know what to do. His manner had reversed from the successful young man who'd first greeted us. His cocky attitude had been replaced by uncertainty. Maybe even fear. Was his ego so fragile that being bested in a handshake competition by an old man burst his self-confidence? I couldn't believe the he-man test had happened. It had to have been just another mind game. I knew about those from experience with the old guy. I just wished that I'd seen how the old coot put Billy down.

He slid as close to the door as he could to let Merlin, then me, stride through. He made a wide path around us, and then rushed down halls painted in the magenta and cobalt blue of agate. We passed offices labeled *Personnel*, *Accounting*, and some others I didn't catch. At the back we burst into a cube farm, but it wasn't like any set of cubicles I'd ever worked in. The petroleum industry, where I'd spent my whole career, kept pretty conservative office spaces. Casual Friday meant wearing blue jeans and a golf shirt with the company logo. Not here.

A pair of basketball hoops bracketed the room, with a wide aisle running between them. Several soft foam balls littered the aisle, and the trashcans beneath the hoops overflowed with wadded-up paper. Another wall held a dartboard. A man and a woman took turns shooting colored spitballs at a big orange and black sign announcing a Halloween paintball competition.

"Hey, Billy," the spitball man called out. He seemed put out when Billy ignored him.

The nearby coffee bar used those individual coffee packets, but it also had machines for cappuccino and espresso. Cases of soft drinks sat next to a refrigerator beside shelves full of candies and chips and a huge pile of healthy snacks and granola bars. Several twentysomethings chatted at the counter: a man in shorts and two women wearing sweats. Tattoos reigned, appearing on almost every person I saw.

"I got a date tonight, boss," said a woman sporting black spiked hair with orange tips. "But I'll finish the character algorithms this weekend."

Several people stuck their heads out of their cubes to comment or yell "attagirl."

The woman laughed at them. "You're just a bunch of jealous nerds. At least I've got a life."

"Half a life—you work here," someone said. The laughter died down as everyone went back to work.

Billy ignored them all as he urged us toward a corner office. He glanced at Merlin several times, then fixed his gaze on me.

"You first," he said. "Alone."

Merlin stiffened beside me. Billy wouldn't look his way.

"Me? Why?" I was just the chauffeur. *What did she want with me?* I turned to Merlin. He seemed to be thinking something through, and then he relaxed and nodded to me.

Billy seemed to relax, too. He almost smiled as he ushered me forward, then stopped me at the door while he gave it a gentle rap.

"Send him in, Billy," a voice called from inside.

"You go on ahead," Billy said. "She wants me to wait here with Mr. Merlin."

He didn't look happy about that demand. He swung the door open and I sauntered in.

The woman stood staring out a full-length window. It looked onto a green space: about ten feet of closely clipped grass surrounded by trees and shrubbery one step away from being overgrown. When she turned, I recognized Amber Tascosa as the woman who had peeked in on us while we waited in the lobby. She took her time looking me over. I figured I might as well do the same.

She was in her mid-thirties, what Mom used to call a big-boned woman. Not fat, just kind of large at about five foot six. She had the look of a woman who worked out.

I don't think my wife would have approved of her pantsuit. Too mannish, and the light blue color didn't go with her brown hair and brown eyes. She looked intelligent—something about her eyes and general carriage. She exuded a definite sense of control and power.

But it looked like Shirley was right. The corners of her eyes sagged with fatigue.

"Not what I would have expected from Merlin." She had a strong, firm voice, just a little deep for a woman.

"I beg your pardon?"

"Your name is Marlborough? Al, isn't it?"

"Please, it's Alfred. I've always thought Al was, you know, a mechanic or something."

"Alfred, then. What does your friend Merlin want?"

I shook my head, both to indicate that I didn't know and that her assumption about me and Merlin was misplaced.

"Look, he's not my friend. I want you to understand. This guy glommed onto me yesterday, and I haven't been able to shake him. He doesn't know his way around. And, well, frankly, I think he's a bit loopy. So, I'm just trying to help him."

"Loopy." She smiled. A small, pleasant smile. I can't say it made her pretty or anything like that, but she didn't look so severe.

"Yeah. And, well, I'd watch out for him if I were you. He's not as weak as he seems." I figured, better safe than sorry. If he did drug her or something, at least I'd warned her.

"You don't trust him?"

"Not really."

"What does he want?"

"He's looking for a friend. Some guy named Arthur Pendragon. That's why we came here. I told him it was crazy, but he insisted we'd find Arthur here. He thinks Arthur is some kind of king."

"And these names. Merlin. Arthur. Pendragon. Did they mean anything to you before you met him?"

"Well, Pendragon. I've got your game. It's pretty awesome. I like the graphics." *Oh, what the heck, go for it.* "But I gotta tell you, it's almost impossible to win as the Britons. You gotta make it more fair."

Her lips tipped up a little. "My designers wanted to do just that. But fair isn't the way it happened. The Britons weren't ready for self-government after the Romans left. Life had been easy for too long. And of course, the Saxons had their own pressures from the east. Huns forced them out of their homes and put them on the move. Saxons and most of the rest of what we now call Europeans.

"No, it wasn't a fair battle for the Britons. Not in the long run." She sighed, and the small smile went away. "But that isn't why Merlin is here. What does he want with Arthur?"

"He hasn't said."

"And you haven't asked? Aren't you at all curious?"

I shrugged. "I just figured they were buddies. Maybe Merlin thinks he can get a handout from an old pal. He's destitute. You should have seen him before I made him clean up."

"Destitute. Somehow, I doubt that."

She turned to the window again. Her chin rested in one hand with the elbow supported by the other arm crossing her waist. I looked around her office. A large tapestry covered the wall opposite the window: a unicorn and a woman with jewelry. Shelves full of books occupied much of the walls. Several more books rested open on her desk. Knickknacks filled one shelf.

No, they looked too expensive to be knickknacks. At the center, a foot-high bust that I figured must have been old because of the broken ears and nose. Two ancient coins mounted on black material in glass-fronted frames. Pottery shards under glass. I guessed they were post-Roman British, like the game. Maybe for inspiration.

"Billy." When he looked in, she said, "Fetch Merlin."

Billy backed out of the doorway and waved to the old man. Merlin ignored the cowering Billy as he strode into the office. Two paces in, he stopped and planted his staff beside his right foot. He stared at Ms. Tascosa, his bushy eyebrows working up and down as he took her in. His left hand came out and strummed the imaginary threads in front of him. Then he looked at the woman in surprise.

"Merlin," she said. "I gave up on you two years ago."

CHAPTER 8

ALL THREE OF us spoke at once.

I blurted, "You know him?"

I think Billy said something similar. Merlin spoke longer than either of us, but whatever he said, it wasn't in English.

Amber said, "I don't understand the old language."

What a strange thing for her to say, given the circumstances.

"I tried to learn Celtic, but I just can't retain it." She tapped her forehead.

"Ambrosius." He blinked. "Amber. I should have known."

"Have you come to take me back?"

Billy lurched forward, glancing from Amber to Merlin and back again.

"It is time for you to return," Merlin said.

"No! You can't go back there," Billy said. "You're cured. Don't listen to him!" He extended his arms in both directions, as though trying to keep them apart.

"It's all right, Billy." Amber exchanged a long look with Merlin. They seemed to come to a wordless agreement. She looked back to Billy. "Merlin and I need to talk."

Billy edged forward, both arms now outstretched toward her, beseeching. He seemed about to speak, but she raised her hand to silence him. "It isn't what you think."

His arms dropped back to his side, but he started rocking on his heels.

Amber said, "Please take Alfred to your office and show him the new graphics."

Billy caught himself in the middle of a heel bounce and flashed a hard look at me. He turned back to Amber and spoke with more assurance than he'd had since the handshake with Merlin. "That's not released yet. We aren't showin' anyone."

"Oh, don't worry. Alfred's a fan; he's not the competition."

Billy glared at me again, but when he cut his eyes toward Merlin, I thought I saw fear.

"Billy," she said. "It's OK. Show him the upgrade."

Billy rolled his shoulders and motioned for me to follow him. This unexpected turn surprised and pleased me. I'd get to see an unreleased version of one of my favorite games. I wondered if it would be a cosmetic upgrade, or if there would be new strategies and new weapons.

At the door, Billy turned and looked past me at the other two, who gazed at one another like old friends. He opened his mouth to speak, then closed it. He took half a step back into the room and raised his hand toward Amber. I thought that he wanted to stay, and that he definitely wanted influence over whatever discussion loomed ahead. Then I saw his eyes turn toward Merlin, and his shoulders sagged. He looked back to Amber with what I took to be hope in his eyes.

She motioned us out of the room, dismissing us. Neither she nor Merlin spoke before the door closed behind us.

Billy grabbed my arm, hard. "Who the hell are you?"

"Me? Like the lady said, I'm a fan."

"Bullshit. You and that old fart are up to somethin'."

"Hey, I just gave him a ride. I don't even like the old man."

"Yeah, right. So, why's she givin' you the horses and the ranch, too?"

"What?"

"We never show our product to anyone. Not 'til it's ready to release. What'd ya tell her while I was stuck with," his eye twitched, "that geezer?"

I shrugged. "She asked about Merlin. What he wanted. I told her that I don't know, and that's the truth."

He released my arm, and the tightness around his eyes relaxed a little. But he remained suspicious.

I said, "Maybe she liked me because I told her the game wasn't fair to the Britons."

"We all know that." He seemed to accept my changing the subject, but I could tell he still thought I had something up. "Amber kicks butt playin' the Britons. The resta us, well, we win a few battles, maybe even a campaign. But at some point we run outta resources and get our asses whupped."

"I tried turning off plague, and I still couldn't win."

"She wouldn't let us give the Saxons plague. Even when one a the designers found a record of plague in the Anglo-Saxon chronicles, she wouldn't use it 'cause they caught plague much later. After our game time. The Brits caught it through the old Roman trade routes."

He led me to his office in the other back corner. It was as big as Amber's, with the same kind of view through big plate-glass windows onto a man-made wood. Framed prints of sports cars covered his walls. A classic Maserati caught my eye, but Billy waved me into a chair. He sat behind his desk and stared at me across the empty expanse.

I wanted to see the new game, but I kept thinking about Merlin and Amber.

"All this time," I said, "I thought we were looking for some homeless guy named Arthur. Now, the old buzzard has found your boss, and she knows him, too. I'm confused. I know it's none of my business, but you seem to know where Merlin wants to take her."

"She isn't my boss. We're partners. And, no, it isn't any a your business. But..." He glanced at the terminal on his desk, and by the set of his shoulders, I knew he'd made some decision. "Well, it ain't a secret. Sometimes, even she brings it up."

I nodded, hoping he'd go on.

"Until about seven years ago, Amber lived in a home. Mental hospital, ya know? Ding-dong batty place. She'd been in first one and then another hospital for more'n twenty years."

"Twenty?" I stammered. She would have been a child when she went in.

"Before I partnered up with her, my attorney did due diligence. He found out about her history. She'd been in a walkin' coma for like, forever. *Walking coma*, those were his words. She would walk, if someone led her around. Eat and drink, if someone put it to her mouth. Go to the bathroom, if someone remembered to take her and sat her down. If not, well, there was a mess to clean up wherever she was sittin' or lyin'. Mostly she just sat, starin' ahead."

"I can't believe the hospital told your attorney all that."

He waved my concern away. "Naw, they just told him that she'd been institutionalized. He dug a bit for the rest. He told me to run, don't walk, away from the deal. Course, by then I'd known Amber for goin' on a year and a half. Other than the plain fact that she woke up in a mental hospital, she acted like she didn't know why she'd been put in there. Maybe she doesn't.

"But I knew by then that she was...is...one a the most intelligent and dynamic people I'd ever had the pleasure to meet. Very centered. Interested in everthin'. I was teachin' a computer class, just basic Office stuff. That's where we met. She'd never seen a simulation game, so I showed her some. Right off, she begins sellin' me on this idea for a game. Britain after the Romans left, and the Brits had ta fight Saxon invasions. Nope, I saw my future. I couldn't just walk away."

"So you took the risk?" I'd never had the courage to do such a thing.

"I dug a little more. Mostly from a nurse and one a the orderlies at her last hospital." He flashed a small smile. "I have a way with the ladies."

I had no doubt about that. Billy was the type of guy that could talk to any girl, any time, and end up in bed with her. And the rest of us, we'd just watch in fascination and envy.

"Everbody seemed to agree on a diagnosis a walkin' coma, although a couple of 'em implied there was more goin' on up there," he tapped his head, "than the docs knew about. Then, outta the blue one day, she woke up. And it musta been somethin' else, from what I heard. Throwin' her body all around the bed and gruntin' like a stuck hog. When they tried to get her outta bed she collapsed on the floor. A dead drop. She couldn't walk, oh heck, they said her legs wouldn't even hold her up. After a while, she started screamin'. It put the whole place in a tizzy; lots a the borderline cases started screamin' along with her. Fin'ly, the docs put her in a quiet room. I heard it was a padded cell. Restraints. They were afraid to sedate her, since this was the first time since she got there that she'd made any sound at all. It went on for a couple hours, and then she calmed down. Stayed quiet for the rest a the day. After that, she began to improve. They told me that it was like she was learnin' to control her body again."

"Wow." I was stunned.

"Then she started makin' words. That got the docs excited. It was pretty incoherent at first. But with speech therapy, she came right along. And she was walkin' and eatin' and stuff, all on her own.

"But I found out nada about why she'd been put in the loony bin in the first place. She'd been in so many places, they'd lost her old records somewhere along the ol' Chisholm trail. Rumor had it some-thin' happened to her family when she was about eight. They died. Somethin' terrible, everbody figured, 'cause that's when she stopped talkin'. The walking coma.

"The hospital was nice. Real expensive. It took some doin', but I found a lovely young lady that did some a their bookkeepin'. Amber's bills got paid outta some kinda trust. They thought that the parents had lotsa insurance and an honest attorney. He put her into first one home 'n then another and invested the money. Invested well, it seems. By the time she woke up, she had a million. More."

That's why he wanted her in the company. She had the money, and he talked her into going into business with him. *I bet he's on easy street.*

"I wanted to talk to the family attorney, but he'd died a few years earlier. His son took over the practice. He's an honest guy, too. But he knew bupkis. A twister hit their office, spun off from Tropical Storm Frances. It scattered the files up to the Red River, almost into the U. S. of A. And he told me the official records had burned up in a fire, big conflagration in a county courthouse somewhere between here 'n Austin. His old man had been more concerned keepin' her finances straight than in passin' on her story. Client confidentiality, the son told me. Even he hadn't heard it."

"The attorney wouldn't have told you anything, not if he's such an honest guy."

"Amber told him he could answer my questions. He just didn't have any answers."

"She knew you were snooping into her past?"

"Yeah, she said it wasn't her in the hospital. That time has never meant much to her." He shrugged. "I admire her. She overcame a lot."

He started telling me about how they put together the company, and about developing the game. Only after Amber and Merlin came and announced we were going out for dinner did I realize he'd never shown me the new game graphics.

It wasn't just the girls he could razzle-dazzle.

As we passed through the cubicle area, Amber spoke with several workers. After commenting at several workstations, she called for everyone's attention.

"I like what I see, but it can be better. We don't build a fantasy game, our game is based in reality. Saxons, Jutes, Angles, Scotti, Irish, Franks, they all assaulted Britain. The British were on their own after four hundred years of Roman rule. I know better than anyone that it's hard to win as the British. But our fans want to keep trying. This new version has to give them more reality. You have to make them care about this world. Create a *need* to jump into the chaos. Let the gamer-hero bring hope to the game's citizens. Make other game companies envy you, creators of a world that existed and exists again. Go for it."

She excited everyone in the room. Several shouted things like "hoo-ahh" and most clapped for a few beats with great enthusiasm. She made me wish I worked for her. She also made me feel guilty for playing the Saxons most of the time. She was right about how real it felt, even the first version that I played. If they'd improved the new version, well, wow. No. Wow!

Amber drove the four of us to a small Italian place in her Audi. She and Merlin seemed to have come to some agreement, but they weren't talking about it. Merlin remained his usual unreadable self, but I did think that he seemed satisfied with the outcome. Amber acted more resigned than satisfied. Neither would talk about what they'd discussed, no matter how often Billy asked.

Billy made no secret that he didn't like being at the same table with Merlin. A long awkward silence followed after the hostess seated us. Amber concentrated on the menu, pointing out items for Merlin. I eavesdropped on the family at the next table. It appeared to be a couple with their freshman daughter.

"Have you made many friends yet, Rachel?" the father asked.

"Oh, Daddy, stop worrying." The girl put her hand on his. "I've got lots of friends. And I'm still in touch with everyone in Baltimore on Pingpoint and Slambunch."

"That's social media, Grantling," the mother said to the father.

"Yes, Audrey dear. I'm not a dinosaur."

Rachel laughed. "Now that's funny, Daddy."

I wished I'd had a family like that. But we didn't.

Billy couldn't leave a silence for long, so he began chattering. He kept cutting his eyes at the old man, but once started, he didn't let a moment pass without filling it with some story. It seemed to me a nervous reaction, but his bar-hopping adventures from the previous weekend entertained us most of the evening.

I had some Chianti with my veal piccata. It was a better meal than I'd had in months, and it made me feel pretty good. Maybe I had more than a couple of glasses—Amber proclaimed I'd had too much wine to drive back to west Houston. She invited Merlin and me to stay at her place. Since I couldn't seem to focus on my watch to see what time it was, I figured I'd better take her offer.

She dropped Billy at the office. He hopped into a red Miata. Its convertible top descended as we left the lot. I thought about how cool his life must be—young and successful. Didn't have to take anything from anyone. If any firing had to be done, he was the firer, not the firee. A successful small business could keep a man happy. Red Miata!

I paid little attention, but I could tell she drove farther west, out toward Tomball. We pulled onto a private road and drove another quarter mile along a creek. The lane passed through a forest of oaks and pines thick with brambles and up to a big, new ranch-style house.

I had trouble getting out of Amber's Audi and had to lean on her to get to the house. She skipped the house tour and led me to a wonderful guest room. I leaned against the door to get my bearings and stared at a large tapestry in blue and tan on the wall behind the bed. I stumbled by the dresser, flipped on the TV, and turned off the light by the bed. I don't remember any particular show; I just kicked off my shoes and vegged out.

Something woke me. Maybe I heard the click of the TV or the sudden silence when it went off. The open curtains kept the room from seeming pitch-black. In the dim light I saw a figure slide across the room.

"Who's there?" I asked, trying to rise.

"Shhhhh." She tiptoed around the bed. By her silhouette against the window, I figured it was Amber. She sat on the edge of the bed.

"Boys should'n sleep in their clothes. They get all wrinkly." Her voice sounded soft and seemed higher that it had earlier.

"I...I guess I did have a...a little too much to...ah...drink. I...ah...fell asleep."

"That's all right," she cooed. "I'll just take them off for you." She started unbuttoning my shirt.

All men would like to think they're irresistible to the opposite sex, but I knew in my case it wasn't true. Sure, I'd had a few partners, but I'd always had to pursue them. Awkwardly. I'm not the leading man kind of guy that women lust after. Average, at best. A woman coming to my bed in the middle of the night was a new experience for me.

"Uh, Amber." I took her hands in mine. "What are you doing?"

"Call me Lolly." She slipped her hands free and went back to work on the buttons.

"Lolly? Why?"

"Silly," she giggled. "'Cause they'll get wrinkled." She slid the shirt open and stroked my chest.

I was about to tell her I meant *why Lolly* when the moon came out from behind clouds. Amber wore a see-through top; her nipples stood alert under the thin camisole. I watched the material slide across her as she swayed back and forth, her body following the motion of her hands. Her light strokes played across my chest, and they became even lighter as she brushed across my stomach.

The attention made me uncomfortable. I was getting an erection, but it couldn't get straight in my pants. "Amber, why are you in here?" I shifted a bit on the bed, hoping my jeans would shift too, but it didn't work.

"Please, call me Lolly." She bent down and brushed her lips across each of my nipples. The pressure in my groin increased. I tried to shift again, but her weight on my chest held me in place.

"Uh, Lolly, what are you doing?"

She gave a coy sidewise glance. "Poor boy, he does'n know what I'm doin'." Her tongue slipped out and lapped at the top of my belly.

"I mean, why?" The pressure became unbearable. I so wanted to reach down and pull myself into line. I didn't know how to deal with this situation. I'd never been seduced before.

At the same time, the discomfort got better and worse: she unzipped my pants. I tried to sit up, but she pushed me back down and slid one hand inside my underwear. I think I moaned.

"Shhhh. I like you. And it looks like you like me." She exhaled a stream of warm air under the waistband.

What could I do? No woman had ever come on to me like this. Even with my wife—ex-wife—I'd had to take the lead, sometimes begging her. This was like a fantasy come true. I reached up to stroke her breast, but she put my arm back by my side.

"Not yet."

She raised me up and took off my shirt, and then my jeans and underwear. She put my hands behind my head, like making me her prisoner. Only my erection flew free.

She studied me for a long moment in the darkness. A fear of her laughing at me welled up. She was young and rich, and I was neither. What could she be doing but making fun of me, laughing in her head? I almost sat up, wanting to push her back.

Before I had the courage to do anything, she leaned into me. She began caressing me from my waist up the side of my torso, almost tickling me. It made me hard again, and then even harder. And to my great relief, she didn't laugh at me.

"Oh, I so like havin' your soldier at attention," she said. One hand traced across my stomach, the other hand down the outside of my thigh and then back up the inside. Her fingers met at the tip of me.

I lost track of what happened next. I blame the wine.

I got lost in an exciting new experience that could have lasted two minutes or twenty. I remember after she mounted me, she let me take her top off and touch her. I remember caressing her breasts as they swayed up and down, and then as they rocked before me my hands slid to her sides, until I closed my eyes and lost myself to her and the moment.

She lay on top of me for a long time while our breathing settled back to normal. I heard the thumping of my heart slow and felt hers doing the same. When she rolled off, I became afraid she'd slip out of the room as mysteriously as she'd slipped in. My breathing steadied again when she relaxed beside me on the bed. I reached over to stroke her hair, but she forced first that hand and then the other under the pillow, behind my head again.

"The soldier is at parade rest, is'n he? But look, he got wet." She cupped me with her hand.

"Lolly," I said, "I don't think I can go again. Not yet."

"Silly boy. I know that. But I can enjoy your body while I'm here, can't I?"

I didn't want to argue with her logic, that's for sure. But it made me wonder why she had been in the nut house for so long. I had to know. Was she a sex addict or something?

"Billy told me that you'd been in the hospital."

"Billy's OK. But he wo'n let me puh-la-a-ay," she drew a circle on my belly as she drew out the word, "with the boys at the comp'ny. I think some of 'em could be fun."

"Is this why you were in the hospital?"

"This? You mean Ess Ee Ex?" She giggled. "No, you silly boy. I lived there forever. Before I learned 'bout sex. Actually," she giggled again, "that's where I learned 'bout it."

"How? Weren't you in a coma?"

She stopped stroking me. I wished I could see her face, but the moon had clouded over again. I feared I'd upset her and she'd leave, and I dreaded saying anything to make her do that. She rolled over on her side, facing me. The soft scent of an herbal shampoo displaced the musky sex smell.

"That's what they say. But I was'n in a coma. I jus'…" She ran a hand through her hair. "I jus' did'n wanna talk to anyone."

I started to ask her why, but she put her hand on my mouth.

"I do'n know why. I just di'nt." She sighed.

I didn't know what to say, but since her hand still rested on my mouth, I didn't have to say anything. So I lay there, waiting for her to continue. When she did, her voice was playful again and her hands started moving across my body.

"There was one orderly. I think I was seventeen then—they had birthday parties for me ever year and they made a big deal a the next one so it was prob'ly my eighteenth. Anyway, this orderly was about my age, maybe a couple years older. Kinda cute, in a still-pimply kinda way. He had sparklin' eyes—got right in front a my face and talked to me. I did'n respond. Oh no, then they'd know I was payin' attention. I never let them know I was watchin'. If I did, the doctors would want me ta talk, but I would'n talk. No, I stayed quiet."

The last bit sounded like something she had said before. Like a litany to herself. As she spoke, she'd stopped stroking me, and I felt like she was thinking about something.

"I do'n know why I'm tellin' you this. I never have. But it feels good, somehow, tellin' it to you." I saw her teeth sparkle in the low light—a smile, I hoped. "You're special, somehows."

She continued after a few seconds, her hands becoming as playful as her voice.

"Most of the orderlies knew I could read. I guess I'd been doin' it all along, I do'n 'member startin'. There was always one or two of 'em who'd put a newspaper in front a me, or a book, and come along ever once in a while and change the page. This boy, he did. But the books he put out for me ta read," her hand traced down to the hair below my belly, "they were'n like what the others put out. It was'n *Treasure Island*, you know? At first, they were the ones called romance novels. I saw that on the covers. But then, he started bringin' in really nassssty onessss." She stroked me from base to tip as she said the last two words. I was already semi-erect.

"One night, he came inta my room. He talked for a while, tellin' me it was time for me ta be a woman and all. Then he said," she giggled a bit, "that I should tell 'im when I wanted 'im ta stop." She giggled again. "He knew I would'n talk. But I would'na stopped 'im, anyway."

"Lolly," I said, my penis deflating. "Did he…molest you?"

"No, you silly boy. He was nice to me. He took off my gown and gave me a sponge bath. He spent a long time, you know, between my legs. I did'n know what ta think. I'd never had feelin's like those when I was bathed before. I wanted ta look at 'im, but the lights were on, so

I kept starin' at the ceilin'. It was real hard ta keep from moanin' out loud, at the end. It was real confusin'."

I said, "It was criminal."

She ignored my comment. Her hand rested on my chest.

"He came back the next night. But this time, after another sponge bath, he got up on the bed. When he rolled onto me, his eyes met mine. I tried, really, really hard, ta keep my eyes flat. I'd been doin' it for years. But I could'n. And he knew. He knew I was there. And he knew that I enjoyed what he was doin'. An' I did enjoy it. Much more'n the night before. I did'n scream, like the heroines do sometimes in the books. I was able ta control that, at least. But my body convulsed. I came, and he knew it.

"That was the beginnin' of a long and," she took a deep breath, "truly wonderful relationship. He did'n tell anyone that I was, you know, aware. And he came to me often." Another giggle. "He came with me often. Until he got caught with me one night, and I never saw 'im again."

She sounded wistful. She thought she was a teenager losing her first love. Not a rape victim being rescued.

"The doctors really wanted-a get me ta talk, so I guess he spilled the beans. But I stayed quiet."

Her hand grazed my stomach. My penis responded. It didn't know that she'd been damaged. Anyway, years had passed. She'd grown into a woman. She knew what she was doing to me. Better than I did, in fact. I stiffened again.

Lolly rolled on top of me. She lowered herself onto me, leaning on my arms, pinning my hands behind my head. I got harder inside her. She began moving on me again. She raised up until my tip remained barely inside her, and then eased down to the very base. She repeated the motion several times with excruciating slowness. My breath got shorter as the salty smell of our sweat filled the room. She moved faster—then with shorter strokes. Her hair flew around my head. Her breasts rubbed against my nipples with each oscillation, and when her convulsions started again, mine did too. I thrust upward, my back arched in the air for half a minute as she continued to ride up and down. Neither of us cried aloud, but I felt a silent scream from her matching my own.

She dropped onto me, panting. She released my arms, and I placed them around her, hoping she'd let me. She didn't move. Our breathing slowed, and I fell asleep holding her atop me.

CHAPTER
9

I AWOKE TO a dull thud pounding in my head, a sour, groaty taste in my mouth, and alone. Not even an aroma of her hair remained on the pillow beside me. I got a brain-whack when I sat up that took half a minute to fade. The thought that our tryst had never happened seized me. That I'd imagined her visit in the middle of the night. A very wet dream.

Lolly...Amber...didn't need me. OK, now that I thought about it sober—with a huge head that proved last night's loss of sobriety over and over in a pounding rhythm—I knew she wasn't all that pretty. Yeah, OK, she was far from ugly; she could get most any man she wanted. That just proved the point that I'd hallucinated. She was rich, she was used to getting her way. Her whole demeanor emanated power. And last night, well, whoever I'd imagined didn't have that same power about her. She was... sweet, innocent in a funny way. She must have fulfilled some deep psychological need I had for an innocent, almost virginal woman.

Yeah, right. Real innocent. I can't forget that phantom out and out seduced me. Like a succubus. That's what she was. A succubus. An imaginary demon that sucked my soul out. Through my penis.

I got out of bed and showered, berating myself for letting a dream get to me. I looked around, but the guest bath didn't have a shaving kit. I hadn't planned to stay the night, so I lacked shaving gear. Well, time for me to head home anyway. I could leave the old man here; he'd found what he wanted. I figured they wanted me out of their hair. Him and that woman, Amber.

Time to get back to my life. Friday wasn't the greatest day for job hunting, but I'd wasted half of it with this fool's chase. At least I got a good meal last night. And twenty bucks, now the birdshit's off of it. I could fill up my car with gas and maybe have a few bucks left over. Yeah, yesterday wasn't a total waste.

I picked up my clothes to get dressed. Her camisole slipped out of the pile.

I dropped onto the bed holding the sheer material to my face. I sniffed it: just a faint scent of her.

I sighed. "Lolly."

After a moment, I dressed. I thought about stuffing the camisole in my pocket, but it made an obvious bulge. With regret, I placed it on the dresser and smoothed it down. Then I left the room, feeling better.

Loud voices echoed down the hallway. Someone sounded angry. Billy. No, he wasn't yelling, more like pleading for something, but the tiles and the stark walls in the hall distorted his words so I couldn't understand. I had almost reached the great room before I could distinguish his words.

"…never, ever do anythin' to hurt you. You know…" He stopped when he saw me. He had the look of a beaten dog. Lolly turned from him to me with cold, angry eyes. I'd stepped into some kind of bad shit here.

"Uh, morning, Billy. Is everything OK, Lolly?"

"Lolly!" she exploded, whipping around to Billy again. "You told him that, too? What kind of chamberlain are you, anyway? Am I surrounded by treason?" She stormed past Billy toward the front door.

He whined to her back all the way to the door. "Amber, never. I know how you feel about…C'mon, I didn't—" The slamming door cut him off. He threw himself into an overstuffed chair. "Shit."

"Did I do something wrong?" I asked, certain that I had. I just couldn't figure out what. I dropped onto the matching beige sofa on the other side of the coffee table.

Billy sat head bent over and studied his hands. Palm up, palm down, and then just the thumbs. Then he took several deep breaths. When he looked at me, he'd brought himself under control. His expression didn't seem normal—if I even knew what that looked like for him—but he'd lost the beaten expression. He shrugged and gave me a thin smile.

"She wanted to know what you thought a the new graphics."

"You didn't show me."

That answer animated him. "Damn straight, I didn't. Fuck that shit! I don't care who she thinks you are. We don't show development to anybody."

I knew it was my fault, somehow. And it had made him angry at me. "She got pissed? Because you didn't do what she asked?"

"Yeah. Well, no. Aw, shoot, it wasn't like I was tellin' you any deep, dark secrets. Besides, you were *her* new buddy, not mine. Look, man, she isn't embarrassed about her past. She doesn't talk about it, but when people ask, she tells 'em. Like it's somebody else she's talkin' about. But today, oh man, somethin' about it, or about me tellin' you…it set her off."

"Sorry." It was me. I was sure of it. Was she so sorry that she came to me last night?

"You didn't do anythin'," he said. "It was me."

No, I did a lot last night.

"Man, with her history I've come to expect odd behavior sometimes. But this damn thing with Merlin…" His eyes studied the corner of the room, like he was thinking something through.

I wanted to know more about Lolly, so I waited until he continued.

"She used to talk about somebody comin' for her, when we first met. Said he'd take her back to where she belonged. And it sounded like she wanted it, looked forward to it. I always thought it would be some shrink. Or maybe somebody from her childhood. Nope. Merlin's the one. He ain't no doctor, is he? How's he know her?"

I shrugged. "I met him the day before yesterday. He latched onto me."

"Is he still lookin' for Arthur? I mean, since he met Amber?"

"You heard him last night. I don't remember him talking about Arthur. Not only that, but he and," I almost said Lolly, "your partner seemed as comfortable as old friends."

There didn't seem anything else to say. We were both clueless. I began thinking this would be a good time to get unstuck from this mess. I didn't know how to bring up Lolly with Billy. Anyway, she'd gotten mad at me for some reason I couldn't fathom.

But now, Merlin had found someone else to pester. He might know approximately where I lived, but I didn't think he'd try to get back to my place again. I could go find a job. Now I'd seen an object lesson in what happens when you're unemployed for too long: Merlin, an unkempt old man who used drugs to take wild trips. Of course, he'd sent me on two of them, so I'd have to avoid any drug tests for a few weeks. Let the hallucinogens run through my system.

"So, you met Lolly?"

Billy's question caught me off guard. He tried to look nonchalant, but he glued his eyes to mine. He'd raised the exact subject that I wanted to talk about, but now I didn't know where to take it.

"Well, Amber stopped in to…uh…talk to me last night."

"She didn't call herself Amber, though."

I nodded, unsure what else to say.

He hit the arm of the chair. "Man! I shoulda thoughta that when she invited ya over. I made her promise not to seduce the employees, but she doesn't meet many other men. Except at those charity things she gives money to, and I've never seen her act up at one a those."

"She said you wouldn't let her…uh…play…with the men at work."

"Amber's a great motivator, a leader. A real Dale Carnegie. Wonderful concepts. But she doesn't know her ass from a balance sheet. So I run things. And sometimes that means keepin' Amber in line. When she gets horny, she likes to call herself Lolly."

He saw my unasked question and shrugged. "I don't know why." He shook his head. "I can't believe I'm tellin' you about this. Especially after she accused me of treason."

"Odd word." *Go on,* I thought. *Tell me more.*

"It's her fascination with this Pendragon stuff. She calls me her chamberlain. Sometimes, she calls me Chamberlain Kaye." He shrugged again. "Look, I don't know you, and I don't particularly like you. I dislike your…companion, a lot. I'd love it if you'd just take that old bastard and get outta Amber's life."

"Forget that. She can keep him."

"That's what I'm afraid of. And what about you, now that you've met Lolly?" He studied me for my reaction.

"What do you mean?"

"I mean, can ya walk away from her? Get outta Dodge?"

"She rejected me. Seemed final to me."

He didn't answer for a long minute. I began to get uncomfortable, the way he looked at me.

At last, he cleared his throat. "I guess there's stuff you need to know. Since I made her leave all the other men around her alone, I guess it's my fault she went to you. Well, as much as it sticks in my craw to tell ya about Lolly, I got ya into this and so you need to know."

He thought she came to me because she couldn't have any other man around. That hurt, but I believed it.

Billy said, "In the daytime, she's Amber. She acts like she couldn't care less about men. Sometimes I've see her lookin' at a pretty woman, and I thought maybe she, well, swung that way. But then she came on to me. Said to call her Lolly—and she didn't act a thing like the woman that I knew. Amber. But the sex was in-cred-ible. You know what I mean, don't ya?"

My face became warm.

"Yeah, I figured. The next day, I did the same thing you did. I thought we'd moved to a new level. So when we were alone, I called her Lolly. She acted clueless. When I…mentioned…the night before, she denied even seein' me. When I pointed out we'd gone horizontal, she cold-cocked me! Slugged me."

"Wow," I said.

"Yeah, wow. I was on edge like a November turkey for weeks, but we did get past it. A few months passed, and then she came to me as Lolly again, wantin' sex. As tempted as I was, and believe me, I was tempted..."

I nodded. I understood.

"Anyway, I told her that I couldn't handle it. Our partnership was too important to deal with a crazy relationship. She pouted for a while and went home. Amber never said a word about it."

"And the employees?"

"When I heard she'd slept with a coupla the programmers, I told her not to do it any more."

"You told Lolly?"

He looked rueful. "Big mistake. I told Amber. She works out. I think if she'd wanted to, she coulda beat me shitless."

I hadn't thought about her physical strength, but she had enough to secure my arms without effort.

"I had to learn her rules," Billy said. "Amber is Amber and denies she's Lolly. As you saw, she's more than a bit sensitive about it. Lolly is a sex fiend. She knows she's Amber but won't talk about it. I may be a slow learner, but I do learn. So, I waited until she became Lolly. Late one night she came on to one a the coders back in the server room. I sent him home and told Lolly she had to leave the employees alone. She cried. I mean, really flat-out bawled. She didn't mean any harm, she said. When the tears stopped, she promised she wouldn't do it again."

And that forced her to me, in desperation. That's the only reason she came to me. Because I wasn't off-limits. Lucky turn for me. It was fantastic.

"I hope she stays away from them," Billy said. "Diddlin' employees can get us in trouble."

I realized that, regardless of the reason she came to me, she could diddle me all she wanted. Left and right. Up and down. I wouldn't mind. And that maybe leaving wasn't such a good idea, after all. If she accepted everyone else as off-limits…well, I hadn't even tried dating since Janet left. And Amber…Lolly…this could get confusing.

But worth the try. Lolly was so good in bed.

"What the heck is that?"

I guess I'd been daydreaming. It took a moment for me to realize that Billy wasn't talking about Lolly any more. He'd bent over, hands on the floor and his head almost there too, looking under the sofa.

"It's a damn mouse. Look at that thing. Like he's sittin' high in the saddle."

I bent over beside him. Sure enough, a brown mouse rested beside one of the legs, in the sofa's shadow. Its eyes slid from Billy to me and back.

"Watch the critter. I'll be right back."

"What?" I looked at Billy as he turned to walk away.

"The mouse. Don't let it get away. We'll smash it."

The mouse cocked its head, its eyes following Billy as he left the room. It didn't seem to be afraid of us. When Billy moved out of sight, it looked at me. I thought mice ran when people saw them. I'd never seen one just watch. My neck tingled.

"OK, here's the plan." Billy handed me a broom. "I'm gonna chase that damn mouse out from under the couch." He brandished another broom. "It'll run along the wall there, so you pound him when he runs by."

I moved to where he pointed, not sure I liked his plan.

He swatted his broom at the mouse, but it just moved farther back under the couch. He bent down and swung again. I couldn't see the mouse now, but it didn't come running out. Billy swung again, losing his balance and falling onto the floor. Then the mouse came to the end of the sofa closest to me. It cocked its head at Billy, then studied the whole room.

Billy poked his broom at the mouse and it bolted. I waited for it, but it didn't go along the wall. It ran outside the front leg of the couch. Then it veered toward Billy as he lay on the floor. Billy rolled away, screaming, dropping his broom. The mouse streaked across a throw rug to the other side of the room. It stopped in the middle of a wall, with nothing to either side.

"We've got that little turd now. He's so confused, just look at him. We'll rush him from both sides and bash his brains to bits."

That sounded like a plan. We came at it from the two sides. About a 60 degree angle with the mouse at the vertex, I'd say. Being an engineer, I notice things like that.

We rushed the mouse. We both stepped on the throw rug at the same time, about three feet apart and moving fast. Just then, the mouse bolted between us. Bisecting that angle. We both tried to stop and turn to hit the mouse as it ran between us.

The rug slid.

My broom slapped Billy in the head.

His whacked me on the ass.

We both tumbled to the floor—arms, legs and broomsticks entangled.

The mouse was back under the sofa where it had started. Watching us.

"What do you fools do with my mouse?" Merlin called from the patio door.

Billy muttered, "Dammit to hell."

I wouldn't have heard if his head hadn't been half under my shoulder on the floor.

He slunk up off the floor, and then picked up speed heading for the front door, calling back over his shoulder, "I gotta get to work."

I sat up on the floor. "Your mouse. Why am I not surprised?" I thought about how unkempt his beard had been when we first met. *I bet that's the mouse house.*

Merlin ignored me, stooping to reach under the sofa. The mouse jumped onto his hand, and Merlin stroked it as he walked to the fireplace. He placed the mouse on the mantel. It rose on its hind legs and, I kid you not, bowed to the old man.

"You can't leave that filthy thing in the house. Women don't like mice."

Merlin regarded me with downturned brows. "Are all people so foolish in this time? Or are the two of you exemplars of the extreme?"

"What?" He hadn't insulted me in almost half a day. Seemed like he'd been saving up. Even the mouse looked at me like I was stupid.

"I shall need your help tonight. I will perform a ceremony to send Arthur back. It shall be much easier on the eve of Samhain."

The old man's conversation gave me mental whiplash again.

"You found Arthur? Where is he?"

"Ambrosius."

"Amber knew where he was?"

"Ambrosius is Arthur."

"Oh, bullshit! Amber, Lolly, Arthur, what kind of game is this? You're crazy, old man, and there's no way I'm helping you do shit."

Merlin raised his eyebrows and grimaced. "I have no time for you. The mouse shall explain."

He flipped his arm at me and I fell to the floor.

CHAPTER

10

It's dark and close. I'm comfortable, curled inside something like a big bag. Muffled sounds, loud and unrecognizable, come from outside the cloth bag. They don't concern me, though.

What am I this time? Oh, right. "Let the mouse explain," he said. I'm a mouse.

A crack of light appears above me, and the sound level rises. Then something blocks the light; the thing comes into the bag and squeezes me around the middle. I have a moment of panic until I recognize a familiar smell, an aroma of dried grasses. And beneath that, a faint smell of fish. I relax. The grip on my body is firm, but not tight, while it lifts me out of the sack.

When I break into the open, I'm suspended high above the floor. This is like the hawk flying over fields but without wings. I want to scream in terror, but another part of me feels no fear, and I don't make a sound. I'm lifted onto a long, narrow platform with a wall behind it, and the hand—the huge gnarled thing that holds me—the hand opens. I scurry out of the open palm and run to the end of the platform, dodging several large objects. Then I turn and run to the other end. It seems about a forty-foot sprint, but it can't be that long. My mouse legs are grateful for the exercise. I settle in the middle of the platform and turn to face the open space beyond.

The noises have coalesced into voices, a man and a woman. I recognize the man as my master, but I don't know the woman.

Master? No, that's Merlin. That old crank is anything but my master. And the woman is Amber. This is her office at Pendragon. I'm sitting on the display shelf with the bust and plaques and framed coins.

Why can't I control my body?

Oh, this is like the hallucination where I occupied a bird. I'm just along for the ride. This is his idea of explaining Amber-Lolly-Arthur to me. Well, I'm not playing.

Let me out. Now.

I didn't make any noise, did I? I screamed as loud as I could, but no noise came out.

A playback. Not like the fish. This is a playback, and I can't influence it. And if Merlin can hear me, he's not going to let me out anyway. I should've killed his damn mouse.

Merlin mentions my name and something about threads. Always with the threads.

Well, I'd better listen. He might say something else about me.

"There are so many threads in this time, but so little magic," Merlin says. "I followed yours across the ocean. It stood out from all others. In this city, the quest grew more difficult. Yours entangled with his. It led me to him, but I could not follow the thread from him to you. I had to command his help. That effort drained the little reserve I had rebuilt."

Amber perches on the edge of her desk. "There are people who claim the power, but I've yet to see anyone turn the weather."

Turn the weather?

"Even for one attuned, it required all my power. All my reserves. I had no place to replenish. I am spent."

"You survived. Fifteen centuries. Why didn't you come to me sooner?"

Survived fifteen centuries? What's she talking about? Are they both crazy?

I rise on my haunches and sniff the air. No, that's the mouse moving. I smell a faint aroma. Food. Where is it?

Merlin bows his head. "Sorry, my liege. This sleep lasted much longer than any other. I had not anticipated a need to persevere for such a long time. A body must revivify after such a long sleep, and I had little reserve. All my power went to turning Nimuë's spell from death to hibernation. The time of sleep did not contravene her intention, but the waking did. After that came the matter of nourishing the flesh and restoring enough power to travel. Some years passed before I could leave my cave."

"Nimuë. That bitch."

A bittersweet smile crosses Merlin's face. "You speak ill of the woman I loved."

"The woman who wanted to kill you. And if I understand what you've told me, she wanted to kill me too."

"No, Nimuë would not kill a king. That is the task of the warrior, not the druid. She could not heal you, and she feared your mind would die before I arrived to help. Nimuë thought to help you, Arthur, her High King."

OK, I heard the name Arthur. A king. Someone wanted to kill the king and Amber, too?

"She did not act alone."

"True. Morgayne and Elaine joined with her. It took the three to complete the magic, and each contributed to the spell."

"Morgayne hates me," Amber says. "Rather, she hated me."

"Had Morgayne acted alone, I agree that woman would have killed you, or tried such. Her bitter hatred exceeded her bonds to druid philosophy. But never would Elaine have harmed you, nor would Nimuë. You were their king."

What? Wait. Amber, the king?

Merlin thinks for a moment, and then continues. "The spell comprised a song of three voices. To me Nimuë explained what she knew of it, and I have since spent over a millennium decoding it. The ladies cast your essence into the Aether to preserve it from the severe damage to your head. Nimuë left a clear path back to your corporeal body and taught me the triggering spell. Morgayne made your exit from the Aether difficult—she perhaps hoped her conditions could never be fulfilled, but as we both perceive, they have."

What's this new age gobbledygook? Who are these women?

Amber brings her hands up to the level of her chest, and then lowers them to her thighs, presenting her body. "And why am I a woman?"

You're Lolly! I know you're a woman. Why do you think you were this man King Arthur?

"I had not foreseen that. My first thought credits Elaine. The curse is subtle; she possessed a wish for you to learn a lesson."

"What would she teach me?"

My mouse nose twitches again. Now I know what I smell: cheese. My eyes dart around the room, searching for the food. I don't see it.

"Consider. In this trio, Nimuë provided healing. Her portion of the spell concentrated on protecting the mind and keeping the body safe. Morgayne's power removed your essence and cast it into the Aether. She also composed the conditions for return from the Aether to the physical world. Over a millennium, I came to understand her conditions and to realize she hoped they would not be satisfied. She stipulated a requirement for the body that could draw you from the Aether. That body had to be functional, but without a commanding presence—without a mind in control."

Ether? Are they talking about some kind of medical procedure. Is Amber transgender?

She says, "I would call that an impossibility. Without a mind, how does the body remain functional? Yet, here I am."

"I have examined the song they sang for you many times over the centuries," Merlin says. "Only now do I understand the descant which Elaine wove into the refrain. This mindless body must be that of a mature woman."

"But why? What did she wish to teach me?"

"Elaine wished for you to live as a woman. She wished for you to learn the result of the changes you wrought."

I wander along the shelf, sniffing. Where is the cheese I smell?

This mouse has a one-track mind.

"I still don't understand," Amber says.

"She did not like the role you created for women."

Amber pounds on her desk and rises. "That's absurd. I protected women. It occupied an important place in the code for my warriors."

Merlin shrugs. *"Some did not see it so. For the female druids, Elaine in particular, your protections removed ancient authority. The new Christ church persecuted druids, and in particular it objected to female druids. As king, you supported, even encouraged that church."*

"I didn't hew to everything the church said. I valued the old ways, too. Our relationship is ample evidence of that. But the old ways of the druid were disappearing. Blame four hundred years of Roman rule. They brought the new religion. Elaine and Nimuë had no quarrel with me. And Morgayne's anger ran deeper than a simple turning of the tables, making me a woman."

I reach the end of the shelf. No cheese this way. I turn and scamper to the other end, sniffing for food.

Merlin says, *"You were a great warrior and Arthur, a great king. But you chose not to examine certain things. For followers of the ancient ways, women had been equal leaders. Druids and queens. Surely you see that women lost a large part of their role in society? Their station changed."*

There it is again. He's calling Amber Arthur.

"Look at me, Merlin." Her smile is ironic. *"I am a woman in this society, with money and power, and no man controlling my destiny."*

"I see that. But you are a man in a woman's body."

Still that. How crazy are they?

"True. And I was a king, accustomed to wielding power. But had these changes Elaine disliked not occurred, it would have made no difference. After all, there are other women in positions of power. In government and in industry."

"Equal to men?"

"Some. Not all, but reaching for it."

Merlin strokes his beard. *"I have awakened many times through the years. Never to full life; I could not bend Nimuë's enchantment that much. But I could become conscious enough."*

He walks toward me and reaches out a hand to stroke the back of my neck. Despite myself, I thrill at the contact.

"I could captivate mice, other rodents, and, on occasion, birds who ventured into my cave tomb. And through them, I watched the changes

history brought to our beautiful land. Every hundred years or so, I became more aware for a time. Always, your thread remained in the Aether, so I cast my attentions to my surroundings. I learnt this damnable Anglisc tongue that displaced our own and the Latin of our Roman overlords. I learnt of the Norsemen who came later, and the French who came later still and conquered the English. And I mourned the loss of magic in the land. Even magic atrophies without use and attention."

Feed me, master.

He sighs, turning back to Amber.

"But I saw the treatment men gave women. Many times they had less status than a milk cow. You say things are different now. Perhaps they are. But you could have kept their status in your own time. Who knows what changes that would have wrought over the centuries?"

"So," Amber says, "I'm a woman to experience my own degradation of the fair sex?"

I'll just roll with this and see where their delusion goes.

"I now believe such was Elaine's desire," Merlin says.

"I'm pleased to say that she failed. I'm a successful businesswoman in this time. I have created a good life." She stares out the window. "But now, you're here to take me back."

"You have a destiny to fulfill in your own time."

She turns back, reaching to the old man. "I wanted you to come and take me back. I thought of nothing else during the first days here, and you remained my hope for months leading to years."

He nods. "And now I am here."

Amber collapses back onto the edge of her desk. Her sad voice entreats Merlin. "Tell me what happened to my kingdom."

"You do not know?"

My master removes something from his pocket. Yes! Cheese! As Amber talks, he crumbles a piece of hard cheese in front of me. Oh, glorious food. I eat. My human mind recognizes the sight of bleu cheese, while the mouse delights in the strong aroma.

She says, "I've searched. There are no records of my rule. A few mentions here and there of battles I led. I found scant information about my time as Ambrosius, before I became High King, Arthur. But about that time, about the name Arthur, nothing, despite the enormous assets I've had to expend in my search. Not just personal wealth—because of my game, I had the resources of my company. We paid academics to look. How can there be nothing about me, about my reign?"

"Have you read the work of Geoffrey, a monk of Monmouth? He wrote of you in the twelfth century. No? Or a scoundrel named Mallory, who created fantasies later?"

"I've seen many obscure works, but I know neither of those names."

"Curious." Merlin's eyebrows rise and lower several times as he rotates his staff in one hand. "When I awoke through the years, I heard their tales. Their stories had a bare grain of truth to them, but they were oft repeated. Your story inspired generations of young men. Yet, neither you nor anyone else I have asked in this time knows of that life you led, or of these old tales. I have to think on this. Perhaps your very presence in this time has distorted history."

"So, tell me. After you send me back, what becomes of me? And my land? What is my lifetime?"

Merlin lowers his eyebrows and squints at Amber. "That will I not tell you."

"I am your king. I could command it."

"No. There are things a king may not command of a druid. You must consider this to be among those things. You shall not know your own future from anything I say or do."

"Is there glory in my destiny? You learned to speak English, so the Saxons won, anyway."

"Then already have I said too much."

"Must I give up the good life I've made here? What difference does it make?"

"It is your destiny. It is already done. This is the interim."

"When will you send me back?"

"Samhain approaches. That is the night to send your essence to rejoin your body."

Amber nods. *"Yes, Halloween. It shall be easier when the doorway between worlds opens."*

CHAPTER
11

MY HEAD HURT. I must have cracked it on the floor.

Damn Merlin, sending me into these visions without any warning. Where'd that old bastard go?

At least I landed on the rug. If I'd fallen on the tile, my head might've popped right open.

Why did he do this to me?

The room was empty, and I couldn't see the old fart out the patio door. I roamed through the house. Noises drew me to the kitchen. A Latina wearing an apron stood at the stove. I didn't smell anything, so she must've just started cooking.

The kitchen had a full complement of appliances, but with an impersonal decor. Only the hired help cooked in here.

"Um, where is everyone?"

"The lady, she is in gym."

"Anyone else around?"

She smiled and shrugged her shoulder. The oven timer dinged, and she turned back to her cooking.

"The gym? Which way?"

She didn't turn to look at me but reached behind with a spoon extended, and then tipped the bowl of it downward emphatically.

"There's a basement?"

The spoon waggled up and down. I took that as a yes.

I hadn't seen any stairs when I left the bedroom this morning. The only option seemed to be to check by the front door. The spacious foyer opened two stories tall, unlike the rest of the house. Beveled glass panes rose on both sides of the front door, the full height of the room. A crystal chandelier dominated the space, reflecting in mirrors on the sides of the room. The surfaces without glass or mirror were heavy, dark mahogany. Display cabinets faced the door, filling the upper section of the wall. They contained swords and shields polished to a high sheen. A heavy wooden table commanded the space beneath the cabinets, topped with a huge bouquet in a crystal vase. Opulent. I couldn't think of a better word.

The room was symmetric. Another passage balanced the one I stood in, and I followed it to a half bath and, beyond that, to steps leading down to the basement. I saw another room farther down the hall, but I didn't snoop into there. As I turned the corner at the stair landing, I heard thwacking. The sound repeated twice before I got to the bottom of the stairs and saw her.

Amber wore a heavy leather vest and leggings and wielded a sword, swinging at a leather-padded mannequin. She struck it on one of its outstretched arms, and the mannequin spun on a post.

Other equipment filled the room. I recognized an iron horse, parallel bars, rings suspended from the ten-foot ceiling, a treadmill, several other dummies in various poses, tumbling pads, weights, but also some devices whose names or uses I couldn't even guess at. A few swords in scabbards hung from a wooden rack. One entire wall of glass faced onto a small grassy area surrounded by thick bramble-filled woods.

She continued to whack the mannequin, sometimes hitting twice in rapid succession. I detected no wasted movement. I'd never handled a sword and wouldn't know how to swing one. But I could tell that she was skilled at this. Efficient, powerful strokes pummeled the dummy.

When she stopped for a moment, I cleared my throat to get her attention.

She spun around, sword at the ready. "You! What are you doing here?"

Still pissed. And I still didn't know why.

"Uh. No car, remember? It's over at your office."

"You should've gone with Billy. He left over an hour ago."

Right. I could've gone with Billy. It'd never crossed my mind. Because, I realized, I wanted to talk about last night. About Lolly.

"Merlin wants me to help him tonight." *Coward. Ask about Lolly.*

She began thrusting the sword at the dummy closest to me, this one suspended by chains. I felt ignored, like she was accustomed to having people around and had grown indifferent to their presence. My presence.

"I'm kind of confused about something."

She didn't react, just parried as the dummy swung her way.

"Merlin says you're this person Arthur that he's been looking for. The king."

She danced around the swaying mannequin, thrusting first at the head, then the heart.

"Who are you? I mean, one minute you're Amber, then you're Arthur, and sometimes you're Lolly. Which—"

She reacted before I could register it. She spun from her stance toward the dummy to face me, and after two rapid steps the sword sang toward my head. Before I even sensed danger, she'd buried the sword in the plasterboard with an edge resting against my left ear. The ringing sound of the steel made me realize how narrow the boundary between existence and not could be.

"Were I lord in this dominion, you would be dead." Her eyes blazed as she yanked the sword from the wall.

I didn't know what to say, so I said nothing. My eyes had opened wider than they had ever been, so I didn't blink. I feared movement might excite her more, so I didn't breathe.

Anger drained from her eyes, and she lowered the sword.

"I am Arthur Ambrosius, named King of the Britons, Lord of Dubonni, Overlord of the Dumnonii, Silures, Catuvellauni and Cornovii, Protector of Armorica, and on and on." Her recitation trailed out at the end. Perhaps because she knew the litany of titles meant nothing to me.

I blinked and I began breathing again. But I didn't move.

She sighed. "I was born Ambrosius Aurelius, son of a proconsul, a Roman military overlord. Some of the soldiers called my family Pendragon. When I discovered myself in this body and not a king, I took back the name Ambrosius. But in a female body I became Ambrosia. Whence Amber. See how the mighty are fallen."

"I see." I didn't. Well, her gobbledygook sounded consistent with what I'd learned in Merlin's mouse, anyway. But I didn't care about the Arthur part. I cared about the Lolly part.

I took a step up the stairs.

"Please don't swing that thing at me again, but last night," better to stay away from the sex part for a minute, if she thinks she's a man in a woman's body, "you asked me to call you Lolly. Why?"

Her back stiffened; a bit of the fury returned. "Did Billy tell you to call me Lolly?"

"No. No. After you stormed out—uh, left—this morning, he told me not to. But I have to know. Aren't you also Lolly? I mean, in addition to being Arthur and, uh, Ambrosia Orleans."

"Ambrosius Aurelius. Names are important." She glared at me. "Merlin said you were a fool. How he picked you to help, I cannot fathom."

"You made yourself clear last night. *Call me Lolly.* I remember. You told me several times."

She turned from me, pacing among the practice dummies. I wasn't sure whether she would answer me or ignore me. Or attack me. But I felt a need to know.

She stopped behind a mannequin that held a round leather shield. With the dummy separating us, she turned and faced me.

"Who are you? I should throw you out of my house, but something prevents me. I should thrash you for your effrontery, but I do not. Why? What power do you have?"

I couldn't help laughing. Perhaps not the best idea, because her eyebrows dropped to a mean line and her sword arm flexed.

"Sorry." I held up my hands, palms forward, to calm her. "To me, it's such a strange question. I'm an unemployed petroleum engineer, recently divorced, pretty much dead broke, with so few friends that no one would even notice if I left town. Except the apartment manager, but she'd just rent to someone else. I'm so far from anyone important, or powerful, that your question made me laugh." *Otherwise, I'd cry.*

She thought about this for a minute. "There are other kinds of power. You have something."

I shrugged. "So, let me apply this power of mine to ask you again. Aren't you also called Lolly?"

"Pestering ass, aren't you?"

"I guess it's important to me."

"OK. You aren't the first to call me Lolly. Nor was Billy."

She leaned against the iron horse. "There are so many things I don't understand about being here in this time; I've always just thrown that one into the mix. I guess it's something else those witches did to me when they sent me here."

She pushed away and stared at her sword. "And now, I don't know why I'm telling you this. I don't even talk to Billy about it any more."

"Let's just chalk it up to this power I have over you." I smiled, hoping she'd take it as a joke.

She didn't like the joke. But, she kept talking.

"I've read about multiple personalities." She looked at me across several pieces of equipment. "Of course, I've studied it. I guess being sent ahead fifteen hundred years into another body does qualify as a trauma to the psyche. But it just doesn't seem right. I'm not some teenager going through puberty. I'm an almost fifty year-old man. Well, I was. Now I seem to be a woman in her thirties, but I still have the mind of a mature man. Split personality just doesn't seem to fit."

"So you don't remember talking to me last night. You don't remember asking me to call you Lolly?"

"I never have," she insisted. "Never with anyone else, either."

This was one screwed up lady. Lolly acted free and happy. Amber claimed the title of most uptight bitch. Seemed like a classic split personality to me. Not that I knew much more than what I saw in movies.

"Can I talk with Lolly now?" I don't know why I said that. I guess I thought I could just call her.

"What?" Her eyes shrunk to beads, framed by lowered brows above and the grim line of her mouth below.

Merlin called me a fool. Maybe I am. But for once in my life, I felt something important happening to me here, and I felt compelled to play it out.

"Let Lolly come out. I want to talk with her."

I saw her weapon arm flex again. I didn't think she'd hurt me, but I couldn't be sure. She stood partway across the room, behind several dummies and the iron horse. I was already on the first step of the stairs. I thought I could get out in time if she rushed me. I backed one more step up the stairs.

Then I couldn't help it. I pushed it too far. "Last night, the sex with Lolly was incredible."

Raw fury. Her face screwed up and she spun at me, flexing her arm as she had the first time she threw the sword. I backed up another step.

Her arm stiffened awkwardly and her face roiled with uncontrolled anger. Rage interfered with her battle grace as she strode toward me, some steps smooth and others stiff. She stumbled into the dummy's arm and then smacked it out of the way. I took another step back up the stairs. Before I could turn to flee, she threw the sword at me. It went wild and I ducked to one side, but it ripped across my shoulder, knocking me onto the steps. My shoulder hurt like blazes, and I couldn't get any purchase with my feet. I tried scrabbling up the stairs, missing because I couldn't take my eyes off the danger streaking toward me.

Now Amber moved like a cat. Deadly purpose had replaced the boiling fury. Her eyes held no pity, only insulted anger. She reached for my shoulders, dragging me back down the few precious steps I had managed to get up. Her incredible strength overwhelmed me. She shook me and then threw me against the wall. My head banged, and by the time I could focus again, she had pulled the sword out of the wall again and held it two-handed with deft precision, ready to strike me.

Her arms drooped before they began to swing. One arm fell away from the sword handle, twitching. Her mouth twisted to the left, then to the right, and her eyes lost their death-giving focus on me. The look of raw fury returned, replaced quickly by a soft look. Then her eyes hardened and her left hand floated toward the sword. Before she could reach the haft, her face relaxed and she looked at me with softened eyes. I hadn't seen her face well in the dark last night, but something about the look made me think...

"Lolly?"

The out-of-control, raw expression returned. But for some reason, she turned the anger away from me. She flailed at the dummies, but with none of the efficiency I'd seen before. She hit them hard. But she drew back too far, off balance, and when she swung at a dummy, her arm flew wild. She hit a dummy's arm, the stomach, the head. Glancing blows mixed with dead-on strikes. She knocked things over. Her recovery lagged. Her anger had stolen the finer points of her skill.

I tried to get up, to get away from this feral fury, but my legs had gone limp and my arms still quaked from her throwing me at the wall. At least she seemed to have forgotten about me. I slid to the floor, watching her mad display.

I really was an impulsive fool.

I rubbed the shoulder the sword had hit. It had ripped my shirt from the neck to my upper arm. There didn't seem to be blood anywhere, but I knew I'd have a huge bruise. I'd be lucky if any part of me wasn't black and blue. This lady embodied danger. I've never been close to death before, but I'd been there twice in ten minutes.

She pounded the sword time and again on a padded bar, similar to the iron horses but covered with leather. I could see now why my arm, or head, hadn't been sliced off. The blade was dull. Despite her slicing at the horse with the edge, the tough leather showed only small dents.

In profile, with her face screwed into a scowl, I didn't recognize either Amber or Lolly in this woman. With one last harsh strike at the leather, her fury was spent. Her arms dropped to her side, the sword fell to the floor. Her breath came in rapid gasps and her face began to relax. But who would she be? I hoped for Lolly. But as I thought that, I knew it wouldn't be her. I'd been more foolish than I thought in asking for her. She'd come to me last night, and Billy said he'd seen her at night. When Amber slept.

Lolly must be the weaker personality. And was this furious person Amber? It didn't seem to be, but what did I know?

The woman looked around the room. I recognized the focus and power that I'd seen in Amber. I tried to rise again, to leave her presence, but I couldn't. My movement drew her attention.

"Did I do this?" She waved her arm at the room. Most of the equipment had been pushed out of place; several of the lighter pieces had been knocked over.

I nodded, ever so slightly.

She slumped against the leather-clad horse. "I am bonkers. Stark raving mad."

I was inclined to agree, but kept my mouth shut. Maybe I'd spent my foolish streak.

She looked at me closely for the first time since her wild assault. She gathered herself and strode toward me. I tried to scramble back up the staircase.

"No, it's OK." She made calming patting movements in the air.

It didn't reassure me.

"Did I do this? Yes, it's foggy, but I think I remember. Throwing the sword at you. I remember bouncing you into the wall. I am so sorry. It's unlike me to attack an unarmed man. I'm not going to hurt you."

She stooped down, pulling my hand away from my sore shoulder. She examined my body. Quick but practiced. She had experience with wounds. "Bruised, but not broken."

I had felt her strength before. I was in no condition to fight her now.

She tilted my head back and looked at my eyes, having me look left and right. "Shock. Your head is also bruised but not broken. Anything else?"

"My back. When you threw me against the wall."

"Lean forward. Does that hurt?"

I shook my head. The ache ran deep, but I felt no sharp pain where she pressed.

"What's this?" She put her hand on my shoulder blade. I knew what she meant, and I felt her hand cupping around it like she didn't want to touch it.

"It's a birthmark." I shook free of her.

"Has it always had this shape?"

It formed an acorn that pointed to my shoulder. It even had a larger splotch at the wide part that resembled a woody cupule.

"So my father told me. His uncle had it, except it pointed a different direction. Dad told me it shows up every few generations."

"Now I see why I am restrained from throwing you out. And why Merlin keeps you around."

"The birthmark? Merlin's never seen me without my shirt."

"Perhaps not. But Merlin can see things others can't. The acorn, it's...well, not exactly sacred, but special to the druids. They say it has power."

"Druids?" *Crazies who play at magic.*

"Merlin hasn't told you? He's an important druid. Well, he was in our day."

There we had it. Amber had multiple personalities and Merlin was delusional. They must've spent a lot of time together back in that hospital.

"I guess I'll have to put up with you, for Merlin's sake. But, no more mention of the other woman to me."

"I think I'll just be going." Yep, time to get out of there.

She shrugged and left me lying there. She called back down the stairs. "Lunch should be ready. You're welcome to stay and eat."

I stayed for lunch. I didn't want to, but what else could I do, call a cab? I had no money. Twenty birdshit bucks.

Merlin got into an argument with Amber, but he called her Ambrosius, and sometimes he called her Arthur. It seemed that she...he...oh, what the heck. She looked like a woman, so she was a she. I let their conversation roll over me. I caught the gist but wasn't in the mood to pay close attention. It seemed that Amber had second thoughts about going back.

"Life is easier here, more settled," she told him. "There isn't a constant threat of war. Here, I have money and enough power to be comfortable. And frankly, being a king isn't all it's cracked up to be."

She drank her tea.

"I've done that," she said with a wry smile.

Merlin kept interrupting, telling her that her destiny wasn't here and now. That the world wasn't right with her here. She scoffed at that. She was here, she said, so the world must be how it must be. And it would have to stay that way, because she planned to stay here.

I thought the whole argument went beyond the verge of crazy, but I'd come to expect that from them. They had the air of old friends who always bicker. Loony-bin friends.

I began to think that maybe Amber got savvy enough to fake her way out of the hospital. Billy sure seemed to think she was on the up and up. Of course, she came to him with lots of money and an interest in investing in his company, so he could be biased.

As for Merlin, I figured he just escaped. I could see him running away because the hospital found his mouse and threatened to kill it.

Thoughts of the mouse made me look around. I found it sitting in the corner of the room, nibbling on a piece of bread. It looked like it was watching Merlin and Amber argue.

I wondered what it would be like to have a mouse hallucination, but not a playback like before. The mouse looked at me and I mouthed, "How about it, mouse?"

CHAPTER

12

I'm chewing something soft.

No, that's not right, I'm eating tomato soup.

How did I get onto the floor? There's Merlin and Amber, still arguing, and on the other side of the table is…omigod…that's me! Staring into my soup. Head supported by an arm, just staring.

I'm in the mouse.

I swallow the bread and, without thinking about it, start licking my paws. The little crumbs in the fur taste pretty good. There's an underlying flavor of cheese. Must've been from Merlin. I guess the mouse finished the cheese first, because it left a strong smell on my fur. And now, I'm tasting it. Neat.

I lift my nose and sniff. Amazing. I can smell the tomato soup from over here. And an aroma that my mouse brain identifies as its master. Merlin's sweat smell is distinct. And there, it's faint now, but I recognize the fishy smell he had when we first met.

I'm going to take this slow and easy. Don't want to panic like I did with the fish. I'm not going to think about how to do things, just what to do. Like, I want to run to the other corner.

Wow, I'm off. Skittering along on four legs. I run fast. What a great feeling. There's none of that discomfort of trying to scamper on hands and knees. All four legs move in harmony. Running is good.

I touch my nose to the wall, sniffing a bit of ammonia on the baseboard. Must be nice to have a maid to keep the place summer fresh year-round.

Now, back to where I started. I spin around and fly across the floor. My muscles are all working together. My four legs, not two legs, are doing just what they were designed to do.

Hey, it'd be neat to slide into the corner.

My legs go limp and I tumble over, rolling into the wall. Not what I had in mind. I guess I tried too hard.

I let the mouse sit back up. My adventure didn't interrupt the bickering between the loonies. I'm still staring into my soup. I can see that my body is breathing, so I decide not to worry about it.

Can I understand what they're saying? I haven't been paying any attention to them, but in the other visions I could understand the people. I concentrate on the noises they're making and try to turn them into words. Sure enough, I can understand them.

"Fate, Merlin? How can you argue for fate? You've always agreed with Pelagius. We have free will. We make our future; there is no inalterable plan."

"Pelagius would have been a wise druid. He took our concepts and translated them for the Christians." *Merlin bends down and tosses a crust of bread toward me.* "But the issue is more subtle than that, and you know it."

I sniff the bread. What a delightful aroma. It's coated with toasted sesame seeds. I crunch into one of them with a passion, and then take my time chewing the rest of the crumb.

"This is a different time, Merlin. And a different country. Here and now, people are taught to think for themselves and to make their own future. A man—a woman—can be anything she can make herself into."

"It is a different time, Arthur Ambrosius. But it is not yours."

"So you say." *She sops up the last of her soup with a slice of bread. I watch her to see if I'll get another treat. She eats it her selfish self.*

"Are you happy, Ambrosius? In a woman's body?"

Amber glares at him.

He continues, "You cannot make love to Guinevere. Even were she here, you could not."

At this, her gaze softens and she smiles at the old man. "There are things women can do with women, Merlin. I know that you are aware of that."

"Have you?"

Her smile fades, and she looks down and shakes her head.

"I thought not. It is not in you to be a woman with another woman. You are a man, but more. You are Arthur, the High King. You command men. And yes, you lead them to war. But you win."

She speaks to the table, a hint of anger in her voice, "I did not win in Gaul. I almost died."

Gaul? That's France. How did she almost die in France?

"Perchance you would have died, had not Nimuë interceded."

She looks at Merlin in defiance. "In that time, I did die. I felt it."

"You did not. I spoke with you, both before and after your return to Britain. After the treachery in Gaul."

"Impossible. I came here instead."

"And back shall you go, to fulfill your destiny."

"Again, fate. What is my destiny?"

"To go back. Beyond that, I cannot tell you."

Amber sits for a minute, thinking something through.

"Tell me, Merlin. In your view, I came here and went back. That means that I knew Nimuë would trap you in a cave and leave you in a sleep near death. Did I warn you?"

The old man looks into her eyes. "When I asked what happened, what Nimuë and the others had done to you, you told me that they sent you away, but I brought you back. And you told me: persevere."

"Persevere?"

"Fifteen hundred years is a long time. Had I known, I might not have woven my own spell in with hers. Then, truly, you would remain here. And I should sleep as though dead until the world ended."

"One word, huh? Persevere." She exaggerates the word, like she's rolling it over in her mind.

"I had no more right to know my future than you have to know yours. You will remember that."

"Merlin, I cannot count the number of times you foretold the future. Even your own."

"Prophecies are not fact. You should know that. They are intentionally obscure."

"Intentionally? Now you tell me." Her lips form a rueful smile.

"This time I do know your future, because I have lived it. And you, yourself, must go live it."

"And I will be happy there? And make love with Guinevere?"

"You shall fulfill your destiny."

"Damn you, Merlin. You are as maddening as ever."

That makes me laugh. Except, coming from the mouse's mouth, it doesn't sound much like a laugh.

Merlin looks over at me. At the mouse, I mean. He looks confused. He glances back at Amber, and then at me, I mean, my body.

Crap, he's about to figure me out. I'd better get out of here.

CHAPTER 13

THE SOUP HAD formed a scum on top while I controlled the mouse.

Oh, wow! I did that on my own. Into the mouse and back again.

No way. I'd just been sitting here, daydreaming the whole thing. Letting my soup get cold.

I looked at the mouse. Just in case the vision had happened, I sneaked it a crumb while Amber had Merlin's attention.

"One thing more, druid." Amber rose from the table. "Why did you keep your…friend's power a secret from me?"

Amber glared at the old man, who looked from her back to me. Deepened lines around his eyes showed his uncertainty.

He turned back to Amber. "What power, my king?"

"I saw the mark on his back." She waved an arm in my direction.

Merlin looked at me once more, then back at Amber. His utter befuddlement broke through her anger.

"By the lady." She chuckled. "You don't know, do you? I was going to throw him out, but in the circumstances, I suppose you'll need him. I'm going to the office." Amber left the room, still laughing and shaking her head. "He didn't know. Some magician."

Merlin pushed his chair back and came around the table toward me. His lips moved, but no sound came out. He clenched and unclenched his left hand, while his right seemed to be forming sign-language symbols.

I didn't know whether to laugh, like Amber, because he looked ridiculous, or shrink from his intensity. By the time he got to my side of the table, my body decided for me. I shrank. He didn't look like the frail old man I'd met two days ago.

He pulled my shoulder forward and pushed my torn shirt away. I heard a quick intake of breath, and then his fingers began probing my back, at and about the birthmark.

"Did your father have one of these?" he asked.

I didn't want to answer, but he gave me one of his intense looks. "No."

His eyebrows shot up.

I sighed. "His uncle had it."

He stopped poking my shoulder and stared at my face. "And the varicolored eyes? Also the father's uncle?" He began stretching the skin around my eyes, first one, then the other.

His presumption overcame my uncertainty. I pushed his hand away from my face. "No."

His hand hovered where I left it. "Others of your father's kin?"

"Never heard of anything like that in my father's family." His interest in my deformities annoyed me.

He straightened up, hands dropping to his sides. "You are certain of that history?"

"Of course. It's not the kind of thing that goes unnoticed, and I wouldn't have forgotten."

He continued to study my eyes from a distance.

I sighed. It wasn't a secret; I just didn't like it. "The eyes came from my mother's father."

Merlin dropped into a chair, sucking in his breath as he hit.

"So," he said. "So you are a confluence. Most fortunate."

"What's that? Some psych-ward term for freak? Because I remember how the kids treated me growing up. A freaking confluence. The only thing fortunate about my life is that I've survived it. It was bad enough with the eyes. Can't hide that, but eventually the kids get bored with it. Not the acorn. I tried to keep my shirt on all the time, but can't do that in gym class. If it had been just a blotch, they would've dropped that, too. But it is so clearly, so cleanly, an acorn. Nut job. That was me."

"This explains many things."

"Explains…Piss on you!"

The crazy old man didn't even listen to me. He held a deep—and I'm sure, insignificant—discussion with himself. His mouth moved and his hand made signs. Must be how he managed both sides of the conversation.

Amber came through the room, tossing a blue pullover shirt at me. "That should fit," she said. She went to the foyer, but I didn't hear the front door open.

This is ridiculous, I thought as I changed shirts. *What am I doing still hanging out here?*

No cab fare. No, that wasn't the only thing. Lolly. That's why I stayed here. I had connected with one of those split personalities in that woman's body. More than just sex. Well, the sex was great, but the connection went deeper. It was crazy. I'd just met her. We had sex. Well, twice. Still…

Maybe the old fart could tell me more about her.

"You want to explain something? Then explain your friend's split personalities." There. Couldn't get much more direct than that.

"What?" He stopped signing.

"Arthur. Amber. Lolly. Tell me about her."

"Interesting. I feel coerced to answer. I do not understand how I could have missed it before. I knew the compulsion could work both ways, but there is so little magic here that I did not expect any ripples from your side. I should have examined you better. I should have seen your sigils. But it is easy to resist, now I know of it."

"What are you talking about?"

"And yet, I explain to you that which I have no intention to discuss. Perhaps the compulsion is not so easy to resist."

What a frustrating old fool. "Are you trying to change the subject? I want to know about the personalities in that woman's body."

"You would like an explanation. It seems that I must," he said. "Momentous times. The great Roman Empire was falling. You know of the Roman Empire?"

"Of course. What kind of uneducated fool do you take me for?" I thought again that he wanted to change the subject.

"Gaul, what later became France, became overrun by barbarians. Rome found itself threatened. Of course, later she fell." He paused. "Rome left Britain to defend herself against enemies in every direction. Into such a world was Ambrosius born."

The two of them had developed an elaborate fantasy world. I wasn't interested in any of it.

"What about Lolly?"

"Ah. Cut to the chase. Billy said that last night. It means to tell the end, yes?"

"Close enough. Tell me about Lolly."

"There is so much between the start and the chase to finish the game. It is in many ways the most interesting part of the hunt. Yet you wish to fill your belly with the fruit of the hunt. Very well. Ambrosius won many battles and became king. He took the name Arthur, the High King. Arthur Ambrosius won many more battles. But the last one that this king entered was nearly fatal to him. Enemies betrayed him and routed his army. Arthur received a dire wound while effecting the retreat of his army. His closest knights carried him off the field to a town nearby."

"You call this cutting to the chase?"

"It is a new concept for me. I do not like it."

"You've told me about Amber and Arthur. What about Lolly? When did Arthur become Lolly?"

"Three powerful druids were staying in this town. One had great healing power. The knights sought them out."

"Amber said my acorn formed a druid symbol."

His gaze caught mine. "And so it is. A powerful one." He looked down at his empty plate. "These druids were subjects of Arthur, but they were not his friends. Nimuë, Morgayne and Elaine.

"Nimuë the healer could not repair the hurt without killing the man. I saw his wound later, and I could not have done so either. Perhaps the two of us working together could have accomplished both tasks." He seemed to consider that thought.

"So he died?" I asked.

"I have wondered many times if they did the only thing they could to prevent his death. It is what they said. But their goals differed from Arthur's. The three dispatched Arthur Ambrosius from his body and sent him into the body of the person you know as Amber."

"Where is *his*," I almost laughed using the pronoun, finding it difficult to keep a straight face, "body, now?"

"Rotted, you fool. That happened fifteen hundred years ago."

Aargh. I should wring his outlandish neck.

"Don't call me a fool, you crazy old man! Just tell me about Lolly."

"I know nothing of Lolly."

I hit the chair with my fist. "Amber is Lolly," I shouted. "She seduced me last night."

Crap. Hadn't meant to tell him that. Not any of his business.

He sat still for a long moment, and then nodded.

Nodded! Like he agreed with me. I couldn't believe it.

"I did not know about Lolly. Perhaps she is the original occupant of this body. I must rethink Morgayne's spell. Perhaps another path out of the Aether existed."

Lolly was the first. I liked that thought. But then why didn't she dominate? Why did Amber control them? "How do I bring Lolly out? I need to talk with her."

Merlin stood, picked up his mouse, and strode toward the patio door.

I said, "How do I talk with Lolly?"

"I have preparations to make for tonight. You must help me prepare."

"Lolly?"

"Tonight I will send Arthur Ambrosius back to his time. He shall be gone. If Lolly shares the body, she shall remain."

"So if I help you do this thing you have to do tonight, Amber will leave and Lolly will be left?"

"That is the future." He said it flatly, with finality.

I chose that future. "I'll help you."

CHAPTER

14

THE OLD COOT was getting a lot for one birdshit-splattered twenty dollar bill. For less than I used to earn in half an hour, he'd taken a full day of my life. And I'd just agreed to let him take more. I couldn't figure out why. I told myself I might get another chance with Lolly, and that was a part of it.

Now I followed the fool through the woods behind her house. Or was I the fool for following?

I didn't believe that these two characters came from another time more than fifteen hundred years ago. Nor that one of them had been a king of Britain. I like science fiction as much as the next engineer, but it's fiction. Time travel works only one way. One second follows the next, adding up to another minute, another hour, another day. We live through the whole time. Nobody jumps around in time.

No, I'd gotten enmeshed with a couple of loonies. That seemed certain.

Their lunacy had an internal consistency. I banked on that. If they both believed that this ritual would exorcise Arthur, or Amber, or preferably both, from the troubled lady that I chose to think of as Lolly, then perhaps it would happen.

I had to admit, though, that something else was going on. I'd never been much for introspection, but I realized I'd been drifting for a long time. I wasn't contributing to the world. Oh, sure, while I had a job I fed my little family. I helped the company make money, producing more oil and gas and fueling the great Texas economy. *Energy For The World.* But the company treated me like a trained monkey doing a mindless job. And then when they were through with me, they treated me like disappearing ink.

No, I hadn't done much to improve the human condition. Although I'd never thought about my uselessness, I began to realize how it had dragged me down. My wife had recognized that long before I had; Janet didn't hang around for the bottom she saw coming.

Maybe if we'd had kids, I could've found some reason for my life. But after several years, we found out I had a low sperm count. Not zero. The doctor told us it would take only one strong spermatozoon to complete the trek. We kept trying, but no success. She left. And now, without her, I wasn't even supporting a marginal Texan family.

Then, the merger came. Being on the lesser side of a merger means you have no power, your boss has little power, and when the names drop onto the new org chart, you wind up…somewhere else.

Now, without a wife, without a job, without meaning of any sort in my life, my uselessness became so obvious that even I couldn't avoid seeing it.

I had refused to look at myself, but then this crazy old man showed up with his threads and his stories of a lost king and his hallucinations. Somehow, I had importance for his quest. Crazy as it was, I grabbed hold of the sense of purpose that he brought. My life had some meaning, some purpose in the grand scheme that the old man had spun.

I felt a sense of certainty that I was doing the thing that had to be done. I would make a difference, and through my efforts, something that had gone terribly wrong in the life of the lady called Lolly could be set to rights. And maybe—just maybe—we would find a way to nurture the connection between us.

"Alfred! Why do you stand there? I need you here."

I was standing beneath the umbrella of an enormous old live oak. Merlin gestured to me from about a hundred feet away, near the other side of a gentle slope across an open expanse. I had only a vague memory of walking along a path through woods to get here.

Someone had run a brush hog over the clearing between us. Although a few weeds had grown to four or six inches, stumps and drying vegetation covered most of the area. Gentle rolls separated dry rills draining the clearing into the stream.

I ambled over to Merlin. He planted his staff in the ground and began pacing in a spiral centered on it. He held his arms a few inches away from his body, hands splayed out with fingers parallel to the ground. He paused a few places to dig his heel into the ground, and then continued tracing the spiral. When the far side of his loop reached the steep slope down to the stream, he stopped.

He signaled for me to wait just outside his final loop, and then he retrieved his staff and returned to the three places he'd marked. At each one, he stood on the mark, held his staff at arm's length and parallel to the ground, and closed his eyes for a moment. He seemed most satisfied with the second place, and called me over to it.

"We must remove these plants. Flatten a circle large enough for a man to lie in it."

I looked around. "We didn't bring a shovel. Or a hoe."

"We do not use iron for this. Find a stout branch and begin." He strode to the incline and followed a cleared path down to the water.

I hadn't expected manual labor. I guess I should've known. He was an old man, what else would he need someone else to do for him?

He didn't leave his staff for me to clear the circle. There weren't any branches in the brush-hogged area, so I wandered to the edge of the woods. Tough bushes and brambles filled the space between the trees around the open area. It would require serious tools, best a chainsaw, to cut into them. I walked the edge of the clearing looking for a stout enough branch on the ground.

I'd become surprised at how much anger I'd been carrying around. I knew it wasn't normal to fantasize about going postal and attacking your erstwhile bosses with an axe. I'd never done that before the layoff. Just venting, nothing else. Picture the carnage, don't do it.

Now, that murder down the road in Tomball. When I read about it, I could picture the violence behind the attack. The paper left the details pretty sparse, but my imagination filled in the gaps. The police never said what had been used to cut the victim up. They said he had defensive wounds. I knew what that meant. He'd held his arms out, trying to block the blows. I pictured an axe raining terror down on him.

Merlin interrupted my reverie. "Why do you stand there? Bring the branch and begin."

I stood under the live oak again, leaning on a stout branch I'd found somewhere.

I had no difficulty removing the weeds from the moist ground, wet from the foggy nights and overcast skies the past few days. When I finished, he sent me for wood. Dry fall, he said. Wood that had been on the ground awhile. I found plenty of twigs and small branches.

Maybe if I could help Lolly, I'd feel a sense of purpose, and these melancholy thoughts would go away. Until this morning, I hadn't thought of myself as moody. I had a vivid imagination, for sure. And the TV news gave my thoughts plenty of ammunition. Helping the old man these past days had kept me from thinking about the morbid stuff. Like atrocities in the ongoing Chinese civil war and the second murder in Brenham—I hadn't even had time to read about it, much less to create a scenario of what happened. I figured it resembled the first. After all, the cops had already linked the crimes. Maybe I was getting over my negativity.

Of course, I couldn't ignore that hallucination Merlin induced where I became a hawk or whatever. Eating the field mouse seemed pretty gross. But, it wasn't me doing it. I mean, even the old man said that he'd replayed one of his memories. So it was the hawk, not me, that relished the taste of blood on my tongue. Well, that is, on the bird's tongue.

I jumped when something touched my back.

"You have chosen this place?" The old man stood beside me.

It seemed that I'd been piling the wood under the oak tree.

"Oh, I guess I haven't been paying attention. I'll move the wood."

Merlin cocked his head and squinted at me. He looked up at the tree and then over toward the stream.

"Go to the dirt circle. Stand there until I call you."

I shrugged. Whatever. When I got to the cleared place, I turned and waved, but he ignored me. He planted his staff and then held his arms out again, hands parallel to the ground, and swung them back and forth. After a full minute of this, he motioned for me to come back to him. He repeated the process with me at his side.

I had no idea what he was doing. I figured it made up part of the ritual that I'd agreed to help with.

"Remain here." He went back to his cleared spot and repeated his hand motions for another minute.

"Come."

Once I reached him, his hands danced again.

"You must be under the tree for the ritual. Your power is there."

My power? What was he talking about?

"So, where do you want the wood?"

"Ah. Where should the fire be? It must be between. But where?"

He paced from his clearing all the way to my spot under the tree as I trailed along.

"Can you find the point midway?"

"I'm an engineer. Of course I can. How precisely do you want it placed?"

"Midway." He disappeared down the slope, and I heard the splash of water.

There are several ways to figure out the point midway between two places. A couple of them occurred to me. With a long rope I could determine a bisecting line. Of course, I didn't have a long rope with me. Or, I could use the geometry of angles to find a point that made equal angles to the endpoints. But the ground wasn't flat and I had no compass.

Geometry having failed me, I realized the task had little need for so much precision, since he planned to build a bonfire. I decided to use my own stride length as a measure. I paced off the distance between the two points. I had about a six-to-five pace, and at thirty-five and a third paces, my original estimate of one hundred feet was a little high. I traced back seventeen paces and scooted forward a bit more, and then dropped a rock to mark the midpoint.

Not precise, but good enough for a fire. I cleared a three-foot circle and lined it with large rocks I gathered near the stream. Then I moved the wood from under the tree into the stone circle.

Merlin continued to play in the water, so I went back to my spot under the tree and took a nap. I dreamed of Lolly. Both of us. Naked.

CHAPTER
15

LOLLY WAS SITTING on me, lifting and lowering herself at a glacial pace. I watched her breasts rise and fall in counterpoint to her body movement and listened to her soft, rhythmic breathing. The warmth in my loins spread throughout my body in a calm contentment I hadn't felt in a long time—if ever.

She lowered herself on the next stroke, but when she reached the bottom of the motion, her fingernails sank into my left breast and she beat my head with her other hand. Her voice rose into a fierce shriek. I shouted in pain, my cry joining her keening. My arms jerked up to push her off of me, but my hands swooped through empty air. Lolly's image disappeared, but the scratching, beating and screeching continued.

I opened my eyes. A confusing mass of brown and white flailed at me. I raised one arm to protect my face and swatted around my chest with the other. I made contact, but the stabbing pain in my breast got worse, like a knife being twisted. I groped for its hilt, but missed. Instead, something like an ice pick sank into the back of my right hand, over and over in a rapid tattoo. I swatted with my other hand and got hold of something solid. It didn't help; the knife in my chest twisted harder. The rapid stabs from the ice pick switched to my left hand. I found a grip on the knife handle and pulled it out, but it was soft and compressive in my hand. The keening screech shrilled louder, and whatever whacked my head beat faster.

A sharp *thud* sounded by my ear. *What else?* I wondered. Glancing to the side, I saw Merlin towering over me, pounding his staff on the ground beside my head.

"Help me!" I shouted.

"Stop hurting my hawk!" He thumped his staff on the ground with each word.

His tone shocked me. I let go of the knife, realizing I held a bird's leg. I covered my face. The flailing didn't stop until Merlin's murmuring calmed the bird. After a few moments, he reached down and gathered it in his arms.

I rolled away and jumped to my feet. "What the hell! Were you trying to kill me?"

Merlin cooed at the bird and stroked its feathers.

I was incensed. My already injured shoulder flared in pain, and I feared I was bleeding where the damn bird had sunk its talons into me. I saw blood on the back of both my hands.

"Answer me, old man!"

Merlin scowled at me. "I sent the bird to awaken you. He is young yet. You should not have excited him."

"You what? Sent the damn thing to attack me?"

"I have answered, as you demanded. Now I will calm the bird. You must find Ambrosius."

"Fuck that. I've got to find some bandages."

He flicked his hand at me in dismissal and continued muttering to the bird, stroking its back. I got a good look at my assailant. I don't know much about birds, so I had to take Merlin's word that this was a young hawk. It seemed a good-sized bird, several shades of brown on its back, chest white with streaks of brown feathers. The hooked beak provided a sharp reminder that I'd better deal with the torn skin on the back of my hands. I felt lucky the damn bird hadn't used its beak on my face.

I found Amber's cook in the kitchen. She got some alcohol and gauze and bandaged my hands and shoulder without asking anything. She wasn't gentle, and the alcohol stung like heck, but she got the job done.

This had not been a good day. Billy brained me when we played mouse hockey, and then Amber almost took my head off with the sword. Now the bird. I thought about going to the guest room for rest and recuperation. Then I remembered the plan: exorcise the extra personality of Amber from the body of the woman I liked. Lolly.

I dithered. But helping Merlin seemed the only way to see if she could become a part of my life. I got Amber's work number from the cook and called. Someone else answered and told me that Ms. Tascosa was out. I asked for Billy. The line clicked and he picked up.

"Yeah, she came in for a while," he said. "Her head was in the clouds, though. What's goin' on over there?"

What could I tell him? I couldn't tell Amber's friend and business partner that Merlin had devised some complex…rite…to send her personality to, well, wherever it came from.

"Merlin's got some Halloween thing planned for Amber. From back in the old country or something. He hasn't told me what they're going to do. All I know is that it involves a bonfire. The old fart made me waste an hour clearing a space and gathering wood."

"Bonfire? Is that legal out in the county?"

"Got me," I said. "Know where she went? When she's coming back?"

"No. But she acted royally pissed when she left. She almost knocked Hoshi on his butt."

"Hoshi?"

"He renders backgrounds."

"Cool. Did he work on the version I play?"

"Yeah. Part a our first crew. Renders buildings, other structures."

"Does good work."

"Thanks. Hey, man, if I hear from her, I'll have her check in."

"Say, Billy. How can I get my car?"

"Not a problem. I can send someone over to pick ya up."

"'Preciate it."

I didn't know what worried me. It was still early; Amber had plenty of time to get home. But I felt something had gone wrong. Or maybe I just felt the effect of all the beatings I'd received.

The cook offered me no help. She pretended not to understand when I asked her about Amber. She'd spoken to me and understood earlier. But now the only thing I could glean from her Spanish was "Señora Tascosa." She enunciated that three or four times. The rest sounded like just so much gibberish.

I knew she could speak English. She just didn't want to talk to me about her boss. But we live in the great nation of Texas. Steve Austin and Sam Houston stole it from Mexico for a reason—so we'd all speak the same English I learned in America.

Of course, the oil companies brought in a bunch of us from outside Texas, even from overseas. I had immigrated to Texas and had gotten my citizenship, but a lot of my colleagues just had work visas. They canned us together, didn't matter. It's that whole management attitude that having years of experience means nothing. They didn't need us.

Oh, like heck they didn't. They fired a bunch of us to make the analysts happy, but the stock price still went down. And they wonder why they can't produce oil. They go out and buy some other company and call that replacing reserves, then outsource the engineering. They don't understand it, anyway. Next upturn, they're going to be sorry. They'll need all the bodies they can get. Then they'll pay for it. Salaries will go through the roof.

I must have drifted to sleep on the couch, because the doorbell woke me up.

The man at the door stood about average height, which I took to be tall for a Japanese man. He introduced himself as Hoshi. He'd cut his straight, black hair in a style that I associated with Moe, the head stooge. Like a bowl had been put on his head to do the cut. But this fellow had dyed a red streak down the center. Twentysomethings. Who could understand them?

He had a bright yellow Cooper Mini that he drove like a sports car. Even buckled in, I had to brace my hands against the door and the dashboard to keep from getting thrown around every time he took a corner. He played country-punk swing from his iPod, but I guess in deference to me, the old man, he'd turned the volume low. During the refrains of this unrecognizable song, his head bounced to the beat, tossing the red streak back and forth in the midst of the black bowl-cut.

"Any news about Amber?" he asked.

"I hear you've seen her since I did. Billy said she decked you."

"Nah, it wasn't anything like that. She was in a hurry and I got in the way."

His tone sounded apologetic. He was making an excuse for her.

"She almost cut my head off this morning," I said.

"What? What did you do?"

"Nothing!" *I asked about Lolly*, I thought. *But that's not for him to know.* "We were just talking while she exercised. Then she threw a sword."

"A sword? Which one?"

"Which? I don't know. One with a dull blade, fortunately. It wasn't like the ones I saw in her display cabinet. Those didn't look like they'd ever been used."

"Oh, she's got lots. I've seen eight or ten. She practices with all of them. Hey." He turned to me with a smile. "I even helped her pick one out. A samurai sword."

"This one was long and straight, no curve in the blade."

"What kind of hilt?"

"I guess you'd call it a cross shape. Long handle with an ornate cross piece where it met the blade. A big gemstone, or maybe a piece of glass, sat at the middle of the cross."

"Not the samurai sword."

"Are you an expert on the samurai?"

"Nah. Mostly I translated from a Japanese book she found. And I asked around, friends and family, to find a couple for her to try."

He braked, throwing me forward. A stop sign. He sped off again.

I settled back in the passenger seat. "I love your work."

"You a fan of *Invasion*?"

"I waste many delightful hours with that game." I grinned like a fan boy—self-conscious and foolish.

"A labor of love. Version one, just the eight of us."

"Not like now?"

"Price of success, I guess." He stopped bouncing to the music and looked over at me. "Look, no offense, but Billy's real paranoid about us talking shop with outsiders."

This company began to sound like a cult. But who led it? Billy or Amber?

"Billy seems like a nice guy. Is he a pretty good boss? Or is that shop talk, too?"

"Nah, he's OK. If it weren't for him, we'd never meet a deadline."

"What about Amber? Isn't she your boss too?"

"Boss? Nah. More a spiritual leader. She's got the vision. She knows how to rally the troops to extra effort. Knows how to deploy her assets. I mean, us programmers. But she's got no business sense. She leaves that to Billy."

"Look, I've only known her a day, but there are some weird things about her."

Hoshi didn't look at me or respond. His head bounced to the music.

"Like this morning, when she went berserk and threw the sword at me."

Hoshi's head stopped bouncing. He signaled to change lanes. Once the car settled in the next lane, he glanced at me.

"I'm sure you're mistaken. She probably made a new move and the sword slipped from her grip. Maybe you surprised her?"

"No. She went berserk. For several minutes she just flailed about, beating on the exercise mannequins and stuff."

"There, you see. The sword slipped because she moved so fast."

"No, berserk came after the second time she threw the sword at me."

"You are mistaken. She would never do that."

He spun the wheel into the parking lot and stopped behind my car.

"Yours?" he asked.

He wasn't going to talk about Amber since I wasn't saying nice things about her.

"Thanks for the ride. Do you think you could take me in to see Billy?"

He gave a quick smile and nodded his head. "Saturday. We're closed. But wait here ten minutes. If he can see you, he'll be out." He nodded again, the red streak flowing forward and back.

"OK. Well, thanks for the ride."

He raced the yellow Mini around the building. I figured employees parked in the back.

Yep. Some kind of cult all right. Amber knocked Hoshi on his butt earlier today rushing out of the building, but he made excuses for her. He refused to believe that she had attacked me. Or worse, he believed me but wouldn't admit it.

She was bonkers, but he defended her. A cult.

The air had reached a pleasant temperature today, and the gurgling water had me calmed down by the time Billy came out. Despite myself, I responded to his smiling greeting as we shook.

"Any news?" he asked.

"I hoped you could give me some."

"It's that damn Merlin. She's been weird as locoweed ever since he showed up yesterday."

I nodded. "I think they're both crazy."

He studied me for a long moment.

"So why are you hangin' around?"

Be careful, I told myself. *If you start talking about Lolly, it might lead to telling him that Merlin's trying to exorcise his friend's personality. Don't go there. Say something else.*

"Good question. I can't seem to get away from Merlin. I seem to be bound up in his *threads.*" I signed with air quotes.

"Threads?"

"It's like fate, somehow. I don't get it, either. But every time I think about leaving, something happens, and I stay."

He shrugged. He hadn't heard about the threads.

"I'll go look for Amber after work. I know a few places she might hang."

"Can't you call her cell?"

"She's funny about that. Won't carry one."

I didn't either, but that was economics.

"I'll wait back at her place with the old man. He's got that thing going tonight."

"Appropriate."

"Huh?"

"Tonight's Halloween. That crazy old fool probably thinks there's some power in the night."

I nodded as though the idea were crazy. But unlike Billy, I was willing to play along with him in the hope for an unobstructed chance with Lolly.

I said goodbye, knowing that he'd be pissed at me the next time we saw one another because I'd helped eradicate his friend. I almost pitied him.

But he was a boss. He had everything, and now my turn to get something had arrived.

CHAPTER

16

I PUSHED THE doorbell button a fourth time before the cook opened the door. I don't know what she said, but she said it fast. Her tone and hand gestures made it clear that her job did not include opening the door for people. She continued jabbering and stabbing at the air all the way back to the kitchen. Then, she stuck her head back around the door and spoke in a conversational tone.

"Dinner. Seven."

She left me alone. I didn't expect to find anyone else in the house, but I checked the gymnasium anyway. Apparently, the cook didn't clean, either, at least not down here, because the mess hadn't been addressed. I pulled one of the swords from the rack and almost dropped it. I had no idea how much those things weigh. I lifted it two-handed and put it back in place.

The smaller one next to it still weighed more than I expected, but it balanced pretty well in my grip. For a few seconds, anyway. How did warriors wield these things? I struggled to hold it out in front of me; I couldn't imagine fighting with it.

It raised an even bigger question: how did Amber handle them? I looked around for the one she'd thrown at me twice, but I couldn't find it. In fact, several slots in the rack stood empty. Maybe she set it aside to clean or repair. She'd buried the damn thing into the wall, dull edge and all. Surely that did something to it. The woman must have muscles that I hadn't felt last night.

Last night. I thought about Lolly. Could multiple personalities exhibit different physical traits as well? I mean, like heaving muscles when one dominated and gentle smoothness for the other? I didn't know anything about psychological disorders.

I hefted the smaller sword, almost grabbing the blade with my left hand before I noticed that this one held a keen edge. I hung it back on the wall, taking great care not to cut myself or have it drop on my foot.

I gotta get into shape. My muscles hurt from that small exertion.

A sliding door led into the small yard, a ten-by-ten grassy area. I couldn't get through the surrounding bramble if my life depended on it. Not without an axe or something. I locked that door and went upstairs and out the back patio door.

From the back yard, I couldn't even tell the gym had a yard. The thick bushes from the stream grew all the way up to the house. I walked around to the front yard. A side door there looked like it led to the office. Even from this side, the gym yard remained invisible. *Woman likes to work out in private.*

I strolled out to the bonfire clearing, relieved that Amber mowed the path through the brambles, because the clearing sat almost a quarter mile away. The path looked like a cross-country hiking trail. I hadn't seen any fences near the house, so maybe Amber left the way accessible for joggers.

I enjoyed the Houston Halloween weather, not too warm, not too cold, pleasant for short sleeves. The sky remained overcast, but the clouds didn't look like they'd drop any rain. I missed Baltimore, where I'd grown up and gone to college, but I didn't miss the winters. The best part of Houston was its winter. Every year I enjoyed watching neighbors in shorts string outdoor Christmas lights while batting away mosquitoes. Texas was a strange country.

People here decorate their yards for Halloween, too. In some neighborhoods, people go all out. Hay bales, pumpkins, giant spider webs strung in the trees, giant plastic spiders on the shrubs. Witch dolls on their brooms smashing into trees.

The clearing sat empty. Merlin had added a few things around the bonfire circle. Several small piles of plants, some green and others dried, awaited his ceremony. A few freshly harvested dandelions topped one pile. The damn things seem to grow almost year-round here. I recognized a few of the other plants from my walk through the woods, but I couldn't name them.

I heard a sharp keening from above. A young hawk perched in a pine tree. It looked like the same one that attacked me. It scrutinized the clearing, occasionally raising its head to look in the distance, then turning back to its vigilance. It stared at me a few times. I watched it on its branch for a couple of minutes, and then it dropped from the tree and rose into the air. It gained altitude and soared in a circle.

Seeing it made my injured hands itch. My anger at the damn bird flared briefly for its attack, but I fell back to envying its ability to fly above everything. To see far into the distance. And hawks had to have great eyesight to spot a field mouse or something else from so far up. I was sure he could see Merlin from up there if he tried.

Hey, I could see Merlin from up there! I'm getting pretty good at the mind meld trick. I did it with the mouse. I bet I could do it with the stupid bird! After all, I have that druid mark. I can use that power.

I laughed over the thought. I had no power. I hated that. But this vision thing? I ended the fish one when I got bored. Me, not him. That surprised the old fraud. Then, with just that one lesson, I controlled his mouse. Yeah, I commandeered *his* mouse. Why not hijack *his* bird?

I liked that idea.

But not leaping into a bird in mid-flight. No, that wasn't good. The experiences with the fish and mouse taught me to allow a bit of time to orient. So I sat down in the clearing, just beyond the crown of my live oak, and waited for the bird to land. The whole time I thought about what fun it would be to fly under my own power and spy on that sneaky old man. I'd show him sly.

The bird settled back on its pine branch and resumed its watchful waiting.

I concentrated, and when the hawk looked at me, I repeated what I'd said to the mouse.

"How about it, bird?"

CHAPTER
17

Oh yes! I can see way up the stream. Just beyond the clearing, it splashes over large rocks, and, beyond that, it bends left. It's lined with trees on both sides, a few of them changing to fall reds and oranges.

This is wonderful. Beyond the wood I see houses, distant neighborhoods. It feels like I'm almost up in the big blue sky. Wow!

I wonder if I can find the old man.

I turn my head to look around, and an overpowering sense of fear rushes through me. Someone is attacking me. I hear a loud keening. I feel great danger, but I don't know its source. I try to look around, but I can't move my head. The fear switches to anger: someone is trying to overpower me. The keening becomes a cry of rage, a series of shrill, angry screams.

The trees and sky and stream disappear—everything goes black. It takes a moment to realize that my eyes are closed. I try to open them, but instead everything goes from black to violet. What's going on?

Oh. It's the bird's fear, because I moved its head. And it got angry when I tried again. I'm experiencing its reactions to me. How interesting. That didn't happen with the fish or mouse.

Well, the damn thing should fear me. I'm taking control, and I'm going to go hunt for Merlin. Show the old bastard that I can do anything he can do.

I think about seeing. I won't worry about the mechanics—how to open the eyes—that's the bird's job. I just concentrate on what I want to do: look around.

It doesn't work. The formless, violet vision becomes dark, swirling shades of purple, black and maroon. I'm getting dizzy, and the shrieking hurts my brain. I shout "Shut up!" and the angry keening stops.

See, I can bend you to my will. Stupid bird.

I want the colors to be green. I demand the bird see the green leaves and the brown tree stems around me and the light blue of the sky. I recall the last image I had before the violet, insist on seeing that, and then, to my great delight, it's back. I'm up in the tree, and far below, my own body lies on the grass.

My heart races. The bird's heart. I'm panting. I tell myself to take deep, slow breaths, but the panting continues. Again, I concentrate on breathing slowly. I insist on breathing slowly.

A vile, rotten taste fills my mouth and I gag; the smell of days-old death overwhelms my nose. Sounds well up around me, a cacophony of unrelated noises. I'm reeling; I'm about to fall. The greens and browns around me merge into a putrid, muddy mess.

I try to pull away from the volcano of sensations, but the horror keeps coming. The swirling colors become brackish swamp mud with sulfurous methane bubbling up. Bile rises in my throat and I heave out my stomach's contents. It splatters on me. The smell makes me retch again. I'm floating in a pool of vomitus.

A booming thunder swells from the general din, making my head pound. Mixed in is another sound, a shrill and high-pitched shriek.

The damn bird. Screaming again. And somehow it's making me feel sick.

It's playing mind games with me. Fuck that. A stupid bird will not make me feel sick. I'll fight back. I'll get the damn bird under my thumb. I'll show that arrogant Merlin what I can do.

Crap, it's hard to think with that horrid smell and the thumping and the keening and the dizzying swirl of color.

Take control, Alfred. You can beat this birdbrain. Think calm. Think placid. Think quiet and still.

The noises fade a bit. I feel like I've put a layer of cotton between me—my consciousness—and the bird's ears. I still smell vomit, but not sulfurous eggs.

I'm getting it under control. I just need to concentrate a little harder. Without warning, a scene emerges.

Three boys come at me, each from a different direction. The biggest one wears a worn and ragged sweater. The weave has a brown and white diamond pattern, but holes and tears make it a stringy mess.

The big, dumb, angry kid has caught me between him and his two equally stupid pals. They don't want me to run away. The big dummy plans to force me to understand how much stupider I am than him. I'm willing to admit that and call it a day, but he has his own ideas about how to make his point.

One pal pushes me into the big kid. He slaps my head and throws me back at the others. The three of them play pass the patsy for a while, and I get dizzy and sore from the slaps and punches. Then the big boy decides the game can be more fun—for him. He flips me onto the ground and sits on my stomach, pinning my arms beneath his knees.

He whips out a shingle knife with a curved blade. Now I'm terrified. He swings the hooked blade around, threatening my eyes, my nose, my ears. The other boys shriek with laughter every time the edge comes close to my face. After each dangerous swoop, he taps my chest with the point, first on my right breast and then on the left. Each prick draws blood. For variety, he starts cutting buttons off my shirt, one by one, between pricks. But he laughs loudest when thrusting the knife at my face, staying his hand just before he slices my nose or ears, then pricking my chest again.

No! I'm not a child; I'm a grown man. That never happened to me. Just a childhood nightmare. Bird is messing with my brain somehow. Damn it. I'm more powerful than this stupid bird. I have to get on top, again. I…

"Just get out, Alfred." *Janet stands in the kitchen, arms crossed, staring at me with tired eyes. I don't hear anger, not like last night, last week, last month. Her voice leaks tired resignation, and that frightens me more than her anger.*

"Look, I brought you flowers." I offer her the pale peach roses. A dozen. I paid extra to add baby's breath and feathers. I hold the flowers out to her. The movement wafts an aroma to my nose: the worst smelling roses ever.

She shakes her head, ignoring the bouquet.

"Why do you want me to leave?" I ask, dropping the stinking flowers. They shrivel and rot on contact with the floor, leaving only feathers.

"We've had this discussion. You never listen. Just leave."

"I'll change. I'll do whatever you want."

"You're a weak, spineless man, Alfred. You've got a grandiose vision of yourself, but it isn't reality, and it never will be. You live a worthless life, and you've always thought you deserved a different one. You'll never be satisfied with yourself, and you'll never stop sniping at me. Go away."

Janet, you bitch! Always the perfect girl next door who married beneath...

Damn, it's the bird again. Found a real memory this time. That hurt. Time for me to hurt you, shithead bird...

"Sit down, Alfred."

My foot catches on a chair leg and I stop my fall by grabbing the edge of the desk. I try to smile as I take a seat across from my new boss. For the first two weeks of the merger, we pretty much lacked any lower level management. Now, they've named the bosses. This one is mine. He came from the other company. The group met him this morning, and now it's my turn for orientation.

"I have some information for you here." He holds out a large envelope.

"What's this? New procedures for reservoir simulations?" I'd thought it would take some time before we'd have to change to new software.

"No. These are policies. And the package. Your numbers are in there."

"Package?" I know what that word means. But I don't believe it. Not me.

"You'll have until Friday to clean your desk. I've scheduled an appointment for you to talk with..." he looks at his notepad, "Sophie? Yes, Sophie, to get her up to speed on your projects."

"I'm fired?" My stomach drops to the floor.

"Alfred, we aren't firing anyone. But with the merger, we have duplication. We have to get to the right number of people for the work."

"So, I'm not fired? Am I being transferred?" The package has my name on it. No return address. Just the company's leaping whale logo.

"That's your package. You were with the company more than ten years, weren't you?"

I nod. Sixteen years in a few months.

"Then you'll get the full six-month package. And the outplacement service, too."

My head floats above my body, my stomach on the floor. This is happening to someone else. I'd always been loyal to the company, did whatever they needed me to do. And now they're cutting me off. I want to say something, some magical phrase, to make it all go away. An employment abracadabra.

Damn it.

That was real. Bird's hitting close to home. How in blazes is it tapping into my pains and my fears? It's a stupid bird.

I'll pin your wings and throw you off the branch, you shitbird. Then I'll leave you to deal with the pain.

At last, the keening stops. I still don't see anything except a confusing mass of ugly colors. I concentrate on opening the bird's eyes. Nothing happens, so I command them to close. Again nothing. The damn bird still dominates.

Shit, what's it doing now? I'm so disoriented, I can't tell up from down. I feel like I'm tumbling about. Up is down, then down is down, and then it's up. What game is this?

Ooof! Now I feel like I've been slugged by a baseball bat. Pain sears up and down my side.

I open my eyes. Trees spin above me. I can't focus and my eyes close again, but not because I thought to do it. I roll my head to the side and my nose bumps onto something. I taste blood and grass. The pain in my side lessens, but I feel bruised.

How's the damn bird doing this to me? I ought to roast it over a slow fire. Cook it, eat it, enjoy it. Oh yes.

All sensations cease. The pain stops. I don't taste grass, or blood, or anything. I'm not disoriented any more, but I don't feel oriented either. I try to open my eyes. There's no sense of resistance, not like I'd been feeling before when the bird fought me. I guess my eyes open, but I see nothing.

No, that's not it. It's more like I'm not seeing.

I try to sense my body. Any part of my body. No sensation. No pressure on my feet, so I'm not standing. No pressure on any side, so I'm not lying. My chest doesn't rise or fall with my breath, nor does air rush through my mouth or nose. No sounds. No sight. No smell or taste. Nothing reaches me.

My god! The bird has cut my mind off. Where does a soul go when it isn't in the mind? Is this nonexistence? Limbo? Is time passing?

With no sensation, the only change is thought. Is my life over? Has the bird killed me somehow? I don't know the rules of this possession crap; Merlin didn't tell me much. I didn't have any trouble at all with the mouse. Have I made a fatal error? Jeez, how do I get out of this?

Well, I don't feel anything, but I have to assume that I'm still in the bird's head. The alternative is that I'm dead and it doesn't matter what I do anyway. OK, shitbird. You gave me pain, I'll give you pain.

Leg in a trap. Steel trap. Snap your leg. Can't get free. Fox comes along, snaps at you. Bites your wing off.

Ouch! My side hurts like hell. Oh, jeez, what a great feeling. It's pain, but it's a feeling.

I've got to take charge of this situation before I get lost in limbo again.

Thunder and lightning flash, but it isn't raining. Just as I become aware of a battle raging around me, a tall, bearded man throws a short sword at me. Before I have time to react, it slices through my collarbone and into my chest. I black out.

When I come to, the tall man is sparring with another, but even I can see he's commanding the pace of the fight. They talk together, but the important sound is the gradual slowing of the beat of my heart. I crawl toward the two men, feeling that my fate depends on the outcome of the fight. As they dance around one another, I'm not sure which one I want to win. The tall man has taken my life, but somehow I feel the blame lies with the other. That shorter one fights with crazed desperation, sensing his own death nearing.

Streaks of black and violet wash over me, and then I experience no sensations for a time. My vision returns, but it's like looking down a tunnel. The tall man's face seems to be far away, but his eyes are clear to me so he must be close. He's sad, and he looks at me with remorse. For an instant, I see a shimmer of light, a ribbon connecting him to me. But then it's gone.

My heartbeat slows. I can't concentrate long enough to count between the beats, but they are few and far between. My death is near.

No! Damn you, bird. That wasn't my life. You need to quit that.

My left side flares in pain again.

I think I made the bird hurt before, when I was cut off. I'll try again.

Your mother abandoned you, bird. Your father threw you out of the nest. Worms crawl in your stomach and eat their way out.

Oooh. That worked. I feel like throwing up. Again.

This mental fighting doesn't work so well when I experience the same thing the bird does.

I'm surprised when another hawk swoops down beside me. It's huge, but I don't feel afraid. The bird leans in to me and I open my mouth wide. Something drops from the other bird's mouth into mine. Food. Wonderful, tasty food. I'm so happy, so contented.

These feelings come from the bird, but after the ordeal I'd been through, the happiness helps me, too.

The big bird turns its head away from me and the hawk, and somehow at the same time I see it turning toward me. But now it has bushy, white eyebrows and slate-gray eyes.

"Get out of my pet," the Merlin-bird says.

It morphs again. An infuriated Merlin holds the hawk under his arm, keeping it immobile.

I shake my head. "You aren't real. I will control the bird."

"You fool. You ruin this bird."

"I'll make it obey."

He turns to walk away.

"It is worthless to you now." He brings his hand over the bird's head, covering its eyes. With a rapid twist, he snaps the bird's neck.

CHAPTER
18

"WHAT THE HELL?" I stammered, rolling across the ground. I lay alone in the clearing.

I staggered and stumbled along the path to the house. The crazy old loon killed his pet bird. Just like that. Squitch, a little twist of the wrist and it died.

I couldn't grasp the casual violence. The matter-of-fact way he ended its life.

His fury was directed at me. I knew that. I guess I was lucky the bird took the fall. I couldn't control it, anyway. In that struggle, it scored more points on me than I did on it.

I didn't feel like giving up, though. I remembered what Merlin had said. Fish were easy, mice easier than rats, birds of prey were tough, cats impossible. The hawk was harder than I'd expected. I didn't want to be another fish, so I looked around the back yard for something else. I had about half an hour before sunset, plenty of time to try again.

I rejected all birds, even if I'd seen any close enough. My crashing through the woods had frightened any woods animals away. What could I try?

There—what's that on the back wall? A lizard? Gecko. Yes. Probably smarter than a fish, but I figured a gecko would be a lot easier than a bird. I thought I could get close to it before it ran off.

I edged toward the little green lizard. It waited for me like we had an appointment. I stopped an arm's length away, and then tilted my head toward it.

"How about it, gecko?"

It stared back at me. That didn't work. Oh, both the mouse and the hawk had already been trained by Merlin. But...could I capture an animal? Could I tame it?

I cooed and stretched my bandaged hand toward it. The gecko cocked its head at me, but didn't flee. My fingertip made contact. I stroked it with the lightest touch. After a moment, it responded by moving its head against my finger in time to my strokes. Its eyes watched my hand.

"I'm not going to hurt you." I tried to use my voice to reassure it, thinking that the animal would respond to tone rather than words. "I just want to share. Would that be OK with you? It'll just be a few minutes, that's all. Maybe it'll be fun for you, too. What do you think?"

I took a deep breath and thought about what it would be like to be one with a gecko.

Something huge hovers over my head. I flinch.

The gecko jerked its head down. Oh, that was me reaching. My arm. I scared myself. But the lizard didn't run away. It seemed to be in my thrall, at least somewhat. I tried again.

I feel a slight pressure on my torso. My finger. The pressure stops. The hand starts to pull away. I look at my body in front of me and realize it's gone slack.

I came back into my body. I didn't want to fall. I sat on the ground, and then looked back at the gecko. It clung to the wall, watching me. I rested my chin on my hands and knees, eyes on the lizard.

I see myself sitting on the ground. My own head slumps into my hands, but my body doesn't fall over. Gecko-me looks left. The wall surface is smooth. Hmm. How does a gecko stay on a vertical surface? I examine one of my feet. Each finger has ten or fifteen scaly looking pads. There's nothing sticky on them. In fact, they're dry. I don't understand how I'm hanging head down on this wall, but I guess I'll let the gecko brain worry about that.

I scurry down the wall, turn around, and run back up. This is pretty cool. I thought that being a lizard might feel icky, but it doesn't. Who wouldn't want to be able to walk up walls? There's no real sense of unsticking my foot at each step. The toes release without effort, but when I stop moving, they adhere to the surface.

My own body is beginning to slump. I know Merlin's body doesn't sleep when he's in his mouse. He controlled it when it played brooms with me and Billy, I'm sure of that. The mouse didn't have the brains to figure out how to make us slide into each other on the rug. And at the same time, the old coot was walking to the house from out here in the clearing. Can I be in two places at once like him?

I sat up straight and lifted my head from my hands. The gecko had moved down the wall, but it still clung a bit over my head. This time, I concentrated on being in the gecko and staying in my body.

I see the gecko turn its head when I turn my gecko head. I watch my own mouth form an excited 'o' and in the same instant see the lizard take a few steps down. I smile and lift my arm and hop off the wall into my palm. I hear a happy shout as I say, "Hoorah!"

Gecko-me lifts my head and tilts to look into my human eyes. I see both my greenish eye and my round black eye with an orange iris. I feel like both sides of me fall into the opposite pupil. I try to move my gaze, but both sides stay in place.

I slide into a world of impenetrable darkness: a deep, dark void that I can't escape. All light, all matter, everything falls into nothingness.

The sun had set, and it was dark in the back yard. The gecko dropped from my hand and scurried away.

How long had I sat there, staring at myself? Fifteen minutes? Thirty? I'd lost track of time. I don't remember any thoughts—just deep, dark blackness. I didn't like that.

The patio door opened at my pull, but my calls echoed in the empty house. My disorientation faded as I wandered through the house. I found dinner on the stove and the table set for three. In my state, food sounded good. I filled a plate and ate alone, surprised when I first discovered the jack-o'-lantern napkins.

My mind latched onto simple, mundane thoughts about Halloween.

I wondered how many trick-or-treaters had come by my apartment that night. Do they knock doors in apartment complexes? I wasn't there a year ago. Lots of kids lived in the complex. I guess they'd be disappointed.

Who was I kidding? If I were home, I'd be hiding in the bedroom. I couldn't afford candy for them.

Amber had built her place out in the country. All alone. Not a house anywhere nearby until the other side of the thick woods. No little witches or goblins coming here. Just a crazy old man who thought he could send someone fifteen hundred years into the past. And a woman with multiple personalities wielding a mean sword. Nope, no Halloween monsters out here.

I thought about going home. I'd gotten Merlin so pissed at me he wouldn't notice. It looked like Lolly, or Amber, would miss the big ceremony anyway.

I took out my car keys to go. Twice. The second time I even stepped out the front door. The third time, I was determined to go. I went to the toilet in the bedroom to pee before the drive home. Then I saw Lolly's camisole on the dresser. I smelled her on it.

So, in the end, I stuck around. I sensed something happening out here, and I had a part in it. I couldn't say that about anything else in my life.

So I stayed. I watched TV.

By the time the ten o'clock news came on, I had gone into a zone. It all washed right over me. I noticed little of what the local news anchors reported. The bellicose new Kaiser and wars in Arabia and China. Kids with Halloween costumes. Candy. The weather lady brought me around. The overcast conditions would break by morning. Clearing and cool tomorrow. Good news after days of mostly cloudy October skies. Sun.

Still no sign of Amber. I left a note on the table and went outside to tell Merlin. I hoped he'd gotten over the bird by now. After all, he killed the damn thing, not me.

I wandered around the deserted clearing. It looked like he'd been busy. He'd made even more piles of weeds and added more stuff to them. The piles surrounded his spot. A bench that looked like it came from a park sat by the bonfire circle. Leaves and grass and green pine needles covered it. It looked pretty comfortable.

I saw a few weed piles under the tree where he said I had power. Faint light from The Woodlands reflected from the clouds, but not enough to tell what made up the piles, even when I stood among them.

A few minutes later, I saw a faint glow floating down the path. Flashlight. I hadn't thought to bring one. I waited for Amber to join me. As the halo of light emerged onto the clearing, I heard two soft voices—women laughing. The circle of light played on the ground just ahead of them. I could tell from the silhouettes that neither was Amber.

The two women had proceeded well into the clearing before they saw the unlit bonfire. They stopped. The light circled the piled wood and then surveyed the leaf-covered bench.

One of them called out in a clear voice, deep for a woman, "Neve. Someone's been here. There's a fire circle." I detected a hint of a French accent.

Another flashlight flicked on at the edge of the clearing. The third person—Neve, I figured—strode toward the two women, stabbing the beam from place to place around the clearing. She stopped beside them. I heard soft murmuring. Both flashlights began probing the dark places around the clearing, and one, then both of them, found me. I sheltered my eyes from the bright lights. Neve took a step forward, putting herself between the others and me.

"You don't belong here," she called out.

"Just who are you?" I accused back.

"I'm Neve, a guest of the owner. I think it's time for you to go."

I laughed. "I've been staying with the owner. You're no guest here."

She stepped toward me with slow and deliberate paces. The other two women stayed behind. She stopped just at the edge of the oak tree's crown.

That's right! This is my tree. Mine.

"If you are the owner's guest," she said, "what's his name?"

"Leave before I turn you in to Ms. Tascosa."

Her shoulders relaxed a bit and some of the bravado drained from her bearing. "Ah, OK. I've known Amber for several years. She lets me come here for Samhain. It's a good place to be on Halloween night."

I figured we'd both established our bona fides. "I'm Alfred. Alfred Marlborough." I stepped forward to shake her hand.

"Neve Drake." She lowered the beam from my face and shook my hand.

The other women took this as a signal that I'd checked out and strolled toward us, chattering together. In the light of their approaching flashlight, I stole a look at Neve. The tallish, handsome woman appeared in her sixties. There could have been some salt-and-pepper left in her gray hair. The only wrinkles in the clear skin of her face clustered around her eyes and mouth. It may have been a play of the light, but her nose seemed sharp considering the softness of her other facial features. She seemed comfortable in the dark, confident.

"These are my friends, Vanesa and Carla."

I took Vanesa's hand. Her soft handshake ended almost before it began. She looked about thirty, a blonde with a round face, wearing white jeans and a flowing white top. The bottom of the blouse formed an angle, showing about an inch of skin between it and her jeans on the left side and none on the right.

Cute, a little exotic. She reminded me of a Polish woman I'd known in college.

"Good evening." She ducked her head in a shy greeting.

I almost stuttered my response. "I'm Alfred." She was so pretty.

Carla wore leather pants and a leather top that looked a size too small. The leather pieces didn't meet in between. Not nearly. Her long, brown hair hung unkempt, naturally wild and curly. She seemed a few years younger than Vanesa.

"*Bonne nuit,* Alfred."

French? She had the husky voice I'd first heard. She took my hand in both of hers, and I became aware of a stirring in my groin. I guess I'd have to call it a soft-on: just a little firm, but ready to stiffen on demand.

Oh, man. I've been spending Halloween in the wrong places.

I wish the rest of me were so prepared. I'm not good at small talk with pretty women. I tried to think of something to say, and decided to ask what brought them into the woods so late at night. But I didn't get the chance.

Neve's flashlight jerked up and focused on Merlin, standing at his spot near the stream. He didn't flinch at the light or attempt to cover his eyes. Nor did he say anything to the ladies. Neve kept her torch on Merlin, but glanced to me.

"Don't mind him. He's crazy, but harmless. Unless you're a bird."

Neve cocked her head.

"In fact, he's the one that's Amber's friend. I just kind of came along for the ride. His name's Merlin."

Neve gasped. "Are you *the* Merlin? That Amber's been waiting for?"

He called back, "You know me."

When Neve moved, she really moved. She covered half the distance to Merlin before I realized she had started. Vanesa and Carla drifted toward him after her.

Neve's light pointed toward his chest. For an instant, I thought he'd changed back into his threadbare old robe, but the resemblance was superficial. This robe had the same general lines, but the material looked in good shape. Not new. No, well worn, but not ragged like the other one. This one also once had a shadow of something more around the collar, something that had worn off. Faded ribbons looped through the buttonholes.

Amber must have given him another robe. She probably knew his taste.

"You're the reason Amber and I met," Neve said. "She came to me, thought I could help her find you."

He didn't respond.

"That doesn't surprise you," Neve said.

"I felt your power the moment you arrived at our circle."

"I couldn't help Amber. I found your aura, far away and weak. Fuzzy. Somehow disjointed from us. I see now that I was wrong."

"Not wrong," he said. "Perhaps had you checked again you would have located me."

"That's why I came tonight. One of the reasons. To scry for you in a fire here."

"Then your quest is successful." He spread his arms wide, one holding the staff. "You have found me."

I couldn't believe it. The old man was flirting with her.

"Amber said you were the most powerful magician she knew."

"Yet, I could not bring her to this place this night to fulfill her destiny."

"We checked at the house. Not there."

"No. She is many days travel from here."

"No way, old man." I turned to Neve. "She left here this afternoon."

He bowed his head to Neve. "Sorry, my lady. My concept of distance is somewhat…outdated. I think of the time required to travel afoot. I must adjust that. She drove one of those machines—a car."

"Can we light the campfire?" Carla asked.

Merlin replied, "Do you need light and warmth, magnolia blossom?"

Damn. The old man was flirting with her, too. Even in the meager light from the two torches, I saw her blush.

But she didn't look away from him.

"*Mais non*," she said. "But the wood. It is already there."

Merlin motioned me toward the pile of wood. "Remove most of that from the circle. We shall not need such a large fire for this night."

What am I? His gopher? I'm not here to help him; I'm here for Lolly. To get rid of Amber, or Arthur.

"What about Amber? What if she comes? Isn't this all to…" I glanced at Neve. "To help Amber?"

"Ambrosia is too late," he said, "if she returns at all this night. Prepare a smaller fire."

Make a fire. Tote that bail. Lift that barge. I said nothing, but I noticed he didn't call her Ambrosius. Curious.

I cleared away most of the wood, and Merlin lit the rest. I'm not sure how he did it. I didn't see a match.

He and Neve drifted to his spot near the stream. The younger women settled onto the bench Merlin had decorated. I sat on the ground in front of them. My feet almost touched theirs. I hadn't forgotten Lolly, but it sure felt nice to be in the company of pretty young women.

"Is Merlin really a powerful magician? A great warlock?" The flickering firelight gave glimpses of Carla's eager expression.

I felt my body thrill at her attention. "I've only known him a couple of days."

The brightness in her eyes dulled, and she glanced at her friend.

Wrong answer, dummy.

"Well, I have seen some strange things since I met him."

Her eyes came back to me. I had to spin this for all it was worth.

"What have you seen?" Vanesa had a quiet, almost coquettish tone.

"Well, for one thing, he was just an emaciated scarecrow when I first saw him. And that was only day before yesterday. It's hard to see him in this light, but he's gotten mighty healthy in, like, forty-eight hours."

Both of them looked at Merlin, trying to figure out how strong he looked.

No, don't talk about his *virility, you idiot.*

"He says that he draws some of his power from me. Because of my birthmark."

Carla's skepticism showed on her face. I started to unbutton my shirt, but looked up when I heard a faint gasp. Both women had stiffened.

"No. Look. Sorry. The birthmark is on my shoulder. Here."

I had a couple of buttons undone so I could pull the shirt away. The fire lit my shoulder, showing the mark. Carla turned the flashlight back on, and they both peered at the acorn shape.

She asked, "Can we touch it? You are bruised."

I didn't think it would be a good idea to mention that our mutual hostess had thrown a sword at me. So I just shrugged. "It'll be OK. You can touch the acorn."

A finger pressed on my shoulder. Carla, I thought. After a moment, her hand pulled away, and softer fingers stroked the skin over the acorn. I tried not to show how nice Vanesa's touch felt. They acted a bit skittish, out here in the woods. Their attention felt too nice to spoil.

"This has power?" Vanesa circled the mark with her finger.

"So Merlin says. And that circle over there under the live oak? That's my place of power. So he says, swear to god."

"Did he discover it for you?" She sat back on the platform.

"No, I found it myself, Vanesa. See, I came out here to help Merlin set this up," I swept my arm to indicate the whole clearing, "and the place drew me. Several times. Merlin just confirmed that it was my place."

"*Tres* cool," Carla said. "Your own place of power. And it's a tree. I'm a vila. That's a forest nymph. Vanesa, she's a limoniad, a meadow nymph. That's why we like to come here. Trees, meadow, and a stream. Neve isn't a nymph, but she gets her power from running water."

Nymphs? They're sexy enough.

"Merlin told me about three powerful druids. Nimuë, Elaine and Morgayne. Are you three like them?"

"No, no. Neve is powerful. She's a potent healer," Vanesa declared. "We have just a little touch of power."

"Are you in a coven or something?"

The women looked at one another and giggled. "We're not that organized," Carla said. "She's teaching us things about our power. Like a private Hogwarts."

"What's a Hogwarts?" I asked.

"You don't read the Harry Potter stories?"

Vanesa giggled. "Neve calls him Harvey Porter."

I shook my head. Sounded like fiction. I didn't read much non-technical stuff.

"What else can Merlin do?" Vanesa leaned toward me, anticipating.

"Oh, hey. He's got this neat trick. He can make you think you're inside an animal's mind. Like a mouse or a fish." I stopped myself from saying *or a bird.* "Now that's cool."

They both gazed at Merlin, who had his head close to Neve's.

Vanesa turned back to me. "Has he done it for you?"

I heard the excitement in her voice. "Many times."

OK, I exaggerate, but not much. It makes a better story.

I let him have the credit. As much as I wanted to impress these young ladies, my own experiences with the hawk and gecko left me wary.

"Do you think he'd do it for us?" Her voice became wistful, "I would so like to be a dove."

"Oh, you're such a girl!" Carla nudged her friend. "I'd be a big cat. A panther, maybe."

"Merlin!" I stood up and waved. "We've got a great idea."

The ladies followed me over to his spot. He remained concentrated on Neve, ignoring us, until I walked right up to them. He frowned at me.

"Vanesa and Carla want to have one of your, what'd you call them, memories? Visions? Vanesa wants to be a dove and Carla wants to be a panther. Do you have anything with those animals?"

"Impossible, boy. Leave us in peace."

"Oh, please." Vanesa's eyes sparkled in the firelight. "We came out here to learn magic. We planned to help Neve summon you. But we didn't get to do that."

"I am here," he said. "So you see, your magic worked."

"That was luck, not magic," Carla said. "I'd love to be inside an animal's head."

"Merlin." Neve laid her hand on his arm. "I did promise them we'd do something special tonight. I would hate to leave here without spelling something."

"Alas, my lady. I am not back to full strength. I expended what energies I had amassed creating a spell for Ambrosia. And for naught, as she has not returned. I am spent."

"So, you can't let our new friends have any visions?" I taunted. *Of course*, I thought, *the old fraud hasn't given them any of the drugs he used on me. That's it.*

Merlin stared at me for almost half a minute. With the fire in the distance providing the only illumination, I couldn't read his face at all. All I could see were his bushy brows pulled down over his eyes.

I probably wouldn't have been able to read his face even in the full light of noon.

"There is a way." His eyebrows relaxed upward. "It is an easy thing to do."

From the corner of my eye, I saw the young ladies brighten in anticipation. I said, "Then, do it."

"I must use your power."

"My power?" My stomach gripped in a quick flash of fear. Then I realized that this had potential. The great magician using my power. I hoped that would impress the ladies. I liked their attention.

I smiled to Merlin. "What do I have to do?"

He took hold of his staff and stood. He put his other hand on my shoulder. "You must be sure that you want to do this."

"Let's do it, old man."

His lips formed a smile, but even the dark shadows couldn't conceal that the rest of his face held no humor. The old man had something in mind, but I couldn't figure out what. Typical.

"Your wish is my command," he said. "We shall move to your place of power."

Merlin led the way to the live oak. Along the way, he had Carla and me pick up the bench, which he called a bier, and place it on my spot.

"Lie yourself upon the bier. I do not know how much of your power I shall need to use. It could be awkward for you to falter this time."

I protested. "The ladies should sit."

Neve took my shoulders and sat me on the bier, smiling at me. "Please do as he says. We're quite comfortable on the grass."

Merlin pressed me onto my back on the wooden bench. It felt more comfortable than I'd expected, and the wide variety of aromas from the plants he'd woven around it refreshed me.

"With your permission," he said, "I shall enter your mind and direct your energies outward to each of the women."

I sat up. "You're coming into my mind?"

"It is the only way."

"I thought you said you couldn't enter another person's mind."

"Without the person's permission, it could be dangerous for both. But this shall be a light touch."

"Dangerous? Should I be worried?" An opportunity to impress the girls excited me in ways I hadn't felt since I was a teen. But despite all my daydreams, danger scared me. I didn't want to lose my mind.

"With your leave, there is no danger. I shall be able to speak with you, if necessary."

That set me wondering. "Was that how you'd planned to use me tonight if Amber had come?"

"No. For that ceremony, I would draw on your energy to trigger spells I had already placed. But directing memories into four people's minds requires control. Now, lie back."

He looked around our small circle, making sure everyone had found a comfortable position. He leaned close to Neve's face and stared into her eyes for a few moments, then repeated the process with each of the young ladies.

Why do they let him do that, but get all squirrelly if I get close?

He leaned far into my space. "With you shall I begin."

CHAPTER
19

The sunset is spectacular. A last sliver of brilliant vermillion slips behind a distant hill. Two sunbeams stab upward through shades of red and yellow. As I wing to the left, I see soft pastels rising from the horizon toward the half moon in the southern sky, fading to the color of eggplant and then black with a few stars in the east.

I recognize a now familiar taste of blood in the air, and looking down I see a plain covered by a confused melee. Men run toward me in a panic, chased by other men who slaughter them as they can. I resist the blood lust, knowing danger for me rides with so many men.

"You shall see Arthur's last battle before coming to your time."

Merlin?

"Watch. I will start visions for the ladies."

The sound of a blaring horn draws my eyes to the edge of the field, where a narrow valley lies between a heavily wooded hill and an escarpment. A few men on horseback call out, trying to rally fleeing soldiers to their position. A banner waves back and forth. Many of the panicked footmen disappear into the woods on the other side of the hillock. But some, then more, turn to the horn.

I soar downward toward the banner. The man in the middle is an older version of the man I'd seen in my first vision. Arthur.

I settle onto a branch and peer into the gathering dusk. The vanguard of the retreating men has reached Arthur, and he orders them to stop and hold their ground. Several of them continue past him, but when another horseman—it looks like the man called Cai—slaps the first one on the chest with the flat of his sword, the others stop and turn.

"Form a line. Everyone with long shields move to the front." *Arthur directs the nervous men to face the approaching battle.* "We must form a Saxon shield. Interlock arms; overlap your shields in front. No gaps. We have to hold until full dark or we all die with swords in the back."

"Do it!" *Cai shouts.*

Under Cai's direction, they form two lines, one to either side of the narrow valley, in an open V-shape. Spearmen and those with long swords stand behind the shield wall.

Their fleeing comrades continue to race through the gap, to be stopped and turned by Cai and other knights. The shouts of the pursuing army grow louder. Arthur prepares his men to close the gap.

"The others are Visigoths," Merlin said.

The name sounds almost familiar, historical, somehow. "Who are they?"

"Barbarians. Invaders in Gaul. Watch."

A tall, blond horseman pounds toward the wall, stopping fifty feet out. He turns back and rallies men to him to slow the first of the pursuers. His horse spins from side to side, always putting him where he next needs to be. His presence brings caution and fear to the enemy, winning precious time for his men. He kills three enemy footmen in as many minutes, and the scattered Visigoths give him space. He sends his comrades to join the defense in the valley, and then prances his horse, taunting the enemy. Two men rush him together. Only one can retreat.

"Lancelot," *Arthur calls.* "Come now."

Lancelot looks up from the dead men to see a crowd of fifteen footmen racing toward him, several carrying spears. He wheels his horse and dashes for the shield wall. It closes behind him, and the line of British spearmen and swordsmen crowd as close to the front line as they can. The line is a hard wall bristling with sharp points directed toward the enemy.

"Where is your helm?" *Cai asks Lancelot.*

The man grins and shakes his long, matted hair. "Lost it."

Arthur removes his helmet and tosses it to the other knight.

"No, sire. I cannot take your helm."

"We are in a desperate situation, my friend. I will be at the back, directing our defense. If this line falls, a helmet will not save me. You are my helm." He turns to another horseman. "Bedevere, take some of these men into the edge of the wood. Protect our flank. Hide men behind the briars. In the near-dark, you'll have the advantage. Kill anything that moves."

The enemy charges the shield wall. The British shields were not designed to be used as the Saxons used theirs, but the Visigoths do not know how to exploit the weakness. In the dark, the wall looks formidable.

How do I know these things? That isn't in the game.

"I have opened some of my knowledge to you," Merlin said.

The second line of defenders poke and slash over and under the shields. The force of the attack is slowed, but more men keep coming into the mouth of the valley outside the wall. Some of them are straggling British, lost in the dark. They are killed by the Visigoths.

Bedevere shouts from the woods, directing his men toward a company of the enemy trying to get around the shield wall. Two horsemen dismount and join Bedevere in the woods.

Arthur paces his horse from side to side in the small valley, directing men to weaknesses in the wall. Lancelot does the same, keeping his horse between Arthur and the wall. Cai stays with the wall, moving the mass of his horse and the edge of his sword to support weak spots.

A blaring horn from the enemy pulls their forces back from the British line. Night has fallen, and even with a hawk's vision, it is becoming difficult to see. With a second call from the horn, a barrage of rocks comes flying toward the gathered British. Some of the rocks come almost to the height of my branch, so I soar up to a higher branch.

This battle doesn't seem as heroic as the other one I saw.

After I'm again settled, I see another assault on the British line, but in the dark, the approaching Visigoths stumble and fall into one another. Some of them slaughter their comrades in the confusion. The static British

have the advantage, and the line holds again. A horn blares and the Visigoths pull back into the open field of the earlier battleground.

I fly down to a lower branch to see what has happened with the British. Arthur's horse stands unmanned. Lancelot leaps from his horse to look
at the prone figure of the king.

"Cai, here." He drops to his knees.

Not even the riot of odors from the battlefield can keep me from recognizing the aroma of Arthur's blood. I had smelled it many times in this
campaign in Gaul as I followed the king in service to my master, Merlin.
His specific blood-smell is almost overwhelming this time.

Bedevere slides off his horse beside Lancelot. Cai arrives just after.

Lancelot pulls his hand away from Arthur's head. "Blood. Lots of
blood." He watches it seep onto his wrist.

Bedevere picks up a large stone with a dark, wet stain. "This accursed
stone hit his head. Fate abandoned us today." He rips cloth for a dressing to
slow the bleeding.

Lancelot shakes the blood from his hand. "Why did I let him give me
his helm?" He stamps the ground.

"You obeyed your king," Cai responds. He looks around at the milling
men and knights. "We are not safe yet. He asked you to protect his life. Now
you must do so. Get him away from here. I must stay and save the remnants
of our army. You and Bedevere carry Arthur away."

"Where?"

"You know Aballo?"

"To the east."

"The healer, Nimuë, is there. Take Gawain, too. Go now."

They lash Arthur to his horse and tie the halter to Bedevere's saddle.
The four horses trot down the valley, passing the line of men already heading
out. Cai remains with the rearguard.

I feel a compulsion from my master to follow the horses. To scout
ahead. I launch into the dark night sky and overtake the horsemen as they
struggle through the underbrush in the narrowing valley. I see that the vale
opens up, so I rise to scan the distance. The track from the valley becomes a
trail, then a path, and at last a road.

This is what I wanted. I wish I could fly the bird myself.

The horses move at a cautious speed, even on the open road. The men keep close watch of the wound on Arthur's head. Too much jarring could be as fatal as not reaching help, but a certain amount of jarring cannot be avoided or he'll die on the way.

I see light in the distance. Maybe the bird doesn't feel the wonderful freedom of flight, but I do. It takes me toward a valley full of campfires. I swoop lower, scanning, but my eyes do not alight on anyone that my master recognizes. He sends me a sense of danger. I loop back to the knights, scanning the countryside as I go. These bird eyes pick out details mine would miss. By the time I see the knights galloping toward me, my master has found an alternative path.

I swoop from the sky, diving toward Bedevere, who is moving at the steadiest pace with Arthur's horse.

"Damnation! What was that?" he shouts after I pass. All the men slow, but do not stop. They scan the sky but cannot see me in the darkness.

I rise again, circling to the north. My master directs me to dive again, but to rise toward the moon after I pass. This time I pass just above the horse's nose, and Bedevere swears again.

Gawain notices me. He is much younger than the others and so sees better in the night. "It's a hawk." I hear him as I slow and glide above them.

"Merlin's bird. I would swear to it." Lancelot reins his horse back.

"What's it doing here?" Gawain asks.

"The thing is possessed. It has Merlin's own magic to it."

"Lancelot, why do you think the damn wizard sent it?"

"Merlin protects the king, in his own twisted way. I think it's here to tell us something."

"What?"

"I know not, but keep an eye on the bird. We must to Aballo."

I hover above them when the knights urge their horses forward again. We continue for another ten minutes, then my master orders me to swoop down on them again, from directly ahead. As soon as I move from my position, the men point to me. My master is pleased that they have noticed. At his command, I swoop low enough to spook a normal horse. These warhorses are not fazed, but the men rein them to a stop.

I rise to the sky. They discuss my behavior for a minute, and then start forward. I swoop down, and again they stop. This time, my master directs me to land on a low branch beside a track leading into the woods.

"Gawain, go look at the bird," Bedevere says.

Gawain walks his horse to my position. He halts below me, and I launch from the branch and fly straight down the path, stopping after a few wing beats.

"It's a path. I think it wants us to go this way."

Lancelot guides his horse to the path. "I cannot be sure in the dark, but I think this is a by-way. It follows the top of the hills."

"To Aballo?"

"Yes, but it is longer."

"We trust the bird, or we do not," Bedevere says.

Lancelot stares at me for a long moment. "Follow the bird. And damn Merlin if we are wrong."

"Lead on, Gawain, as fast as we may."

The knights follow me along the path to another, then another, complaining at every turn and at every bramble that grows into the path, doubting the bird, doubting Merlin.

Even I begin to feel the strain of all the flying tonight.

From atop a hill on the narrow track, they see the campfires in the distance, sprawling on either side of the main road.

Gawain emits a soft whistle. "That's almost as many men as we started the day with."

"Merlin's bird has been leading us around them," Bedevere says. "They must be Visigoths."

"Or friends of that treacherous Roman, Arvandus," Gawain says.

"They were supposed to be our allies," says Lancelot. "Where is Emperor Anthemius? Did he betray us too?"

The men muffle their horses and lead them from the hilltop, mounting again only when they are hidden by trees and the crest of the hill is behind them.

A wave of sadness overwhelms me. The vision of the path ahead of me wavers and becomes indistinct. I feel, rather than hear, Merlin's grief.

"I feared an army allied with the Visigoths. In the darkness, I detected nothing Roman about the camp. The men had no Roman uniforms. To my sorrow, I did not recognize that these barbarians formed the auxiliary troops of a legionary army. Their Roman officers had taken refuge in tents. I turned Arthur away from the vanguard of the emperor's army, less than a day's march away from his defeat at the hands of the vile Visigoth Euric.

"Had I not detoured them, a Roman army surgeon would have seen Arthur. Perhaps he could have been healed that night.

"I ought to have been at the battle that morning. But the Gaulish Druid council sent for me; I had not met with them in years.

"I indulged, and lost Arthur.

"The war had gone well; Arthur defeated everyone he met. Except Arvandus. Word of his treason came to me too late. I lost Arthur. First to Euric, then to a wayward stone, and ultimately to the sisters. Fifteen hundred years of penance has not been enough."

The voice goes silent in my head. Merlin's loss, and his guilt, blank the memory. I feel his sadness and spiritual fatigue.

Then my vision clears, and I see that we've stopped near a town. Dawn is near; a fog rises from the stream just ahead. A horseman gallops out of the mist toward us.

"Lancelot. Any news?"

"Aye, Bedevere. Nimuë is here."

Gawain says, "She will heal the king."

"She comes," says Lancelot, "but she comes with two of her sister druids. Morgayne and Elaine."

"Pfah!" Gawain spits and crosses himself. "Morgayne is a witch. And Elaine not much better."

"Still yourself," Bedevere says. "He is Arthur. He's their king as much as he is ours. They will help. And they do have power."

A small bell sounds from the water, displaced in the fog. The men lead Arthur's horse into the haze. I fly to a tree at water's edge and see three women in a small flat boat glide to the bank.

"Place the king in the middle of the boat," Nimuë says. I feel a deep affection for the tall, ebony-haired woman standing at the back of the boat. The other two women remain seated, hoods pulled up covering their faces.

The men pass Arthur onto the boat and then retreat to the shore. Nimuë places her hands on the king's head and nods to one of the women. The boat drifts from shore.

"Where do you take our king?" asks Bedevere.

"To the Island in the Lake."

"Can you heal him?" Lancelot says.

Nimuë's eyes flash toward Arthur's hero. "He has been ill abused. We will do what we can do."

Bedevere reaches his hand out. "When shall he return?"

Nimuë turns from the men. "Not soon," she says. "Not soon at all."

The boat begins to disappear into the fog. My master directs me to follow, so I launch into the haze, following the vague shapes. The woman sitting on the landward side of the boat pulls back her cape and stares at me.

It is Morgayne. She raises her hand and says, "Begone, bird."

I fall from the sky; there is no fight left in me. I cannot stay aloft long enough to get back over land. I splash into the water. Brave Gawain wades in and takes hold of me, a wild, thrashing hawk, saving me from drowning.

CHAPTER

20

I AWOKE COUGHING water from my lungs. No, that was the bird. The bird almost drowned, not me. I felt drained, though, like I'd been fighting for my life, too.

Neve stooped over me. "Ah, good. You're awake. Merlin told me I shouldn't worry." She felt my forehead with her cool hand. "Are you tired?"

"Exhausted. Oh man, we almost drowned there at the end, didn't we?"

She smiled. "I believe I had a different vision. A delightful party."

"I thought he channeled the vision through me."

"Visions," she said. "Merlin picked a special vision for each of us."

"I was a mouse," Vanesa said. "I watched a wonderful dance from the rafters. Queen Guinevere. What a beautiful lady. Her honey-colored hair, hanging loose, bouncing to the music. And the dances. They...I don't know...did a jig or something. Not, like, in a castle. It seemed more an old barn, but with tables and musicians instead of hay and horses. Oh, but everyone at the gathering seemed so happy."

I looked to Neve. "Were you at the party?"

"Party?" She considered her vision. "Not that type of party. No. But I felt wonderful."

I heard Carla thanking Merlin as he tended the fire. She turned from him and tromped to my bench.

"He says Bouticca was a queen. A warrior queen."

"Did you have a mouse, too?" Vanesa asked.

"*Non*. A warhorse. I pulled her chariot. An enormous army followed us into battle. We stormed a town, and we won. The people bowed to us when we paraded by. They shouted her name: Bouticca! Bouticca!"

"Bouticca?" I said. "Did she fight with Arthur, or against him?"

Merlin surprised me by answering my question.

"Bouticca was long dead before the birth of the boy who later became Arthur. The vision I gave to Carla came to me from another. It has great power."

"*Moi aussi*." Carla strutted away, laughing. Vanesa ran after her, throwing a handful of grass in her friend's hair as she flew by.

Neve laughed, too, putting her hand to my head again. "I think you are recovering. I have already thanked Merlin for his visions. I thank you, also, Mr. Marlborough, for providing the power. Your shoulder glowed, you know."

I felt like a little boy. *Ah, shucks ma'am,' twern't nothin'.* The only thing that kept me from digging my toe in the dirt was the fact that I still lay on the bench. I gathered my full forty-odd years of maturity about me. "You're most welcome. I didn't really do anything."

"On the contrary, my dear. You pleasured three women in one night. Not many men can claim that."

She dumbfounded me. I guess it showed.

"You don't think a double entendre is beyond a…mature…lady, do you?" She teased me and let out a free and hearty laugh.

Adding to this night of surprises, Merlin laughed with her. "You are a delight. I feared this time had drained such freedom from women."

"Then you have not met many women!" She smiled like a young girl.

It all got a bit thick for me. I mean, she looked old enough to be, well, not my mother. A younger aunt. And who could tell how old Merlin was. Seventy? I wasn't out here to watch a couple of geriatrics flirting. I came here to cast the Arthur persona out of Lolly's head. I doubted that she had room in her life for both me and Arthur.

I sat up and interrupted some other inane remarks between them. "What about Amber?"

"What about her?" Neve continued to smile.

"We set all this up to help her. To heal her."

Merlin shook his head. "It is too late to help Ambrosia tonight. We must wait for another night of power."

"Shit."

Neve studied the clearing like she saw it for the first time. She turned to me with suspicion. "What were you preparing here?"

"Don't look at me. Ask the old man. I'm just his ox."

Merlin sighed. "There are things, Neve, that you do not know about Ambrosia. The ritual tonight should have reversed a thing that happened many years ago."

I sensed some of the sadness and guilt I'd heard during the vision. She said, "What do you mean?"

Merlin took Neve's hands in his. "Do you trust me?"

She peered into his eyes for a long time. "I barely know you. I sense you have great power, and I know that power could be deceiving me. Yet, despite that, I do trust you."

"Then do not question this. It is a thing that is destined."

"Is this something Amber has agreed to?"

"Ambrosia must consent, or the ritual shall not work."

Her eyes met his again for a time before she replied. "Very well."

Vanesa called across the meadow. "Neve, it's almost two thirty. Don't you have to work tomorrow? Today."

Neve hadn't broken eye contact with the old man. "Merlin, we must be going."

I said, "Well, I guess we're done here for tonight, too. Can we walk you back through the woods?"

"That would be gallant, my dear Mr. Marlborough." Neve flashed me a gracious smile. "Most gallant."

She gave me her flashlight and I led the way back to the house. The younger women—the nymphs—walked just behind me, chattering nonstop about their visions. I couldn't fathom how they could understand one another. They spoke at the same time, words running one on top of the other. After a time I couldn't keep the grand ball and the chariot battle against the Romans separate. I gave up trying.

I heard Neve tell Merlin how excited Carla and Vanesa were.

"They usually aren't this giddy," she said. "You and Alfred gave them quite an experience tonight. They won't soon forget."

After that, she and Merlin dropped behind and out of my hearing.

Vanesa unlocked her VW. She and Carla thanked me again for my help with their visions. Merlin stretched his hand forward to say good-bye, and both of them reached out and touched it. Then they stretched up together and kissed him, one woman to each cheek.

Geez, Louise! What is it about that old man? The nymphs didn't kiss me.

Neve shook my hand. After again expressing her thanks, she got into the passenger seat, and the ladies left us alone. The lights disappeared down the drive. With the distraction of the young ladies gone, my thoughts returned to Lolly.

"What about Amber? When will we exorcise this Arthur persona?"

And leave Lolly alone in her body. She appreciates me. I have to help her.

"She returns, but it is too late. We are not destined to complete our task tonight. The power peaks in the hour after sunset. We did not start then; now it is too late."

"Can we try again tomorrow…I mean tonight?"

"The eve of Samhain is a time of great power. Yet, it was woefully weak this night. I do not know if I could access power enough, even on this special night, even with your help. I fear this time has drained the earth of its magic. The next chance is Beltane, but its influence is of a different sort. I shall study and think."

"OK, so, Beltane. Is that the middle of the month? Like the ides?"

"Beltane and Samhain divide the year."

"The year?" My heart sank.

"Beltane comes in the spring."

"Oh, crap, Merlin. I can't wait six months. Amber won't let me hang around that long. She doesn't like me." *I need to get to know Lolly now, while we both feel the connection. Who knows what she'll think of me in the spring?*

"I shall summon you back." Turning from me, he strode back in the way we had come, around to the back of the house.

"Wait. That's it? You'll call me? Merlin!"

I ran to the corner of the house, and then to the back. The old man had already disappeared into the dark woods.

"Merlin!"

Crap. How am I going to find time with Lolly if Amber sends me away? And where is she? What's she been doing? I thought she wanted to do this thing with Merlin. Did she get cold feet?

No way I'd drive back across Houston this time of night. Besides, I still hoped for a chance to see Lolly in the morning.

So, I went to the guest room and slept.

CHAPTER
21

I **DREAMED OF** Lancelot. He had power. He dispatched his enemies with ease. A quick thrust, a slice, and his assailants died. But even in my dream, I watched the real hero.

"Alfred?"

I sat up in the bed, swinging my sword arm toward the sound.

"Please, help me." Her voice sounded soft and tentative.

She stood in the doorway, backlit by a dim nightlight in the hallway. Lolly. I rolled out of bed and rushed to her. It didn't bother me that I wore only underwear. Much faster to get down to business.

I reached for her, but she kept me at arm's length. Even in the semidarkness I could see that something was wrong. Her hair stood askew, and her clothes seemed bunched in odd places. I flipped on the light, half-closing my eyes to avoid the sudden brightness. When I saw her, they flew wide open.

Blood covered her whole body. Huge splatters of red. In her hair, on her face, all over her clothes. Dried smears ran from her shoulders to her wrists, and small chunks of something that had an unpleasant look of shredded meat clung to her sleeves. Her hands seemed the only parts clean, as though she'd just taken off gloves.

"Lolly, are you all right? What happened? How badly are you hurt?"

I almost didn't hear her soft answer. "I'm not hurt."

I took her arm, looking for bleeding cuts, but all of the blood appeared to be dry—caked to her skin and clothing.

"Where'd you get hit? Who did this to you? Lolly, what happened?"

She stood in front of me, her head rotating side to side. Tears welled in her eyes. They followed channels through the red from the corners of her eyes; she'd already cried clean lines down her cheeks.

I don't deal well with crying women. My tone might have been too stern.

"You have to tell me—who did this?"

The softness left her face and the tears stopped flowing. A feral anger rose in her eyes and her mouth distorted into a vicious snarl. Even her stance changed, and I had a flash of recognition: in the gymnasium, when she flailed at the mannequins. I shrank away from her.

She raised her arm stiffly, bent it at the elbow, and pounded on her chest. Three times. Then her eyes narrowed, her head bent, and she stared at me, waiting for something. But I had no idea what.

She raised her head and stood straight, then pounded her chest again, and said "Bad!" She stared at me again, angry.

"You're trying to tell me something."

She repeated the chest pounding, then insisted, "Me!"

"You? You did this?"

She tilted her head up, then down. In a reverse of the change I'd seen earlier, the fury drained out, leaving the soft and unsure Lolly.

"Lolly, what did you do? What happened?"

"I do'n know."

"But you just told me that you did it. Didn't you?"

"That was'n me."

"Amber?" *That bitch!*

"No, it was'n Amber."

"Arthur?" *Did she know anything about him?*

She shook her head.

Merlin appeared behind her. He touched her shoulder, and she fainted. I caught her head as she slid to the floor, and then had to follow her down to keep hold of her head.

"Stay with her."

"But...what?"

He was already gone.

I didn't know whether to hold her or not. She seemed to be unconscious, and the bloody mess covered her body. I rested her head on the carpet.

Merlin appeared again, dropping a pile of towels beside Lolly. "Clean her. Remove her clothing."

The white towels looked new, but he left again before I could tell him how pissed she might get.

Now, that's foolish. She's covered in blood and who knows what else is on her, and I'm afraid she'll get mad about dirtying some towels?

Even so, I hesitated another moment before wiping her face with the first towel. The bold, red mess didn't look like it would come out.

I shrugged, nothing to be done about it. I rubbed blood from her hair and her arms. As I began on her far arm, Merlin reappeared.

"That is enough. We must remove her clothing."

Leaning over her body, I felt I needed to protect her from further indignities. Like having an old man ogle her nakedness.

"Why do you hesitate, boy? Are you embarrassed to see her unclothed?"

"No, it's you shouldn't see her."

Merlin began chuffing. The chuffing became a chortle, and then a full-throated guffaw. He slowed enough to catch his breath.

"Before I slept for fifteen hundred years," he laughed again, "I doctored and midwifed and, yes, bedded more women than I would care to count."

He chortled again, then his light mood disappeared.

"Perhaps you should help this person rather than thinking about sex with her. Now, help me remove these garments. Boy."

"You go away. I'll do it."

"Your commands do not move me any more. I severed that thread during tonight's visions, when I could grasp both ends. Neither of us can compel the other." He tapped my head and nodded. "Now, we must begin."

He reached for her shoes. I started with her blouse. I had to give up trying to keep him away from her private areas. It took both of us to move her around to get the shirt, the bra, the pants and underwear off. Merlin stacked all the clothing onto the dirty towels, even the undergarments that had slight blood stains. He directed me to lift her under her arms while he took her feet. The beige carpet had a pink badge where Lolly had lain.

I didn't know where we were taking her until I heard water splashing. By the time we got to the master bedroom, I knew he had the shower running. When did he learn about showers?

"The water is warm," he said. "Clean her."

I backed into the shower. This was a nice, big one. It had a bench along the back and a showerhead on a flexible hose. I sat her onto the bench and balanced her in the corner.

Looking over my shoulder, I saw that Merlin had left again.

I rinsed most of the blood from her hair, and then washed it twice with her shampoo. I soaped a washcloth and cleaned her as thoroughly as I could.

Merlin appeared again with a terrycloth robe while I toweled her hair. He helped me to get her as dry as we could while keeping her propped on the bench. He smelled of something like cut grass, but not like a mown lawn—earthier, like cut weeds and turned dirt.

After I dried myself, we slid her arms into the robe. I stood up with her, and Merlin tied her sash. Then we carried her to her bed.

"Your thread to her is strong. You would like to sleep with her."

It wasn't a question. *Does he think I want sex? Now?*

"I think it would be good for her to be held tonight."

"It is likely that Ambrosius will awaken. Would it be good, still?"

Ouch.

"Retrieve your undergarment from the shower. Sleep in your bed."

He'd removed the stack of towels and clothing from the guest room. It looked like he'd crumbled dried leaves onto the bloody carpet patch and rubbed them into the carpet pile. I hopped over the mess.

I didn't think I could sleep at all, but I was out within a few minutes.

On waking, I had an immediate disturbing thought. *If the blood isn't hers, whose is it?* Her blood-soaked clothes, her blood-matted hair, her blood-spattered face and arms—all those pointed to some violence, but we'd found no injuries, not even a scratch.

What the heck happened? Did Amber snap like she had in the gym? Except this time, she didn't miss? The implications scared me.

I touched my underwear hanging on the nearby chair. Still damp, so I dressed commando. Third day for these pants, but what choice did I have? The buttons on my borrowed shirt didn't feel right; my fingers couldn't seem to fasten them.

The woman had caught my heart, even though the multiple personalities left me troubled and confused. Now she'd done something horrific. But I didn't know what. Or, for that matter, who. Who spattered all that blood on her? Was it Lolly, or Amber? What would happen after Merlin exorcised Amber? Which one of them was the angry one that claimed responsibility for the blood?

The pink badge on the carpet had disappeared. Clean. No blood spots, and no weeds. I couldn't see the telltale tracks of a vacuum cleaner, but someone must have run one to get all the leaf fragments out of the carpet. I didn't think I could've slept through that noise, but I guess I had. No bloody marks tracked through the hall, either.

I padded barefoot to the master bedroom, but found it empty, the bed unmade.

Sounds led me to someone eating in the kitchen. She wore jeans and an untucked, oversized tee-shirt. Even from behind I knew it was Amber, not Lolly, by the way she held her head. Nonchalant and proud. As though she expected everyone to admire her. Maybe not for beauty, but for her accomplishments.

She turned at the sound of my feet slapping the tile.

"I'd hoped you'd left." She turned back to her toast and jam.

How do you ask someone with that attitude why she came home smeared with blood from head to toe? I didn't know. I saw the bread loaf on the counter and put two slices into the toaster. Poured myself a cup of coffee from the drip brewer. Opened cabinets until I found a plate. Then stood in front of the toaster, shifting weight from one foot to the other, waiting for the bread to pop up. Amber ignored me the whole time. Not like she wanted me to feel unwanted. She simply didn't acknowledge my presence. I could have been another inanimate object in the room. Another chair. Even a pet would have received more attention.

I jumped when the toaster popped, but then the smell of toasted bread calmed me.

I joined Amber at the table, pulling a jar of strawberry preserves to my plate. She glanced up with a look of annoyance.

Now that I had her attention, I had to say something to keep it.

"Uh, about last night…"

"Merlin will get over it."

Merlin?

"What did Merlin have to do with it?"

She looked at me like I was a fool. I felt like one.

"He speaks of destiny when it suits him. Free will when that suits him." She laughed. "It seems that free will and destiny were both at work last night."

Now I felt like a confused fool. Free will and destiny? What about blood and gore?

Why did I hang around these people? They were crazier than I could fathom.

I bit into my already-cold toast. The preserves tasted bland, but I was pretty sure it was my problem, not the jam's.

"I decided to stay here. This is my time, now. I've become a twenty-first century…woman." Another laugh. "I accepted that yesterday afternoon. I've been ignoring my gender since I got here. I wore the clothing of women, but dresses fit much like togas and women's blouses look not unlike our tunics. But I didn't think of myself as living a woman's life. Merlin's presence, what he told me about the spell, made me realize that.

"Yesterday afternoon, I decided I wanted to stay here. To do that, I'd have to start living life as a woman, or I would be alone here. I found it to be a strange conclusion."

I closed my eyes, shaking my head, trying to understand her comments. I said, "But when you came home…"

"You didn't bring me home, did you? No? That's good. Did Billy bring me? I fell asleep at my desk. Didn't mean to, but when I decided to stay here and join the world, I got sleepy. Laid my head down, just to rest my eyes for a minute. Next thing, I woke up in my own bed. Was it Billy?"

I shrugged. I didn't understand her concern over who drove. Didn't she know she came home bloody? How could I broach that topic?

"Destiny stepped in. I had prepared myself to come home and tell Merlin that I wouldn't go through his ceremony, but fell asleep at my desk. Destiny. And free will. Both together."

Her talk of destiny left me cold. My thoughts centered on Lolly, standing at the door to my room covered in blood. Poor, frightened, confused Lolly. How could I help her get free of this domineering alternate personality?

Amber seemed to be thinking something through, staring at the ceiling. She must have come to a conclusion, because she looked me in the face again.

"Where is the old wizard, anyway?"

"Listening to a jester whose lessons went unlearnt," Merlin said from the patio doorway behind her.

CHAPTER
22

AMBER SPUN AROUND in her chair to face the old man. "Ah, Merlin. Perhaps the student learned the lesson better than the teacher. But that wouldn't occur to you, would it?"

I didn't understand how she could be in any kind of teasing mood after last night.

"Pfah! You understand little more than the buffoon who sits beside you. He at least has learnt that he doesn't understand and keeps his mouth shut."

I wasn't sure whether he'd just given me another insult or a compliment. I took his comment as advice to keep quiet.

"What have I not learned? The fate part or the destiny part?"

"Responsibility."

Amber laughed, a full and hearty laugh.

"I built and ruled a nation. I led armies, sent men to win glory and sent men to die. Yes, I started wars, but also I forged a lasting peace. Although more mundane, in this time, I run a company and I'm called a pillar of the community. For all that I am responsible."

"You did what your heart led you to."

"Exactly. I've been responsible."

"No, Ambrosius. You have not. You went to war in preference to being attacked at home. You led men in those wars because you did it better than other tyrants and would not submit to orders from an inferior. You became king for the same reason. To whom have you been responsible but yourself?"

She sat back in her chair. "Merlin, is this truly how you think of me?"

"It is time for your actions to be dictated by your responsibility to others."

"Those others are long dead."

"Not all."

"You?"

Merlin gave an almost imperceptible shake of his head. "For me that time is past. For you, Arthur Ambrosius, it is still the future. You do not yet accept it, but responsibility remains for you in that time we knew."

"No. That time's past for me as well."

"I know it is not. But I have no argument to convince you, since you choose not to accept my word that you have changed history by being here."

They seemed to have forgotten about me. That was just as well, since I didn't understand their delusions.

"Ah, yes," she said. "The world you slept through. Was it so much different than this one? Was it better, Merlin? Surely it wasn't worse, even you wouldn't send me back to make the world worse."

He shrugged. "I cannot say. I do know that in that world the name Arthur became famous, the source of stories fabulous and legendary. What is it in this world?"

"Nonexistent. No one's heard of High King Arthur Ambrosius."

"Parents named their children Arthur."

"I don't care."

Even I could tell that wasn't true. She didn't look at him when she answered. It did bother her.

"You have no care to restore the world to the way it was? To the way it is meant to be?"

"How do you know, old friend, that it isn't supposed to have me in it. Now. In this time."

Merlin answered with certainty. "Because I was there when you came back. I spoke with you fifteen hundred years ago. After you woke from your sleep, with head and brain mended."

She shook her head. "Then there'll be another change. Not only the present, but the past, too. Because I'm not going back."

"You shun responsibility?"

"You impose a responsibility I won't accept. It's not mine. That time's past. This present may not be ideal, but it's far from the worst I could imagine. Yes, the Saxons conquered my people, but they weren't destroyed. You know nothing of genetic science, Merlin, but Celtic blood remains dominant in many parts of Britain. The English are not wholly Saxon. I think they overthrew local kings and became new for- eign kings. If I go back, I'm one more king the invaders have to kill. No, that's not a responsibility I want."

"What of the responsibility to today?" Merlin asked. "Do you accept that?"

Amber took a deep breath and then let it out. "Yes. I've chosen to live here. Of course I'm responsible for the things I do in this time."

"Then I will show you the effect of your staying."

"By all means, old friend. Tell me something I do not know."

"Very well. Explain your condition when you came home not long before dawn."

"I was asleep." She crossed her legs, looking uncomfortable. "I don't know who brought me home."

"No one else."

"Nonsense. I can't drive in my sleep."

Merlin looked to me, waited until Amber turned in my direction, and then nodded. I saw that I still had a role here.

"You came home in the middle of the night. You were awake. We spoke. You were covered—"

"That can wait," Merlin interrupted.

"But isn't it the most important—"

"In due time," he said, stamping his staff on the floor.

Amber said, "Your fool doesn't seem to have your story memorized, wizard."

"He speaks for himself. And he speaks true."

Merlin and Amber stared at one another. I felt a frisson in the air, and there seemed to be an unspoken discussion going on. After a few tense, silent seconds, Amber turned back around in her chair. From the set of her shoulders, it appeared that Merlin had won the nonverbal argument.

"So I drive in my sleep. Frightening. But I got home. Is that what you want me to take responsibility for?"

"It is not so simple." Merlin moved to stand beside her.

"Why am I not surprised? Is anything ever simple with you, Merlin?"

"In this life, in this body, do you sleep well? Do you dream?"

She threw her shoulders back. "Do you forget, wizard? Your dream weavings haven't interested me since I became a man."

"Did I offer to interpret? Answer the question."

"You dare command your king!" Amber shot up and leaned into the old man.

I sat as still and quiet as I could. I'd seen Amber angry.

Merlin's massive eyebrows arched high. "You are either king," Merlin said, "or you are a woman of this time. You cannot be both. You have chosen to remain here, in this time. You have abdicated your throne. You are not my king."

His wide-open eyes held an intensity that I sensed in the primitive parts of my being, in the fluttering of my gut and in the jittering of my fingers. He filled the short space between his face and Amber's with a power I'd never seen. His irises had gone from gray to the white of the hottest metal.

Amber held her ground. I could see her jaw working, but whether she couldn't speak or her teeth ground in anger, I couldn't tell. Her shoulder muscles bunched to strike.

Until that moment, I would've thought Amber could pummel the old man to a pulp. Just a couple of days before, I'd half-carried his frail, ninety-pound body to my car. But something had happened these past days. He was formidable, physically imposing without tensing a muscle. I would have run away had he turned that power on me.

After about a minute, the tension in Amber's shoulders slipped away, and I knew she had lost another battle of wills.

"You're right," she said. "I can't command you. Nor can you command me."

"I have not changed. Nor have I released you from your oaths. I am still your druid mage and judge."

Ignored by them, I felt free to roll my eyes. It helped relieve my tension, anyway.

"Times have changed," she said. "Druids don't exist now."

"Perhaps. Perhaps not. That does not change your obligation to me. You have your honor, yet. And you do, in this time, retain a responsibility to me."

Amber turned her chair to face the old man straight on, and then sat down. She sighed, long and deep. Even in profile, I saw a great sadness.

"What would you ask me to do?" She hung her head.

Merlin's eyes returned to their normal, piercing gray color.

"I ask for you to understand yourself. The effects you create here, now, in this time. The continuing influences if you stay."

"I think I can answer that, easily enough. But knowing you, the obvious answer isn't the one you mean." She kept staring at the floor.

"You fall asleep at odd times," Merlin said. "You do not sleep well. Your dreams disturb. You wake unrefreshed."

"It's getting worse." She glanced at him, then back to the floor.

"Do you know why?"

She shook her head.

Merlin looked at me. "Now, you shall tell Ambrosius of this morning."

"Blood." The word burst from me. "Blood all over you. Matted in your hair. Dried blood stiff on your clothes. Blood smeared on your arms."

Amber stared at me while I spoke. Now, she examined her arms, checking for signs of blood or cuts.

"It wasn't your blood."

"Then whose?"

"That is the question we must answer," Merlin said. "And how it spilled upon you."

She asked, "How will we do that?"

"Alfred shall ask Lolly."

"Lolly?"

"Me?"

We both spoke at once. Amber seemed confused, and a touch angry again. I was merely confused.

Merlin said, "Lolly operated the automobile last night. She brought you home. You and she share this body."

"Shares my body?" She didn't want to believe, despite all that I'd told her.

"I suspect it is the other way around," Merlin said. "You came to this time ethereal. Elaine's spell drew your essence to Lolly's body. But she remains in her body as well."

"If what you say is true…"

"It is."

"…then I owe an apology to Billy."

"Oh, much more than that." Merlin motioned for me to stand. "Alfred, call to Lolly."

I didn't like where this was going. There weren't any swords around, but I wasn't sure I wanted to chance her anger again.

"Can't you do it?" I asked Merlin.

"Of course I could, but I should have to pull her to me. I do not wish to coerce her. You and she share a strong thread. To you she shall be willing to come."

"I don't understand."

"That is not necessary. Call her name."

I turned to Amber, the question in my eyes.

She'd calmed down. "Go ahead. If he's right, I need to know. And if he's wrong, I also must know."

"But how will you know she's come?" I asked. "You never know when she's here."

"I'll fall asleep. And that, I will know." She faced Merlin. "You will not be the cause of my sleep, magician."

"Be assured, I shall not."

"OK," I said. "Lolly, come to me."

Merlin snorted. "And I thought you had affection for the woman. Call to her as a man calls to a woman."

I tried to concentrate, to put forcefulness into my voice. It felt odd, trying to format my voice into something different. Looking at Amber, I thought about how different Lolly looked. Not Amber's set expression, but Lolly's softness. Not Amber's direct stare, but Lolly's sparkling, playful eyes. Except for last night, when she was frightened, looking for someone to protect her. And she turned to me. She came to me in the night for help and protection.

"Lolly, talk to me. I want to help you."

An immediate transformation occurred. Amber disappeared; Lolly emerged. It took a bare moment for the set of her shoulders to change, and when she shifted in her chair, her whole attitude was Lolly.

"Alfred, you precious boy. You wanna be my hero, don'cha?" She brushed my arm, her eyes damp.

I'm sure my grin looked pretty silly. I clasped my hand over hers, holding it to my arm. "Yes, I'd like to be your hero."

"Most quaint. Reminds me of that fool Mallory," Merlin said. "Love and chivalry."

When Lolly turned her face from me, I felt like clouds covered the sun. But she left her hand on my arm and squeezed it from time to time.

"Merlin," she said. "The great druid 'n magician. You fiddle with men's minds, don'cha?"

"So. Ambrosius knows nothing of you, but the barrier is not reciprocal."

"I do'n know what *reciprocal* means, but there is'n a barrier to me. I know about him. And I know that he thinks highly of you. I hear it real clear. But you are'n his hero any more."

"He?" I said.

"Ambrosius. He's very male, oh yeah, he is. But he's adapted to our body." She fluffed her hair with her free hand. "I just wish I could get 'im ta wear somethin' a bit more fun. An occasional frill would be nice, would'n it? Some pretty colors?"

"Lolly." Merlin called her attention back to him. "What happened last night?"

She ducked her head and shrugged her shoulders.

"You made Ambrosius sleep yesterday afternoon and took the auto on a long drive."

"What if I did?" She stuck her chin out at him. "A girl can take her car for a drive, can't she?"

He sighed. "My child. I am not going to punish you for driving an auto. Where did you go?"

Dropping her head, she let her hair cover her eyes. "Jus' drove."

"Where, my dear?"

"You know, out in the country. West. I went west." She stared at her knees.

"Did you have a destination?"

She pulled her hand from my arm and folded both in her lap. "Do'n know. I jus' turned when I felt like it."

"Merlin," I said, "what are you doing to her? You're treating her like a little girl."

The old man ignored me.

"Lolly, dear girl. Did you control the automobile?"

She spoke in a small voice. "I drove. At first. Then I fell asleep."

"Where were you when you fell asleep?"

"In the car."

"Yes, my dear. And where was the car?"

"Not on the highway. I would'n fall asleep drivin'." Her open gaze pled for his approval. "But I got real sleepy, so I parked at a gas station. At an intersection of a couple a highways. I do'n 'member which ones."

Merlin looked to me with a question in his eyes. He didn't know what a gas station was!

"It's a place to refuel the car." He still didn't seem to understand. "Power. Energy. Liquid to make the engine run." He shrugged, like it was unimportant.

"Lolly, when you woke, were you at this...gas station...still?"

I couldn't hear her response. I leaned closer.

"Then where were you, my girl?"

"It was real dark when I woke up."

"But you woke in a different place, didn't you?"

"Yes, sir. The car was almos' in a bar ditch, out in the country somewhere." She turned back to me, putting her hands on mine, and rambled along, getting more excited as she continued. "I was so scared. I did'n know where I was or how ta get home. I could tell there was somethin' on me, but I thought it was jus' mud. I thought I'd fallen into the bar ditch, you know, and got muddy? I jus' started drivin'. I finally saw a big street and got on it. It was Highway 105, and I knew that road led home. Ambrosius had driven that way lots, and I recognized the number. I went the wrong way at first, but I was pretty sure I needed ta go east, so I turned around. I passed the turnoff to the Renaissance Festival and through Magnolia and made it home."

She paused, and then continued at a more measured pace. "I saw in the light that it was'n mud. It was blood. That's why I came to you." She looked into my eyes. "My hero." She gave me a small smile.

"We'll figure this out," I said. "Don't worry."

Merlin interrupted. "Humph. Lolly, when you woke up, did you see anyone else nearby?"

She shook her head. "But I did'n really look hard. I jus' wanted ta get home, you know?"

The front door slammed, and we turned as Billy rushed in. He stopped just inside the room.

"Amber, there you are." He almost panted from exertion. "Why didn't ya pick up the phone? I left messages. Where ya been? I've been worried sick." He paced the room.

A glance told me that Amber had returned. Merlin muttered something I couldn't understand.

"Billy?" she said. "How long have you been here?"

"Wha...? I just got here. What's goin' on?"

Amber turned to Merlin. "Did it work? Did you speak with Lolly?"

He nodded. Then he glared at Billy. "This seneschal bumbles more than the last you had."

"You dislike anyone I trust, old man." She rose and walked to Billy, putting her hand on his chest. He stopped pacing, but his arm twitched and he fidgeted as she spoke.

"I apologize for frightening you, my friend. It seems," she glanced back at Merlin, "that I have not been myself lately."

"Well, as long as you're all right." He backed up a pace and began rocking from foot to foot. "But I do wish you'd let someone know when ya just take off like that. You do have friends who worry." He made meaningless gestures with his hands. They looked a lot like the ones Merlin formed, but his seemed without purpose, unlike the old man's.

"You're right," she said. "A woman living alone should remember she has friends. Friends who shouldn't worry unnecessarily, I might add."

"Haven't ya heard the news? It's all over the radio and TV. I was scared shitless that you'd been hurt. They haven't told who it was yet, not even man or woman."

"What are you talking about?"

"Another murder. It's time for the noon news. Turn on the TV."

We followed Billy into the TV room, drawn more by his nervous energy than anything else. The program came on to a commercial so Billy switched to other local channels, but they were all on break. He kept switching until the lead-in music started on one station.

"This morning's breaking news. Another grisly murder in our viewing area, this one east of Navasota. We're going to our reporter on the scene, Javier Escondido."

"That's right, ChaoLinh. The police haven't given many details, but they have told us that this one is like the Tomball and Brenham murders. One officer who did not want to be shown on camera told me it looked like someone had gone berserk with a huge knife. Crime scene experts are combing this quiet farm and home for clues. Could this be a serial killer? Police won't speculate."

The camera pulled back to show the busted front gate of a run-down farmstead. The entry drive led over a cattle guard. On one side a wooden post supported a short piece of a crossbeam above the entry, but the post on the other side had rotted away several feet off the ground. A misshapen pine tree sat a few feet behind the gate. The reporter continued talking about the impact on the neighbors who lived a few hundred yards away.

I glanced at Amber, but saw Lolly staring at the TV. She seemed to be wavering. I took her by the elbow to steady her, and she put her hand on my shoulder and whispered to me.

"That gate. I saw it las' night. After I woke up. Firs' thing I saw."

Her hand went limp and dropped from my shoulder. I thought she might faint. Instead, she glared at me and shook my hand from her elbow. Amber was back.

CHAPTER 23

"SEE WHAT I mean?" Billy gestured at the TV. "There's a deranged wacko out there killin' people, and you shouldn't be wanderin' off without tellin' anyone."

Merlin stepped between Billy and Amber before she could reply. "Your friend is safe. Still yourself."

"Hey, we got along just fine until you showed up. Why don't you just butt out?"

I stepped back. Billy's nervous energy had found an outlet. He looked ready to punch Merlin.

Amber took command of the situation, speaking in a calm and steady voice that demanded obedience.

"Gentlemen. Sit down. Now."

Billy deflated. Merlin just raised an eyebrow, and then turned and bowed to Amber.

"As you wish." He sat on a nearby chair, back straight, gripping his staff in front of him.

Billy plopped onto the sofa.

A now imperious Amber stared at me. I skulked to the other end of the sofa. She turned off the TV in the middle of a taped report about a skirmish between Chinese factions in Peking.

"Billy, stop acting like a child. I'm not your private friend or personal toy. Merlin, stop goading him. And you," she turned to me, "why are you still here?"

I shrugged. "Lolly."

Billy tried to shush me.

"It's all right, Billy," Amber said. "I know about Lolly. I don't like it, but I know."

"May I speak?" Merlin asked.

"Choose your words with care."

He raised a thick eyebrow again, then nodded. "The questions outnumber the answers."

"And you believe I need your special counsel?"

Merlin bowed his head in assent.

Billy half rose to speak, but Amber motioned him back. She stood thinking for a full minute.

"Billy, I have unfinished business with my old friend Merlin."

She again made him keep his seat.

"Rest assured, I won't roam unattended. I'll call you later today. Now you must go."

"But, Amber—"

"There are things that must be resolved. Do not question my judgment."

"Well, crap." Billy kicked at the floor and then left the room. The front door slammed behind him.

"Now, Merlin. What have you learned?" Amber folded her arms across her chest.

"Come. Both of you."

Amber sighed. In a way, it heartened me that I wasn't the only person whose questions he ignored.

He led us along the now-familiar path through the woods. The clearing looked just as it had when we'd left it early this morning, except the bench had been dragged back to the fire circle.

"So this is where you've been keeping yourself. I have a friend who likes to come here."

"Neve?" I asked.

Amber eyed me. "How do you know Neve?"

I shrugged. "Nothing magic. She came by last night while we were here."

"Oh, yes. Halloween. I forgot she was coming."

Merlin cleared his throat. "Your friend is an unexpected treasure. However, we have less pleasant business to tend to."

I noticed a loose pile at his feet and jumped back from it. "Shit, Merlin."

"What's that bloody mess?" Amber asked, curious but not upset by the blood-splattered clothing.

Merlin looked to me and nodded. Why did he want me to explain?

I hesitated. "Last night."

"Oh, damn, Merlin. Did you kill something last night?" Her eyes expanded. "Neve?" Her concern morphed to controlled anger. "Answer quickly, old man."

My words rushed out to stop the threat in her voice. "Neve's fine."

I took a breath and the words I didn't want to say burst out. "Those are your clothes. You wore them home last night. They were bloody then. Merlin didn't do anything. You did."

"Absurd." She leaned over, examining the parts of fabric that weren't stained reddish-brown. "No, it's absurd."

I started to speak, but a motion from Merlin's eyebrow caught me. I stepped back.

"Crazy." She shook her head. "It can't be. But those are mine. Yesterday?"

Merlin eyed me again. "What did Lolly whisper to you? Something about the news on the telly."

"Lolly?" Amber shook her head. "I didn't fall asleep while the TV was on."

I said, "Lolly took over for about half a minute. Remember when I had hold of your elbow? She needed comfort."

Amber blinked; a look of understanding crossed her face.

I said, "She recognized the gate at the farm. Where the murder happened. She was there last night."

"What, exactly, did she say?" Merlin asked.

His steel eyes drew me into them. I blinked a few times and turned away, looking to Amber.

"She fell asleep at a gas station. When she woke up, she was in the country. She got scared and just drove away. The gate was the first thing she saw."

"Lolly? Last night?"

"That's right. She woke up and her clothes were bloody. What did you do?"

Amber ignored my question and turned to Merlin. "You're right. There are things I must know. Proceed with your ritual."

They never answered my questions. Neither one of them.

"I shall do my best to make you aware. I may fail. Either way, you shall accept my judgment as you accepted druid judgment in the past."

It wasn't a question. Amber nodded. The complexity of the world they lived in struck me once again.

"Sit on the bier," he said, and Amber sat.

"Do I need to be at my spot?" I asked, motioning to the tree. I felt drawn to the place, but I also wanted to be close enough to hear.

"Your power is not necessary. Your presence is necessary."

I didn't understand. So what else was new? But whatever was about to happen, I would be close enough to hear.

The old man shifted the bloody pile into the center of the fire circle, one piece at a time. The smell of grassy herbs—the same as last night—floated to my nose. Now the aroma carried an acrid tinge of blood beneath it. The stained towels laid beneath the clothes, the dried grasses matted into the blood. As he moved the last towel, he uncovered a blood-stained sword. He left the weapon on the ground.

Merlin closed his eyes and began chanting. I didn't understand a word of it, but I heard a repeated *ba-bum bum* rhythm in it. After a few repetitions, he began waving his staff over the pile. The refrain changed to a *ta-rah tah tah*, but I couldn't tell whether the main stanzas, if this was a poem, had changed. Later, it became something like *kra kashah*. Several times he walked around the circle of stones. After about five minutes, I lost track.

I thought about Lolly, about how frightened she'd been. I imagined myself as her hero. Then I realized Merlin had stopped chanting and spoke in English.

"…enough power, if she can be convinced."

Amber nodded. "I hope you're right."

"Now, Alfred. You must summon Lolly again. Then step back. You may watch and listen, but do not participate unless I direct you to do so. I am convening what you would call a court of law. Do you understand?"

Hell, no.

I nodded.

"Call to her."

It was easy this time. I'd been thinking about her, about helping her. And despite the craziness of it all, I believed this would help her.

"Lolly. We need you. Come to me."

The change had become familiar. Amber's face softened and her shoulders lost their militant edge. Lolly appeared. "Alfred. I'm afraid. What's he gonna do?"

"He's going to help you. Please believe me." I had to believe, myself.

Merlin placed his hand on my chest and eased me away from her, stepping between us. I moved to one side so I could see her and watch him in profile.

"Lolly, my girl," he said. "I will help you. And I shall need your help as well. Will you help me?"

Leaning on his staff, he looked like a frail, helpless old man. Lolly nodded, hesitant at first, but as he held his free hand out to her, she nodded with greater confidence and took his hand in hers.

"What happens to Ambrosius when you control this body?"

"He goes ta sleep."

"Can you waken him?"

"He takes over when he's awake."

"But he doesn't have to, does he? You know that from experience."

She squirmed, shaking her head and trying to avoid his eyes.

"Lolly, answer."

She peered into his eyes and stopped fidgeting, but didn't speak.

He said, "There are things Ambrosius must know. And things you must know. This step is the first. Help me. I will help you."

She turned her head toward me.

Merlin interrupted before she could speak. "His part is done."

Her head dropped and her arm went limp in Merlin's grip. He waited for her to face him.

"Please, I do'n know if I'm strong enough."

"You are strong enough to make him sleep."

"That's different. It's like…well. When he first came, you know, into my head and my body, he fought. I hadda keep quiet and keep still or they'd figure out. The doctors. But he would'n keep quiet. He did'n know how to do anything, but he fought and fought tryin'. He tried ta talk, he tried ta move, arms and legs. I heard him shoutin' in my head. He was mad, really, really mad.

"I hid in secret parts of my mind, where he would'n know I was there. He could'n make our body work right. He thrashed in the bed, and they put us in restraints. They hurt. He did'n know how he was hurtin' our body.

"I do'n know how long it woulda taken him. I decided ta help, you know, teach him how ta make arms move, words, stuff like that. He never knew it. I was jus' a voice, like in the back of his mind. It was real slow. But it calmed 'im, and when he quit fightin', they took off the belts and it did'n hurt no more. I showed him how ta see, droppin' pictures into his part of our mind.

"I could hear somma his thoughts. Nothin' deep, more like his reactions to things. That was new for me. It was funny sometimes, when he tried ta make sounds into words. I thought, this must be how a baby learns. Pretty soon he was talkin' to the shrinks. Now, that was funny.

"He told them that he was a king. Not a good idea. I whispered that he skip over that part. And about bein' a guy named Ambrosius. He caught on. He's a lot smarter'n I am.

"Ambrosius got us out of the crazy hospital. But then once he took us out into the world, I began ta wanna be a part of it. I never thought I'da wanted that. I figured out how ta put him ta sleep. But if he figures out I've been doin' that, he'll be mad. I'll get hurt."

"Lolly, how can he hurt you?" Merlin asked. "You share a body."

Her eyes expanded. "Oh, that is'n what gets hurt. Rage whips my very soul, and it hurts only me."

"You fear rage?"

She nodded several times, eyes still wide.

"You fear the rage of Ambrosius?"

Her eyes relaxed, and she shook her head. "No. When he first came and fought, he hurt me. He was jus' tryin' ta figure out where he was and why his body would'n do what he wanted." She paused and her face took the look of a pleased imp. "He was so surprised when he figured out he was a woman. His mind locked up for an hour."

"Ambrosius knows about you, now."

"Yeah, I know. He did'n wanna believe, but he does."

"He won't hurt you. Ambrosius is a good man. He knows how to be a gentle man."

"Yeah, like you think you know him better'n I do. I know that he wo'n wanna hurt me, but he's got a strong will. There are still parts of this brain he does'n know about. And that can cause us both pain."

"He needs to know. Only you can tell him. Will you try?"

"How?"

"Wake him and tell him."

Lolly shook her head. "I do'n know how ta speak ta him direct. Before, I whispered to him. Indirect, like."

"When he is awake and in control, you see and hear what he hears, yes? And hear what he says."

She nodded.

"Then you must trade places. Wake him, but leave him inside."

"I do'n know how ta do that, either."

"I believe that I know how. And I can ask him to help."

"What if it does'n work? What if he can't be awake but not in charge?"

"Then we shall try again."

She raised an eyebrow, skeptical.

"And again, if we must," Merlin said. "I shall provide my help, and we shall succeed."

Lolly considered it for a minute, and then she thought of something that seemed to give her hope. "OK, look. If it does'n work and Ambrosius comes back out, here's what you do. Tell him he has to jus' sit back and watch. OK? Tell him it's like watchin' TV. Just sittin' on the couch. Somebody else has the remote control. OK? Tell him that."

"Shall we begin?"

"What do I do?"

"How do you give him control?"

"I send a thought ta wake up."

Merlin considered for a moment. "Send a thought for him to open his eyes and watch."

Lolly sat still for a few seconds, and then her face scrunched up and she shook her head. The softness faded from her eyes, replaced by Amber's clear vision. The rest of her face retained Lolly's softness. Merlin continued squeezing her hand and rotating the top of his staff in a tight circle. All the softness disappeared, and Amber appeared before Merlin.

Amber shook her hand free. He stopped rotating his staff.

"What happened?" she asked.

"We tried to let you see through Lolly's eyes. You awoke too much." Merlin motioned me forward. "Explain this telly watching."

Amber looked at me, puzzled.

"When you're in charge of your body, Lolly can watch. Merlin is trying to fix it so you can watch while Lolly's in command. You should pretend you're on the sofa, watching TV. You have to leave the remote control alone."

Merlin asked, "Do you understand?"

Amber rubbed her earlobe. "Yes. Watching television is a passive activity. I'm to be passive."

"Then we shall begin again."

I started forward. Merlin held a hand out.

"That is no longer necessary. I will summon Lolly."

His hand passed through the space between him and Amber, and her hard features melted. He smiled to reassure Lolly. "We shall try again."

She nodded. Merlin took her hand in his. With the other, he again began rotating his staff.

"Tell him to waken and be at ease."

I was ready this time. The change in the eyes. The struggle. Just like before, so I could pay more attention to other things. Merlin murmured a soft chant, rubbing his thumb on the back of Lolly's hand in rhythm to his words. I saw the effort Lolly made to maintain control, and this time, after a few seconds, her face softened again around the eyes. He continued chanting, and I saw Lolly relax all over.

"Is he awake?" Merlin asked.

"He says that he sees what I see. It's hard for him to...relinkish? No, relinquish control, he says, but he leaves himself...sub...subservint? I do'n know those words."

"Very well. Now you must concentrate: let him hear what I say. Can Ambrosius hear me?"

The muscles around her eyes tightened for a moment, like a wave passing from temple to temple. "Yeah, he hears."

"Can you speak with him directly, in your mind?"

She jerked, almost pulling her hand from the old man's. "I'd rather not."

"Why?"

"It might reveal my hidin' place. He's strong. I might lose me."

"That's fine, my dear. That's fine. One step at a time." He massaged the back of her hand. "You can hear him, so will you be able to tell me Ambrosius's answers to my questions?"

"I can hear him. That does'n reveal any secrets. Wha'cha wanna know?"

"Ambrosius, are you ready to learn the consequences of your presence here?"

Lolly concentrated, pulling her lower lip between her teeth.

"It's complicated. I do'n understand ever'thin' he's sayin'." I thought she looked a little embarrassed, but then she brightened. "That's better. He says yes."

"Lolly, you must trust me as Ambrosius trusts me."

"He trusts you ta do what you think is right."

Merlin nodded. He planted his staff into the soft ground. He passed his hands over the sword that earlier had been hidden beneath the pile.

Turning to the bloody clothing in the fire pit, he pulled something from his pocket. Whatever it was, it fell in tiny bits that floated onto the clothing. Something happened when they hit the bloody areas, like a little spark, and then those bits disappeared. The bits that hit unbloodied cloth just lay there.

Merlin began chanting, but this time I could understand him.

> Power resides.
> Power responds.
> Blood demands.

He picked up the sword and waved it over the pile.

> Sword deeds.
> Vengeance gained.
> Carnage.

He sprinkled some of the bits on the sword. Sparks flew where they hit dried blood.

> Blood demands.
> Power responds.
> Rage.
> Silence.
> Fear.
> Power responds.
> Blood demands.

Merlin turned to Lolly, a terrible fierceness in his face. He pointed the sword at her heart and shouted, "By the blood of your enemy, I bind you. I call you forth. Rage, come to me!"

He spun and buried the sword in the middle of the rags. The pile burst into flames.

CHAPTER 24

WOW! NEAT TRICK!

Those were my first thoughts. Then heat flashed by me. Even five feet away, I felt a searing flare on my face and arms. Not only that, but it warmed the nape of my neck and my shoulders. It even wrapped around and heated my back.

I expected to cringe from a foul odor of burnt blood, but the aroma following the rush of heat reminded me a bit of burnt leaves and even more of hot caramel. The combination of lasting warmth and smell provoked a glow of satisfaction and wellbeing.

The flames consumed the bloodied clothing. The fire emitted intense heat and lasted longer than it should have. Despite the flames dancing over the whole pile, the unbloodied cloth remained intact and unburned.

Then, just as suddenly as they had flared up, the flames disappeared, leaving ragged bits of unsinged cloth.

Merlin's voice boomed. "Stay!"

I turned from the fire pit to see why he shouted. He held his staff at arm's length; the knob on the top blazed with a white light. He leaned the staff toward Lolly. Except it wasn't Lolly. And it wasn't Amber, either.

The delusion Merlin and Amber shared just became more complex.

The woman had a wild look in her eyes. Spittle flew from her mouth as she seethed. She strained to rise from the bench, leaning hard against…well, I didn't know what she leaned against. Nothing held her on the bench or prevented her from moving, but the muscles in her legs tensed, like she was struggling to stand but couldn't. She flailed her arms to the front and to the side. Then she threw her hands palm down onto the bench and tensed her considerable muscles trying to rise. She couldn't.

She screamed and tossed her head, shaking it back and forth until it seemed she had become Medusa, her hair angry snakes.

Every time she strained forward, Merlin's staff shone brighter, and when she sat back, it dimmed again.

What the hell? He's holding her somehow.

If I hadn't been so unsettled by Lolly's sudden transformation into this wild, feral thing, I would have studied his staff to figure out how it glowed. At the time, I concentrated on keeping a safe distance between me and the crazy woman who had taken over Lolly's body.

"You are bound. You cannot confound me. Still yourself." Merlin spoke in a loud and firm voice, but it also held concern, even kindness. It seemed to have an effect, because she stopped twisting about and sat back on the bench, saliva sliding down her chin. Merlin appeared to relax, also, but when she tensed and tried to rush forward, his staff flared again and she stopped like she'd slammed into a wall.

Merlin swept his free hand toward her and then jerked it upward, grasping the empty air as he did so. The motion seemed to drain all strength from the woman, who collapsed back onto the bench. Anger remained in her face and eyes.

"Rage, by the blood you spilled, I bind you. By the fury you released, I bind you. By the powers I command, I bind you."

She sat on the bench panting. Her eyes darted left and right. When she saw me, she held her focus on my eyes for a few seconds. I knew this persona. This woman had almost attacked me in the gymnasium but had slashed the mannequins instead. She told me last night that she had made the blood.

She pushed with her feet, trying to roll backward off the bench. But again, she hit an invisible wall. She thrashed side to side but couldn't move her body more than a few inches in any direction.

"Still yourself, Rage."

Rage. That's what he called her. She sure seemed real.

"Look at me. I am not your enemy."

She did look at him. Glared at him, in fact. And although the anger didn't go away, it seemed to tone down a notch or two. That old man could do amazing things with his stare.

"Speak to me, Rage."

"Pig!" Spit flew from her mouth with the word. Her voice had the timbre of a young child, but her inflection sounded savage and rabid.

Merlin waited.

She shouted, "Man!"

"A man," he prompted.

"Men. Bad. Men." She shook her head with distaste at each word, like a child forced to eat liver.

"Yes, bad men. How many, Rage?"

She squinted at him, head cocked, considering him. "Three. Three bad men."

"Three dead men." Merlin's voice remained steady, calming.

Her rocking head emphasized agreement. "Dead."

Merlin stepped toward her. Rage straightened up, alarmed.

Merlin paused, planting his staff again in the soft ground. Then he took two purposeful steps and sat beside her, a handbreadth separating them. She tried to recoil from him, but an unseen force continued to hold her in place.

"Is Lolly awake? Does she listen?"

Rage regarded him, wariness in her every muscle.

"Did you make her sleep? Is she sleeping now?"

She nodded. The hand closest to Merlin clenched and unclenched.

"Let her waken."

Rage pounded on her thigh. It looked like she tried to resist his command, and then she stopped with an angry look on her face like she had failed.

"Now, let Ambrosius waken."

"Man!" she hissed. "Hate men."

"Wake him. Do not resist, for you shall fail."

The shocked look on her face seemed to confirm his comment. The left side of her face went slack, and I feared a stroke. Drool pooled at the side of her mouth. Then she settled into a sullen funk.

"Does Lolly know what you did to the bad men?" Merlin asked.

She shook her head, not looking up.

"Does Ambrosius know?"

She sneered at Merlin, and then shook her head.

"Tell me about the bad men."

"Bad. Men were bad."

"What did they do? Did they hurt you?"

"Hurt. Mommy and Daddy. Bad. Bad men."

Merlin tilted his head toward her, like he understood, encouraging her to continue.

"You were a little girl. The bad men hurt your parents."

She looked at him like a child being understood by the adult. "Hurt. Killed. Yes. And after, men saw me. Watching."

Oh my god. She'd watched her parents being murdered.

"But they didn't hurt you."

"Would have. Mr. Stives stopped them."

"Mr. Stives chased them away?"

Her head waved back and forth. "Bad Mr. Stives. Bad man."

"He was one of the bad men. You knew him?" Merlin remained calm and still.

"Farm hand for Daddy. Fixed fences. Killed pigs."

"How did he save you?"

"Quiet girl. Saved her. Said, *Be quiet girl. Never talk. Quiet girl lives. Never say a word. If you talk, devils find you. They will hurt you. So girl quiet.*"

A tear rolled down her cheek. She threw her head back and howled.

I wanted to reach out and wipe her tear away, but it might break Merlin's hold on her. I wiped my own eyes instead.

Merlin waited until her cries ebbed to soft sobs, and then said, "People found you."

"Not that day." She wiped a tear away. "Not next day. Quiet girl laid with Mommy. Daddy was broken."

Merlin asked softly, "Broken?"

"Pieces." Her tears streamed down her cheeks again.

I was aghast. No wonder she spent so many years in the hospital.

Merlin patted her hand, and she didn't recoil.

"How old were you?" he asked.

"Seven."

"You didn't talk, did you?"

"Quiet girl didn't talk. Quiet girl laid in hospital." A last tear dripped from her chin. Some of the anger returned to her face. "Rage stayed inside."

"But you were stronger than Lolly. You were in charge."

She shook his hand off and cackled, a bitter laugh.

"What makes you laugh?"

She sang, "Lollipop, lollipop," and laughed again.

"Tell me about Lolly."

"Lolly likes sex." She spat on the ground.

I felt a warm blush in my cheeks.

"You don't like sex?"

"Hospital boy wanted sex. Quiet girl wouldn't stop him. Rage couldn't get out."

Merlin sat back. His eyes dropped to his hand making sign language in his lap.

Sorting his invisible threads again.

He said, "Go on," but his hand kept moving.

"Hospital boy called us his lollipop. His Lolly likes sex."

Merlin's eyebrows jerked up, his eyes opened wider, and he looked into her eyes. Whatever his threads meant to him, they seemed to have provided an answer. I wished I knew the question.

He resumed his conversation with Rage on a new track.

"Tell me about Ambrosius."

"Clumsy man. Crowded in here. Wouldn't stay still. Lolly taught him."

"So she said."

"Lolly doesn't lie."

"Do you? Lie?"

She shook her head. "Mommy said never lie. Mommy said be good."

"Your mommy was right," Merlin said. "When Ambrosius came, he changed your life. Yes? He wanted to be out of the hospital. To be in the world."

She nodded, fidgeting with her hands.

"What did you think of that?"

"Didn't like it. Scary world. Stayed hidden. Let Lolly help. Then he got swords." She smirked at the old man. "Liked that."

"You learnt how to use a sword. From Ambrosius."

"Yes." She thrust an invisible blade, her eyes roving around. "But I don't swing good. He's good."

"Why did you want to learn to swing a sword?"

Her hands dropped into her lap. "Kill the bad men."

"And you did kill them?"

"Yes."

"How did you find them?"

"Mr. Stives. Found him." She glanced sideways at Merlin. "Internet. Like CSI TV."

"He told you where the others lived?"

A feral smile. I thought memories played behind her hard-set eyes. "Not at first."

"You convinced him?"

"I saw what they did to Daddy."

Her distant stare chilled my blood. There seemed little there that remained human.

"I see," Merlin said.

"An eye for an eye and a tooth for a tooth. Mommy read that."

Merlin took her hand and patted it.

"A hand for a hand. Fingers to tell me bad man's name." She plucked at one of the old man's fingers. "A foot for other bad man's name. Another foot for where they lived. Then I gutted him, like he did to pigs. Like he did to Mommy."

"And the others?"

"Slash. Stab. Slice. Cut off dicks they stuck in Mommy. Gut them like pigs. To be sure."

Merlin rested beside her. I found myself sunken onto the grass.

CHAPTER
25

VENGEANCE. IT SEEMS a more just word than revenge. Vengeance is mine, saith the Lord. And if the Lord is on your side, then surely you serve justice. Smiting evildoers. Avenging wrongs done to the universe.

My petty imaginings were always about revenge for small personal slights. Thinking about slapping the person in the checkout line when she doesn't even take out her checkbook until the cashier has rung everything up. The touch of road rage for the ass in the car that cut me off. Taking an axe to an unfair boss.

I had milquetoast daydreams of playing out revenge fantasies.

This woman, this girl in a woman's body, this personification of righteous rage—*she* wrought just vengeance upon vile men.

What a world this is that can create such men. And to exact retribution, to create such a monster of a woman-child.

A monster that I admired, nonetheless. She had endured terrible pain and had found a way to avenge her parents. In the light of her past, my problems seemed petty.

Merlin tilted his head toward her. "Are there others you want to hurt?"

She moved her head in a slight side-to-side motion.

He again almost whispered. "Have you hurt anyone else?"

She started to shake her head, but then spoke. "Him, *almost*." She stressed the final word and pointed at me. "He made Ambrosius mad. Anger made me strong. We fought, Ambrosius and me. Threw sword. Didn't mean to. Both lost control. Lolly put him to sleep. I raged. But I didn't slice Lolly's man."

Merlin glanced at me, and I nodded to confirm her story.

"Lolly stopped me." Then she spoke in a childish—but maca-bre—singsong, "Lolly likes the silly man." She jumped liked she'd been pinched and then whispered, "Sorry, Lolly."

I found myself rising onto my knees and moving toward her. Rage scared me, but I felt compelled to touch her. When she saw me leaning toward her, she tried to shrink away, but Merlin's spell held her in place. Her eyes flared hotter and hotter. My hand touched the back of hers, and then I took her hand in mine. I don't know why. Once I made con-tact, her tension melted away and her gaze cooled.

"Lolly's hero." She seemed almost calm.

I squeezed her hand and then sat back on the grass.

Merlin glanced at me, one eyebrow raised. Then he refocused on the girl.

"Have Lolly and Ambrosius heard your story?"

She nodded. "Lolly might've missed some. Ambrosius held her. Covered her eyes and ears."

Hunh?

"I need to speak with Ambrosius now. You are still bound to my commands, and you shall come back when I call."

"'Kay," she stage-whispered.

The fidgeting stopped and the wildness left her face.

Amber jerked away from the old man. "Damn you, Merlin. That child didn't need to see such violence."

But she'd already seen it, I thought.

"I disagree. She must know her history. Lolly must become an adult."

Oh, Lolly. I started to object that she wasn't a child, but realized that she did act like a teenager.

"You didn't see it," Amber said. "We did. What Rage described, we saw. I tried to protect her from the worst of it."

"How?" I asked. *How do these multiple personalities interact?* "Aren't you just, what, thoughts?"

She looked at me like she'd forgotten who I was. Then she bowed her head in my direction.

"My apologies for almost causing you harm. Rage was right. I became angry and had difficulty controlling myself. I didn't mean to throw the sword. Anger fogged my vision. I think neither Rage nor I had complete control. And then I blacked out. When I woke again, I feared I had hurt you. So I was relieved to find you unharmed, for the most part. Rage and I injured you, but had my own anger won out, you would be dead.

"As to your question, this sharing of a body is new to me. These past years, I remained unaware of the girls that also live in this body. When Lolly woke me a few minutes ago, it was as she said. Like watching TV. Similar to the visions that Merlin gave me as a child, but more immediate.

"I didn't realize that Rage had put us both to sleep. I woke again, and Lolly was sitting on the other end of the sofa in front of that mental TV. Of course, that's just my picture of what we did. My imagination, I guess. At first, Lolly wouldn't talk to me, or even look at me. But as Rage's memories got worse, she shrunk toward me." Amber turned back to Merlin. "I tried my best to protect her, but Rage's memories were too vivid. The smell of blood and sweat and sex. I felt and I smelled the piss that ran down the leg of that terrified little girl. The slimy touch of that man after they killed her parents. Then her revenge.

"I've seen men killed in war, sometimes cruelly. But this was different. Rage slaughtered those men. She was slow and methodical. Lolly didn't need to watch that. She had no experience that could prepare her for those visions. She's shaken to the core. You should have told Rage to put her to sleep."

Merlin sighed. "It was difficult, I know. But it was necessary."

"Why? I've always trusted you before. But this time, I cannot see any reason for what you made her sit through."

Merlin remained sure of himself. "Lolly must take command when you return to your time."

"Return? I can't go back. Not after learning this. Caring for these girls is now my duty. It's why I'm here. This is my task in this time."

"Now you accept fate, Ambrosius?"

"Choice, then. I choose to stay and help them. They need me."

"If you wish to help, you must leave. That is your fate, and it must be your choice."

"That's crazy. Without me, they'd still be in the psych ward."

Merlin's look must have indicated he didn't understand.

"The hospital."

"True. But now, they are out. You did that for them. Your fate changed theirs. Nimuë and the others sent you here, but I doubt they conceived your destiny in this time."

"Nonetheless, I shall stay here."

"Would you have them remain children until this body dies?"

"Lolly's been a teenager for almost twenty years. The other one has been seven for even longer. They need an adult to protect them because they remain children."

"Yes. If you stay they shall remain children. Until you came, they did not live in the world. They did not age. They feared life. And rightly, I must say, since I know their story. But now, the men are dead and the danger is past."

"And a new danger begins. The police will be looking for the killer. They might find a fingerprint. Or DNA." She paused, realizing that Merlin remained unimpressed. "Proof, man. They may find proof that this body killed those men."

"I am better equipped to deal with such things."

"You know nothing of modern science, forensics and police procedures." She glared at the old man.

"True, but you know little more than I."

Amber's stare deflated. "I've been in this time for several years. I can learn."

"As can I. And I possess more potent defenses."

"It will take both of us to protect them."

"Ambrosius, your protection shall suffocate them. They shall remain children. I will help them to grow."

Amber sat silent.

"You must go to your destiny," he said.

Amber shook her head. "We don't need to decide this now. You won't have enough magic for another six months, maybe a year."

Six months. I'd forgotten about that. Rage scared me. Oh, hell. Amber scared me. *I want a chance to be with Lolly, but can I survive that long around Amber and Rage?*

"Tonight," Merlin said. "At sundown."

"What?"

Hunh?

"Samhain is tonight," Merlin said.

"No, it came last night. Halloween."

"The days do not match. Samhain begins tonight. I have felt the familiar magic rising all this day. It is now strong enough that I cannot be mistaken."

"But..."

"Had I seen stars these past nights, I should have known. But clouds and fog hid them many days. This night, at sundown, the magic shall begin to peak. Until dawn, this world and the next shall be at their closest. It is propitious."

"Halloween is Samhain. Neve told me so. She's always sought you on Halloween."

"Perhaps she should have sought me on Samhain."

I said, "It's the calendar shift."

Both of them looked at me, so I continued. "The first calendar, what was it, Julian? Yeah. Caesar's calendar. It wasn't quite right. The seasons drifted out of sync with the calendar. So someone developed another one. Gregory? He was Pope at the time. I don't know when Europe took the

Gregorian calendar, but the Americas did it in the 1700s. Jumped forward ten or twelve days."

Amber looked confused, but Merlin smiled. "Off from the stars by one day."

I shrugged in agreement. Could be. I learned about the calendar stuff back in high school, so the details were hazy. But if they both believed, then I still had hope that we could exorcise Amber tonight. Even I felt something would happen. Or maybe I just hoped it would.

"We must prepare." Merlin scrutinized the clearing. "Much of my work of yesterday remains, but we disturbed some, and it must be replaced."

"No," Amber said.

"I have no time to make new calculations," Merlin continued scanning, "and that is unfortunate."

Amber stood up. "No, Merlin. I won't go back."

He stopped looking around and half turned toward Amber. His eyebrows dropped so low they almost hid his eyes.

"This is my home," Amber said. "This is my life. Now is my time. I wanted to return. For years. But you didn't come. I began to ask myself what I'd left behind. I fought for years. For decades, Merlin. To achieve what? A kingdom fractured by jealousies and petty struggles. With barbarians pressing every border, I rested in winter to fight in spring and summer. How many seasons did that go on, Merlin? You tell me.

"And when, after many years, I had a measure of peace in my land, the province of Gaul began to disintegrate. I couldn't have another border in anarchy, so I rushed to aid the last of the Romans."

She seemed to be fighting tears for a moment.

"But a Roman betrayed me. I died, Merlin. On that battlefield I died. To be reborn, here and now.

"Look at the life I enjoy now. The least of the comforts of my home here are centuries beyond anything in the greatest of my grand fortresses back in our time. I have security, a land at peace and no brigands roaming the woods. I have a successful business and an income that affords me a life of comfort. I never had that, Merlin. Not even as a child. The Roman life disappeared and chaos crashed in. Our lives kept changing and things got worse. I tried to be a great king, but what did I do but slow the advance of decay and rot?"

"That is no small thing," Merlin said.

"If I go back, it'll be more of the same. But I will have lost this life."

"You must go back."

"No, Merlin. I choose not to. This is my life, and you cannot take it from me."

"It is a stolen life."

"It's what I have."

"The body is not yours. It belongs to the quiet girl. To Lolly. And to Rage."

"They never used it. Not until I came."

"That is true. It fulfilled Elaine's spell. And your presence has served a purpose. It has awakened them to the world around them."

"And I must stay to take care of them."

"No!" Merlin stamped the ground.

Amber sat down on the bench, her mouth open in shock at his outburst.

He said, "You have done good for the girls. You have also done them evil. Your heat set Rage afire. Your skills gave her a weapon. Your attitudes gave her leave to seek vengeance. A king may be judge and executioner, but a commoner may not. This girl is not a king. The death of those men may have been just, but Rage had no authority to decide, and none to execute. Nor could you decide. As you have declared, in this time you are not a king. You do not have the right to condemn men to death. You want to protect the girls? Then you must leave them."

"Who will control Rage?"

"You cannot. She is dominant over you. She puts you to sleep whenever she will. Can you do the same to her?"

"I haven't tried."

"You cannot."

"But I can try."

"You cannot. I have seen her power. She is now my concern, not yours. I bound Rage to me. As am I bound to her. As her druid judge, I must seek the best solution for her."

"You're no more a judge in this time than I am."

"I am druid, body and soul, the same person who judged for Arthur the High King. You have the soul, but not the body of the king. My long nap," he snorted a short laugh, "did not dull my judgment. In this extraordinary case, my knowledge better suits me to decide than any other judge."

"You cannot send me back without my permission. I know enough of your magics to know that."

Merlin nodded. I didn't like the direction of this argument. Amber was supposed to leave. She had to go.

"You wish to stay to protect the girls. You believe your presence here is best for them." He waited until Amber nodded. "Let us ask them," Merlin said. "Do they want you to stay?"

"Ask…how?"

"I will summon them. You shall hear their answers."

"No, wait. By your binding, Rage will give the answer you want to hear."

"I shall not influence her."

Amber ran her hand through her hair, and then nodded. "If they don't want me to stay, I shall return. I like this life, but I am not a tyrant."

"Lolly, speak," Merlin said.

She transformed in a beat, but it seemed to take place solely in her face. A few tears streamed down her cheeks.

She sniffled. "I had no idea. Rage's been aroun' my whole life, but I din't figure out she was a person 'til yesterday in the gym. I never knew what made the Rage in my head. Now I do. It was horrid, what they did ta my parents. I never knew them, and now all I know is that they died horribly. I jus' spoke to Rage," she said, her tears drying. "I tol' her, what she did to the bad men, they got what they deserved."

Merlin asked, "You heard what I want to ask, did you not?"

Lolly nodded, answering in a soft voice. "You wanna know what I think about Ambrosius. I owe him so much. I really do. He got us outta the hospital. He showed me that life has ta be lived. I do wanna live. Myself. I'm so sorry, but I want 'im ta go."

"Very well," Merlin said.

Amber came back and frowned. "I'm surprised. I thought she'd want my help."

Merlin's eye twitched, making one brow quiver.

"Now, Rage, tell me what you want," Merlin said, and the wildness took over the woman's face. "And answer your own answer."

"Hate the man. So crowded inside." She slapped her head. "But much to learn. He can stay."

The transformation back to Amber was almost immediate.

"Wow," she said. "A tie vote. I break the tie by voting to stay."

"There is a third vote," Merlin said. "Before yours."

"You don't get a vote," Amber said.

"Nor do you. The quiet girl has not told her choice."

CHAPTER
26

"WHAT ARE YOU talking about?" Amber asked, standing to face Merlin. "Isn't Lolly the quiet girl?"

"You hear, but you do not listen."

I stepped forward, stammering. "What? There's another? Another girl?"

Merlin put his hands on Amber's shoulders, first urging, then forcing her to sit on the bench. As he stepped back, he bumped into me.

"Oaf. Stand away."

I stumbled back a few feet. My dreams of building a life with Lolly were becoming more and more complicated. Unlikely, as well.

Merlin took some leaves from his pocket and crushed them. I smelled caramel again. He grasped his staff, still embedded in the soft earth. The top knob began glowing like before.

The engineer in me wants to know how he does that. Where are the batteries, and why isn't the bulb visible? Is it hidden under a thin veneer of wood?

"Lolly, I know you hear me," Merlin said. "Ask the quiet girl to come out."

Amber remained, staring at Merlin. She tapped her foot.

"Rage. Speak to her. It is her time."

Amber kneaded one of the bench support branches. "This is ridiculous, Merlin. There is no quiet girl."

The old man ignored her, moving the glowing head of his staff in a small circle. When he spoke again, his voice stayed low and quiet. But he did something more than that. I began to feel light-headed.

"You were first. You saw all. You witnessed your parents' deaths. The horror. And you saw the vengeance of Rage. It is time. The circle has closed." He stopped moving the staff. "Come forth."

Amber stopped tapping her foot. Her arm became still in mid-flex, like she forgot to continue. The hand that had been clenching fell open, palm up. The other lay still in her lap. Her thighs sank onto the bench, relaxed. She appeared to shrink, almost to lose her skeletal structure. Her body seemed disconnected from whatever she had become. At the last, Amber's eyes sought Merlin's. Then her face went flaccid and her eyes dulled.

Amber was gone. The woman's skin turned pallid; even her hair had gone limp.

"Hello," Merlin said.

He may as well have addressed a rag doll.

"Do you have a name?"

His head moved a bit as he spoke, but her eyes didn't track with him. He waited, but no response came. After many seconds, her eyelids closed, flowing like a sheet of water down a window, and then opening again in a reverse sequence. I thought it was an automatic reflex, but Merlin seemed to accept it as a response.

"Do you mind if I call you quiet girl?"

I sat on the grass to wait. Merlin spoke in a pleasant voice that reminded me of my first-grade teacher explaining how to make letters.

"Quiet girl. You were first, born into this body. You were there when the bad men hurt your mommy and your daddy. You hid and watched. What they did angered you very, very much, but you were small. You could do nothing to stop them. Then they found you in your hiding place. They told you to be quiet, never to speak, or they would come, find you and hurt you. Kill you. Your anger overwhelmed you. You wanted to hurt them. But you could not."

The woman on the bench didn't react. She blinked at regular intervals, that same mindless, automatic motion. It didn't seem to be in sync with anything Merlin said. But he continued, as though he had gotten through.

"You became quiet girl. Quiet girl does not get hurt. She lives; she does not die. But you had great anger. You had to find a place for it, or you could not be quiet. You might die. You wanted to live. You gathered your anger in one place. You made Rage. She could be very, very mad. You gave her a part of your mind for her tantrums. A small part—you kept the body still; you kept quiet. You kept Rage deep inside."

I felt so sorry for the quiet girl. I could no longer believe this was some shared psych-ward delusion between Amber and Merlin. Rage seemed real and, now, so did the quiet girl. Could the whole thing be true? King Arthur?

Merlin continued. "When the boy wanted your body, you created Lolly. Lolly could have pleasure because you could not. Since Lolly did not know about the bad men, she could react. You kept the secret, even from Lolly. You kept quiet."

He paused for a beat.

"Then Ambrosius came."

Merlin swept his glowing rod between him and the quiet girl. She blinked. Not the flowing curtain of water, but a true blink. I felt a rush of blood in my head.

"You did not make Ambrosius. He just came. He upset the order you had created."

He swept the staff back, and this time she reacted with a quick double-blink.

"You could not control him. Not like you had controlled Rage. Lolly knew about the world; she knew how to help him become part of the world. That made her stronger."

She blinked again, without the sweep of the staff.

"Ambrosius got stronger. Lolly got stronger. And Rage got stronger and watched Ambrosius. Rage learned how to use a sword. Rage learned how to kill."

Her face remained passive, but a tear formed in one eye. She blinked several times to clear it.

"Rage killed the bad men. The bad men who told you to be quiet. They are dead."

He inched the staff to a point between them and began moving the knob in a small circle. As he continued to speak, the circle grew.

"They are dead. All three bad men. They cannot hurt you. You need not remain quiet. You may speak now."

The circle had grown to about six inches across. At some point, her eyes began to follow the glowing tip as it slid left and right. Tears fell from her cheeks and she sniffled.

"I shall continue to call you quiet girl. Would you like that?"

She blinked several times and sniffled louder.

"Is that yes, or no?" Merlin asked. "Do this for me. Close your eyes and hold them for a moment."

She did as he asked, her cheeks wrinkling just a little as she held her eyes shut. When she opened them again, they found the moving glow and followed it again.

"Very good. We shall call that a yes. Now blink twice, quickly."

I noticed her tears had stopped as she blinked twice.

"Wonderful girl. That shall be no."

She closed her eyes and held them closed for a second, then opened them and watched the glow. Merlin slowed the movement over the next few minutes, while he continued to speak to the quiet girl.

"I am glad you have come out. You have been hiding and watching for a long time. Do you know how old you are?"

One long blink.

"Are you older than thirty years?"

Two quick blinks, no.

"Are you seven?"

Yes.

"Do you want to grow up?"

No.

"Do you like Ambrosius?"

A long pause, then one blink.

"Do you want him to stay?"

Her eyebrows dropped and she stared at Merlin, away from the now-stationary staff. She gazed at him for a long time, but when she blinked, it was a normal blink. She turned back to the soft glow of the staff without answering.

"Did you hear me talk with Lolly and Rage and Ambrosius about him leaving?"

Her eyes returned to Merlin and she blinked once, long and hard.

"You must decide whether he stays or goes. This is your body first."

The staff stopped glowing. I leaned forward to observe her reactions.

"If he stays, he will protect you as best he can. As shall I. You shall remain a little girl, and he will live in the world."

She gave no response.

"If he goes, I shall stay to help all of you and protect you. You can stay in the world, or you can go back to the hospital."

No! That isn't an option! I started to rise and interrupt, but Merlin seemed to know what I would do, because he motioned at me behind his back.

I sat.

"You must decide. Shall Ambrosius return to his own time?"

Again, her eyebrows dropped, and she didn't answer.

"This is your body, and you must decide if he remains or goes. Do you want him to go?"

He waited almost a full minute.

"Do you want him to stay?"

She still didn't respond.

"You must answer."

Blood rushed to her face, and she raised her hands to bat Merlin's staff away. She spoke in Lolly's soft voice, but touched with anger.

"Leave her alone. Can't you see? She does'n wanna answer. She's jus' a little girl. You're askin' her ta hurt someone, and she wo'n do that. Leave her alone."

"She must answer."

"No. I wo'n let you bother her. OK, see, I change my vote. He can stay. There. Now we do'n haffa bother her. Two votes. Hers does'n matter."

"That is most noble of you. Did she send you to tell me this?"

"No. She did'n send me. I could'n let you keep pesterin' her. Now, leave her alone."

"Do you know what she thinks? About Ambrosius staying?"

"I know she does'n wanna make such a big decision. You should'n a tried a make her. She's jus' a little girl."

"And you are just a teenager."

"So what?"

"Someone has to be the adult."

"Let Ambrosius. He's grown up." She raised her chin, her mouth set in a defiant pout.

"But he is not in control, is he?"

Her head dropped and she looked up at him. "Wha' d'ya mean?"

"You take over. This is so, yes?"

"He's in control the most."

"He is not in the most control."

"So what?"

"To be responsible means to be in control. How can he be responsible when you have power to put him to sleep and then do anything you want?"

The way he said "anything" made me blush, and it seemed to have the same effect on Lolly.

"But he does'n like sex. Not with boys. He looks at pretty girls."

He nodded.

"I mean, it might be fun with a girl. I've seen a coupla his fantasies, and he makes it look excitin', but I do'n know. I like the boys." She leaned around Merlin to smile at me.

"Rage told me that you do not lie."

"I try really hard not to. I guess I got that from the mother I never knew. That's what Rage said."

"Then tell me the truth. Do you want Ambrosius to stay?"

She folded her arms across her chest and frowned. "It is'n that easy ta answer."

"No, it is not, is it?"

"For me, I want him ta go. But that means you'll pester the quiet girl again. And I wo'n have that. I won't. It's mean a you ta expect her ta make that kinda decision. She's jus'a little kid. And she's had it hard."

"She relives her parents' deaths all the time, does she not?"

Lolly paused, and then her lips began moving as though she were mumbling. But I couldn't hear anything. Either Merlin couldn't either, or could but didn't want to interrupt. She talked to herself for a long minute, her head bobbing from time to time, while we both waited.

"Rage says that they both do. Even now, with all of those hateful men gone."

Merlin nodded. "Thank you, Lolly. Can I speak with Ambrosius now, privately?"

"Wha'dya mean?"

"Can you, Rage, and the quiet girl sleep for a short while? Until Ambrosius wakes you?"

"I guess so." Her head bobbed again a few times. "Yes. We'll do that."

The transformation to Amber began but reversed after a moment.

"You wo'n forget us, will ya?" Lolly asked.

Merlin leaned forward and patted her knee. "I will not forget any of you."

"You'll wake us up?"

"Yes, dear girl. I give you my word."

CHAPTER
27

I SAT STILL, glad that Merlin couldn't see me. I feared his desire to speak alone with Amber would mean I'd have to leave, and I wanted to know the big secret. Either he forgot about me, which I doubted, or he didn't care that I heard.

"Admirable girl. She is growing, already. Tell me, Ambrosius, do you truly wish to be responsible for keeping these girls as they are?"

Amber held her head down, hands running back and forth through her hair. She sat up and looked at Merlin.

"Damn you, old man. You know I can't. Lolly has a chance, but only if I leave. I'm afraid she may not be strong enough to take care of the others."

"Already she is dominant. She pushed the quiet girl aside and took control."

"But can she make them stop reliving their horrors?"

"I will do that."

"How?"

"If you leave, I can make the three girls one. The horrors shall become an old memory, nothing more."

"Which one will remain?"

"Most of her will be Lolly. She is almost mature. Quiet girl does not wish to grow up. Nor does Rage, and she must pay for her crimes."

"She executed simple justice. She has nothing to pay for."

"She had no right to be executioner."

"That is your judgment?"

"So I judge."

Amber bowed her head. "I don't like it, but I defer to your authority in this case. So be it."

"Wait," I said. "What just happened?"

Merlin continued as though I'd said nothing. "And you will return?"

She nodded. "It's best for the girls. Fate wins."

"It was your destiny, but it is also your choice. I must prepare."

"Hey, what just happened?" I asked again. "Are you going to kill Rage?"

Merlin removed the sword from the fire pit and began clearing out the small bits of cloth. Amber's resignation to duty showed on her face.

"I'll be going back to my own time. Lolly will remain. Somehow, our mage here intends to integrate the quiet one and Rage into the Lolly personality. In a way, it will be the death of both of them, I'm afraid. They'll be a memory for Lolly."

I should have been ecstatic, but I felt as melancholy as Amber acted.

No, that's absurd. Do I really believe this? I almost laughed at myself, but that would've drawn attention.

Merlin stuffed the unburned pieces of cloth in the sweatpants pocket and presented the sword hilt to Amber, blade resting on his outstretched left arm.

"Arthur, my liege. I wish welcome back to the noble man that I serve."

Amber grasped the hilt and lifted the sword from Merlin's arm. She looked at it like she didn't know what it was.

"Now," Merlin said, "I must wake the girls and tell them their fates."

"No, I shall. You are judge, but I am king, and these girls remain under my protection. Pronouncing their fate is my concern."

The woman and the old man regarded one another for a few seconds. Merlin nodded. "As you command. Might I suggest you awaken Lolly first."

"Yes. Good."

"Tell her that she and the other girls will choose the parts of them that she shall keep. She should not want the anger of Rage, but the girl's resolve could be useful. And the quiet girl has remained stoic for a long time."

"That will be a blessing to the others, knowing some parts will live on."

"And Arthur? You should decide what part of yourself to leave for Lolly, as well."

Amber's eyes glistened. "Thank you, Merlin."

"Begone. I have much to do here and little time."

Amber strode toward the path to the house.

Lolly. I was going to get a chance to create a life with Lolly. I almost didn't believe it. For the first time in a long time, things were working out my way. I felt sorry for Rage and the other girl, but Merlin said they'd still be part of her. Having Rage become a part of Lolly scared me some, but if they left the anger out, I hoped it would work out. At last, Amber would be gone.

The old man seemed to think that he should hang around and *help* her. Well, we weren't going to need his meddling. I would do what the old man needed me to do until Amber disappeared, and then find a way to get rid of him.

"Begone, I said," Merlin called to me. "You are not needed until sundown."

"Oh, I thought, uh…more wood?"

He held his hand out parallel to the earth. "There shall be power aplenty tonight. I will channel through you and through Neve. The wood we have is sufficient for light."

"Neve? Is she coming back?" Neve was all right. At least after she decided I wasn't some pervert in the woods.

"She presented me this card. With it, I can call to her." He flipped a business card around his fingers.

"I'll phone her." I held out my hand for the card. The old fool didn't have any interest in learning to dial a phone.

He shrugged and handed me the card. "I am done with this. You may have it. She gave no power to you through it."

I turned toward the house, but Merlin called after I took a few steps.

"Alfred, did you feel a connection to the girl called Rage?"

"She scared me. And I felt sorry for her. I admire her resolve. Is that what you mean?"

"A strong thread connects you with her. It pulsed with emotion."

"I don't believe in your threads."

"Do you have feelings of uncontrolled anger?"

I thought about my fantasies of retribution on my former bosses but shook my head. He didn't need to know about those.

"I told you about twinned threads connecting to you. I have discovered they belong to Lolly and Rage. Only now do I see the third one, obscured behind those two. It is almost insubstantial; it belongs to the quiet girl. All of them, including yours, are tangled with the thread connecting to Ambrosius."

OK, I could accept the Arthur crap, but his invisible threads remained pure fantasy.

He took a step back from me. I saw confusion in his eyes.

"Another thread. You bound a creature." It wasn't a question. "I do not recognize its kind."

"What do you mean?" *How could he know about the gecko?*

"Tell me, boy. What did you do? You found something else."

"OK, yeah. Fall off a bike, get right back on."

"Speak sense to me."

"Look, I'm sorry about your bird. I didn't mean to hurt it. I sure didn't mean for you to kill it. It just became a pissing contest, and I didn't like losing to a stupid bird."

"The hawk is no longer your concern. Tell me what you did."

"I tried something else."

"I know that, boy. Cut to the chase, as you say."

"A gecko." I saw that didn't mean anything to him. "A little green lizard. I figured, birds are hard, fish are easy, maybe a lizard would be easy, too. In between, maybe."

"You bound it?"

"I tamed it, yeah."

"Extraordinary. And you shared its mind?"

"It took a couple of tries. And then my own body was falling over, so I had to figure out how to be in both places."

Merlin's eyes flew open and his brows flared upward.

"Impossible," he said. "You have no training. Druids who demonstrate this aptitude require one or two years of training before they can split concentration. Are you certain you saw from both minds at once?"

"Sure. I reached out my human hand and my gecko body jumped onto it. Then I looked into its eyes and at the same time looked into my own from the lizard side."

Merlin waved the top of his staff back and forth between us. It glowed.

"The eyes. Even I look not into my own eyes. They open a portal to the self deep inside. What did you see?"

I didn't like the question because I didn't understand what had happened. But the old man seemed in the mood to tell me more about the visions, and even he thought I did well at it. Extraordinary, he'd said. So I told him.

"I saw both eyes, one of mine and one of the gecko's. Then I felt like I tumbled into a well. Like you say, deep inside."

"What did you see?" he repeated.

"Nothing. I saw nothing. I lost track of time for at least fifteen minutes. When it got dark, the contact broke and the gecko scampered away."

"Nothingness," he said. His staff began forming small circles, and the glow increased. He gazed at me for about half a minute. At the end, his eyebrows jumped up, like he'd had an important realization. He shook his head and turned away from me, muttering.

As usual, he didn't tell me what I wanted to know: what did it mean?

I didn't see Amber—or any of the girls in that body—when I got back to the house. I found a phone in the den and studied Neve's card. To my surprise, she managed one of the big chain bookstores. Hers sat on FM1960, a busy street. She'd written another number on the card. Her home number, I assumed.

I called the work number first; they said she'd called in to take the day off.

Neve answered the other number.

"This is Alfred. You know, from last night…?"

"Yes, my dear man. Tell Merlin I'll be there in about an hour."

That liar. He'd asked her to come back last night. Well, I'd caught him in a bald-faced lie.

"So you two made a date last night?"

"Date?" She sounded amused at the word. "In fact, he's interrupted my plans for a pleasant evening baking."

Not a liar, then.

"Alfred, did Amber get home OK last night?"

"She's…fine. I think she and Merlin better explain when you get here. How did you know Merlin wanted you to come tonight?"

"I don't know. About half an hour ago, I realized he needed me tonight. I've learned to follow such inclinations."

Oh, great. ESP.

But this could be good. Yes, good indeed. If I could link her and Merlin together, I'd get him out of my life. Oh, yes. They liked one another, so it couldn't be too difficult. *I've got to encourage this.*

"If we're not at the house when you get here, come to the clearing."

"Of course."

I had time to rustle up a bite from the kitchen before sundown. I hoped the night would bring great changes and the end of my lonely life.

CHAPTER
28

I ATE ALONE. I was used to it. Things would change tonight, though. No more Amber, no more Arthur. The new girls, Rage and the quiet one, they'd be gone too. I felt sorry for them. They were victims, but they'd never be happy in the world. I didn't care what Merlin planned to do, because Lolly would remain. So long as everyone believed he could get rid of the others, I'd go along with anything.

Merlin and Amber had discussed fate a lot. Free will and destiny. It made me realize that things had happened to me in life, but I hadn't made many things happen. Fate had kicked me too many times. I didn't become an ogre, yet Janet left me. And the merger? The old CEO got a golden parachute and I got the boot. Even Merlin swept into my life like a force of nature and caught me in the backdraft. Well, now I'd found something to choose. Someone. Lolly.

I wandered back into the great room. Looking around, I realized that this could become my home. I knew it was premature—Lolly and I hadn't spent much time together—but we had a strong connection. I chuckled, thinking about Merlin's threads. A rope must connect me to Lolly; only that could explain my intense sense of our entwined destinies.

For the first time, I imagined the room as a place I might live. It had an understated elegance, but it didn't feel comfortable. Decorated all in beige, the room leaned to a tailored look. I decided Lolly wouldn't be happy surrounded by this decor. We'd spend some time redoing this place. Lolly would want fun, for sure. Her playfulness would suffocate in this…somber…room.

I heard the faint sound of a door closing down the passageway that led to the basement stairs. I approached the entry foyer and heard voices. I didn't know whether I should go check or not. It could've been Amber or Merlin, but it could've been Lolly. I decided to just go check. Maybe Neve had arrived already. I didn't know how far away she lived, but it hadn't been an hour yet.

I passed the basement door and followed the hall. The door ahead stood ajar, and I saw an almost rustic room with exposed wooden beams and whitewashed stucco. A rough-hewn door on the opposite side of the room must be the entry I saw from outside. It must have been the door I heard closing. I recognized Amber's and Billy's voices.

Papers and a computer covered a heavy oak table in the middle of the room. Amber and Billy looked at me from opposite sides of the table. She waved me in and indicated I should sit in the massive oak chair next to Billy.

"This is good. Now we have a witness," she said.

He looked back to her. "I still don't get what you're about."

"Billy, you've been my friend, and you've been my business partner. I have things I must do, and I need your understanding in both areas. But as they say, business before pleasure."

Billy shuffled in his chair. "Amber, I don't like the sound a that."

"I've had some problems. Psychological," she said. "No, don't interrupt. I know you're aware of some of them. I've decided that it's time to deal with them. Straight on. I think I can resolve most of them, but I fear it could take some time before I'm ready to be in a position of responsibility. Like I am at work."

"You're goin' to deal with this Lolly thing?"

I saw the rue behind her smile. "Maybe it's the Amber thing that I'm going to deal with."

Billy shook his head, rising from the chair.

"Sit down, Billy. I want to take care of business first."

He sat, but continued to fidget.

"I've written a memo. I'm giving you my proxy over decisions relating to the company, effective today, and lasting one year. It may not be written in legalese, but I've made it as clear and simple as I could. Now, I will sign it, and Mr. Marlborough will witness it."

Amber picked up a quill pen, dipped it in ink, and signed with a flourish. She signed a second copy and pushed them across the table to me. I found a ballpoint pen and signed both pages.

She put one copy in a top drawer and walked around the desk to hand the second to Billy.

He wiped a tear from his eye.

"You're goin' back, aren't you?" he said.

"Not in the way you mean." She squeezed his shoulder.

She looked around him, nodding at me. "Now, if you will excuse us, Alfred, the business is done, and I need to talk with Billy as a friend."

Amber walked me to the door and as she closed it, I heard her start her goodbyes to Billy.

"I've never told you what a good friend you've been to me. I'll never forget."

I was happy with what had happened. Lolly and I would need time to get to know one another, to merge our lives, and Billy seemed a good businessman. He'd keep the company running until Lolly could take over. Plus, he didn't like Merlin, and I could use an ally there.

I went back to the kitchen, found a piece of cake and read the newspaper. I skipped over all the war updates from around the globe. There were too many.

A while later, the doorbell rang. I heard Amber greet Neve. I was about to go say *hi* when they came into the kitchen.

I saw Neve in daylight for the first time. She was a slender 5' 7" and looked in her late sixties, with an active vigor in her movements.

Her deep, black eyes peered over a slightly sharp nose. She had short, gray-streaked, black hair.

"I never worry about you," Neve said. "You're one of the strongest women I know. Your friends caught me by surprise last night, that's all. Merlin is everything you said. He has great powers."

"Billy reminded me today that I take my friends for granted. I should've called when I heard you'd been here. But today has been... unusual."

"How?"

"Neve, I'm afraid that in this case the less you know, the better it will be for you."

Merlin spoke from the patio door. "I disagree. We have need of her healing powers."

"Merlin," Amber said, "in today's law, if you tell her and she does nothing, she could be seen as an accessory after the fact. As are both you and Alfred, already."

"I am unconcerned."

"Well, I'm concerned," she answered. "I'll be gone, and you'll have to clean up the mess."

"Not for the first time. I am well suited to the task."

Neve said, "Could you explain to me what you're talking about? Where are you going?"

Amber shrugged, then nodded to Merlin. Over the next fifteen minutes, he told her about the quiet girl, Rage, Lolly, and then Ambrosius. He related them as individuals, rather than multiple personalities, but Neve was smart enough to figure out what he meant. He explained how each one came to be, except for Ambrosius, who just popped in from "the past." I fought the urge to laugh at that, but Neve didn't question it. Of course, Amber had been telling her the same story for several years, so it wasn't news to her.

Merlin explained that the men who had killed the girl's parents were the ones on TV, the ones brutally murdered.

"It was justice," she said.

Merlin said, "Rage executed them."

I thought she'd be shocked, but she smiled.

"Even better," she said. "Even better."

"Not so," Merlin said. "Vengeance is not justice. Rage must pay for her crimes."

His pronouncement shocked Neve. "Pay? She paid her entire life. She should be rewarded."

"You know as well as I that a community cannot long survive when individuals exact vengeance. That role must remain with the community."

"But, surely, the circumstances…"

"The circumstances call for the most severe judgment."

"Oh, Merlin. You can't."

"I must. Rage was created for one purpose: to hold the anger that poor little girl could not show. Quiet girl controlled Rage until Ambrosius upset the order. Then Rage found that she had the power and the tools to do the one thing she wanted to do but could not for so many years. She killed. She killed them all. Now her life has no more purpose. She could kill again, but for some lesser evil. That circumstance I cannot allow."

"Oh, the poor dear."

"I also must end the quiet girl."

"But why, Merlin? What has she done?"

"Nothing, except endure. But the time for endurance is past."

"Are you so heartless, then?"

"I am a druid judge. My heart and soul compose part of every judgment I make."

"Can I appeal your judgment?"

Merlin raised one eyebrow. "No druid council exists in this time to appeal to. I am the only one."

"I cannot accept your decision."

Amber leaned toward her friend. "The quiet girl and Rage have."

"They know?"

Amber nodded. "They know one person should occupy this body. One. They agreed it must be Lolly. They've suffered enough."

Neve appealed again to Merlin. "But you can't just end their lives …"

"And I shall not," he said. "They will give their best parts to Lolly."

"You said she acted like a teenager. How will she cope?"

"With my help. And yours."

Neve's hand flew to her breast. "Mine?"

He nodded to her with reverence. "You are a healer and a wise woman. I can remove the two girls, but I cannot sew the pieces left behind into the fabric of Lolly. For that, I need your healing power."

She shook her head. "My power pales compared with yours."

"I am not a good healer. For battle surgery and traumas of the body I have experience enough to overcome my lack of healing power. But this knitting of three minds into one, it is beyond me. I shall need not only your power and compassion, but strength that I will borrow from Alfred."

Neve's question to me didn't need to be asked. I shrugged. "The acorn mark."

"You'll let him use your power for this?"

"If I have any, he's welcome to it," I said. "It's never done me any good. I'm glad to help Lolly become a woman. One woman."

"His power differs from yours, Neve. Few who have the mark can wield it themselves. Alfred has shown certain abilities, but more importantly, he is a reservoir that one with knowledge and ability can use. As I can. You have both power and the ability to make it work for them."

Neve took Amber's hands in her own. "Is this truly the best for the girls?"

"It is." Her eyes showed her sincere belief.

"Very well. What will happen?"

Merlin described some mumbo jumbo that I couldn't follow. The gist was that he'd use my power, whatever that entailed, to reach into Amber's mind. He would trigger a spell originated by Nimuë when she sent the king forward in time. That would return Ambrosius back along the thread in the Aether to his own time.

I would be so glad to get rid of that thread. That one had gotten me into this mess in the first place. I'd keep the rope binding me to Lolly, though.

Next, he'd support Neve's healing powers to knit together the pieces of personality to create one. Lolly. Once she became whole, he'd release her mind.

And I'd see to it that he'd keep releasing her. Until he had no hold at all. I hoped Neve could help with that, also.

She said, "Merlin, you told me last night that we should all know about Ambrosius, that people told great stories about him. You said that we didn't know them because he'd come here. Or rather, he'd come to now."

"Through the years many tales have been told," he said. "Those tales call him Arthur, the High King. Most are rubbish. But his fame lasted centuries. As it should in this time."

"After we send him back, will that change? Will I know all the stories?"

"That is my belief."

"What else will change?"

Merlin harrumphed. She'd put him on the spot, and he didn't like it.

"I cannot address certain things because Ambrosius must not know his future."

"Will our world be better? Worse?"

"My lady, I do not know."

She made a guess. "History will change. People could die."

No. History already happened. It can't change.

"Those people would not die; they would never have existed. No one remaining shall know such persons once lived, just as no one now knows the stories of Arthur. Perhaps others who are not here shall exist, and people shall believe that they have always done so."

"I'm not sure this is a good thing," she said.

"It is what must be. This life is the lie. I have considered this since I discovered the temporal oddities. Ambrosius's presence here prevents his completion of tasks in the past. That changed this present. Sending him back shall restore the past and therefore the present."

"It's confusing," Neve said.

"It is a knot in the fabric of time. The druid sisters created the knot when they sent him to this present. The power they unleashed changed this time, knotting it with threads that did not exist in the correct time here. Perhaps there are but a few, but they wrought a magic in this time that requires another magic to untangle."

I asked, "What do you mean by threads that didn't exist?"

"People." He turned in his chair to face me. "As Neve said, some people are here who do not belong. They are bound in the magic of the knot in time. After tonight, the true weave shall continue without those threads."

Neve looked concerned. "Will they just…disappear? That doesn't seem fair."

Merlin rotated his gaze from me to Neve. "They are not meant to be. Their presence is the anomaly, not their loss of existence." He turned back to include me in the conversation. "I would thank them for their sacrifice, if it could make a difference."

What a load of bushwa! But I wasn't the one that had to buy it. As long as Neve did, and Amber did, then Lolly would be left. I hoped. I was glad, for once, that my opinion didn't make any difference.

Neve glanced at her friend. "What of my memories of Amber? Will I forget her?"

"We shall remain within the circle of power. We shall have memories of both realities. If, or how, the rest of the world remembers her, I do not know. I cannot control that. I can merely set things right."

Neve asked Amber, "Will it be right?"

Amber's features softened, and Lolly took control. Neve gasped. She'd been told about the change, and now she saw it.

Lolly held out her hand. "Neve, I'm so glad finally ta meet 'cha. I'm Lolly." Neve took her hand. "You're a really special person, and Ambrosius always thought highly of ya. I asked him ta let me speak, ta tell ya what we think. The quiet girl wo'n talk to anyone but Rage, and Rage… Well, Merlin's the only one who can calm her down enough ta keep her from rantin'. I'm used to it, so I can ignore her anger, but she's afraid you'd take it wrong. The girls want me ta speak for them."

Neve smiled, still holding Lolly's hand. "Go ahead, dear."

"Rage is mad that she's gotta die."

Neve tried to interrupt, but Lolly wouldn't let her.

"Ya gotta understand, for Rage, mad's pretty mellow. Normally, she's howlin' angry." Lolly smiled, a small, sweet smile. "Mad is pretty close ta reasonable, for her. She's not mad at Merlin for tellin' her she's gotta go, or at me for bein' the one ta carry on. She's mad that her lot in life was ta be the one ta carry our anger. She's mad because now that the reason ta be angry is gone, she has no purpose. She's mad because the only way any of us can have happiness in this body is for the rage ta disappear. She's mad because she knows she's gotta go."

She paused, wanting Neve's reaction, but was so impatient for it that she started jabbering again.

"Does that make sense? I mean, it does to her, and it does to me, but does it make sense to you? Ambrosius thinks it will help you ta help us if you understand. Do ya?"

Neve nodded. "I'm a bit surprised. Merlin told me Rage was just a little girl. That seems awfully mature reasoning."

"Yeah. Mostly, Rage is seven. But a lotta what Ambrosius calls worldliness came our way over the years that the quiet girl did'n want, so she shoved it at Rage." Then Lolly smiled real big. "Rage wants ta give me the worldliness. Oh, and cunning. I get ta be clever."

I wanted to tell her that I liked her just the way she was, but I kept quiet. Neve had to believe.

"What about the quiet girl, dear?"

"She told Rage that she's tired. She's ready ta let someone else take over. Everthing."

"Everything," Neve repeated.

Lolly nodded, watching Neve wide-eyed.

"What part of herself is she giving you, my dear?"

"Our mommy. Our daddy. The good memories, I do'n have any. She has loads of 'em that she's kept all these years, and I get 'em. All the good ones."

Lolly bubbled with pleasure, but Neve looked shaken. Her lower lip trembled, and a tear slipped down her cheek.

"OK," Neve said. "I'll help. Thank you, Lolly."

"Ambrosius wants ta talk. Bye, f'r now." Lolly winked at me. "See ya later."

Neve studied the transformation back to Amber, her head tilting from side to side, trying to catch every nuance. I'd seen the transformation enough that I could guess her thoughts. It was like two different people who just happened to look similar. Not alike, not twins. The whole bearing differed. And this hard one, Amber, I would be glad to be shed of.

She spoke, that authoritative tone so contrasting with Lolly's soft voice. "Lolly doesn't understand what it is that I'm giving her, but I think you will, Neve. In fact, you once remarked on the quality in me. I'm giving her a sense of *noblesse oblige*. Merlin accused me of shirking responsibility, and perhaps I've been sometimes selfish, but always I see the needs of others and feel an obligation to act. I give her that."

"She'll be quite well off," Neve said.

"True, but the real wealth she'll receive comes from Rage and the quiet girl. I don't want her to squander that. Lolly should give to the world as she has been given."

"I would've thought you'd give her maturity and wisdom," Neve said.

"Those she'll earn on her own; the noble obligation will hasten their coming."

I didn't care about the *noblesse*. I just wanted to get this over with. The longer we stood around talking, the heavier my lonely past felt and the more I wanted to get rid of it.

I must've made some noise, because Neve turned to me and stared at my eyes. "You have most unusual eyes. I hadn't noticed."

"Hard to see the different colors at night."

She smiled. "I feel that I'm not going to do much tonight. Just a little knitting. Merlin will create one person from four and reconstruct history. Each of the departing personalities will leave something for Lolly. And you are providing the power for it all to happen."

"I would give everything to give Lolly a full life," I said.

Merlin spun on his heel and left the room, calling back over his shoulder, "Come to the clearing."

For an old man, he sure could move fast. He disappeared into the woods before the rest of us got out of the house. It was almost dusk, so Amber retrieved a flashlight from her office before we followed Merlin.

CHAPTER
29

I **HEARD A** cry from the woods. It sounded like the hawk that had attacked me, but it must have been another. I'd seen Merlin wring that one's neck. Then he'd had the gall to blame me.

The bird called again, from farther away.

"Alfred," Neve said. "You seem uneasy. Is something the matter?"

I shook my head and shrugged.

"I'm concerned about you," she said. "You hold a great deal of anger within you."

"Anger? Me? I'm not mad at anyone."

"May I?" She paused in the trail. Her hands reached to cup my face.

I flinched, but the look in her face made me feel warm, her caring concern obvious. I shrugged again, acquiescing. Her touch on my cheeks felt soft and calming. I didn't realize how much I had tensed up until I felt my shoulders relax.

"Oh, my," she said. "Oh, my." Her palms closed against my face.

"What? What is it?" I asked.

"There is much about you that is unresolved. Incomplete."

"Yeah, losing your wife and your job and all your friends will do that."

She nodded, but not like she agreed with me. More like she felt all those tragedies were inevitable. Then, her hands slipped away from my face. Her fingertips lingered a moment longer before she broke contact.

"Alfred, I've had the feeling for several years now that something was wrong. Skewed. When I touched you just now, those feelings crystallized."

I backed away from her. How could she blame me for her woes? I had plenty of my own.

"Please, listen to me. Perhaps you can help me to understand, and then perhaps I can help you. There are little things. People I feel should be around, but aren't. Like the owner of the convenience store near my house. The person who's there, she says she's owned the place for eight or ten years. But I feel—I know—somewhere deep inside me that another man owns the store." Her brows furrowed and she studied my face.

I didn't know what she wanted from me. I glanced at Amber. She held a neutral expression on her face, waiting for Neve to continue.

"And there are some not so little things. This nation Texas. I know that it should be part of the United States."

Amber laughed. "I hope you haven't said that to any native-born Texans. You could be horse-whipped for treason."

Neve ignored her friend. She raised her hands toward my face again, but I pulled back.

"I don't have any idea what you're talking about," I said.

She said, "This life wasn't meant for you."

I stared at her, aghast. How many times had I said that to myself? I wasn't meant to have these misfortunes. Something had gone wrong. I nodded at her, unable to express myself. We followed Amber's flashlight splash to the clearing.

Merlin had a bright fire burning by the time we arrived in the clearing. We wouldn't need the flashlight here. Neve and I warmed ourselves against the slight chill, but Merlin called Amber to his special spot near the stream.

"Neve," I said. "Are you really a healer? Do you have some kind of psychic power?" I saw a touch of a smile.

"You don't believe." Her smile faded.

"No. Well...I don't know. I don't believe in Merlin. Sure, he can somehow give those visions. But I still think he's delusional. All this?" I gestured around the clearing. "I don't know any more. But when you touched me, I felt something."

"Alfred, ever since I can remember I've been able to see what people need to complete themselves. I've been able to heal many of them. Not all, but enough that I believe in myself."

"What about me?"

Her gaze dropped from my eyes. Her hands brushed over my heart. For a moment, her fingers relaxed onto my chest. Then she flinched.

"Oh my."

"What?" I asked.

Her eyes locked on mine. "I cannot heal you."

I felt a flash of anger deep inside, but her gentleness and sincerity continued to wash over me, and the heat dissipated. Her hands remained on my chest.

"What's wrong with me?"

"You love Lolly. At least, you hope to love her."

"Yes. I feel more toward her than I ever have anyone. Much more than for Janet. I know it's silly. I've known her only a couple of days, and it's all been complicated. But when I see her, when I think of her...look, it's more than the sex. At first, it was the sex, I admit. She's incredible in bed." I blushed, but I needed to tell Neve everything. "Maybe Merlin's threads are real. He says I have a strong connection to her. A compulsion to help her. She wanted me to be her hero. I've never been anyone's hero. Not even my own." I touched her hands on my chest. "I want to be her hero."

"What if being her hero meant you had to give her up?"

I winced and pulled away. Give her up?

"No, there has to be another way," I said.

"You are not meant to have her."

I stepped away from the old woman. "How can you know that?"

"It is what I see inside of you."

I refused to accept any more mumbo jumbo. Destiny. *Pfah*.

"You're just like him. Merlin. His damn threads of fate."

"I don't see threads like Merlin. I see your essence. I'm sorry, Alfred, but you don't belong here."

"Damn you, witch. I'm going to let Merlin use whatever power he thinks I have for his damn ceremony and get rid of Amber and Rage and whoever else is hanging around. And when Lolly's left alone, I'm going to ride off into the sunset with her and damn you all."

I saw tears sparkling in the old lady's eyes, but I didn't care that I'd hurt her.

"Dear man." Her voice carried immense sadness. "You need to know—"

"No," I interrupted her. "I don't care."

I turned away from her. Before I could walk off, Amber and Merlin appeared on the opposite side of the fire. Merlin wore a brilliant white robe with a fur-lined collar that extended down the breast of the robe. It had brightly colored ribbons in many hues tied all over it. This outfit repeated the vision I'd seen, just for an instant, when I first met him.

"Now we begin." He planted his staff in the ground. "The power of Samhain is great tonight."

"Merlin," Amber said. "Tell me when I will return. What happened after I was injured in the battle? Up 'til I awaken from this life."

Merlin tossed something on the fire. The flame burned a bright blue for a few seconds. A toasted oregano smell disturbed my anger, but only for a moment. He continued to fuss with the fire while he answered Amber.

"I arrived at the Isle after Nimuë, Morgayne and Elaine sent your mind here. At first, I did not know they had separated your mind and body, so I tended to your wounds. The sisters returned the next day, and by that time I had detected the lack of your essence. Nimuë told me what they had done and helped me heal your body, but Morgayne and Elaine would have nothing more to do with you.

"Arthur, I must offer a defense of Nimuë. It is probable we could not have cured your body had your mind been present. Even you might have given up from the pain and trauma."

Amber nodded, and he continued.

"I left your body in a cave protected by enchantment. Gawain stayed nearby with a few other young knights to watch over you. I returned after six months, and your body had healed."

Amber ran a hand through her hair. "Six months. That's a long time. But I suppose if the healing caused immense pain, it would be better to be away."

Merlin threw more oregano on the fire, and the aroma rose again.

"I set the spells yesterday," he said. "I spent much of my reclaimed power defining the timing to reunite your mind and body after the sixth month."

Amber waited, then prompted, "But…"

"But you did not return last night."

"Another day. What does it matter?"

"Another day here. The preparations I made yesterday could not be remade today, despite the power of Samhain. The spells will work, but the timing shall not be the same. It is much more than a day. You remained enspelled much more than six months."

"Tell me, Merlin. How many months?"

He motioned for her to sit beside me on the wooden bench.

"Ambrosius, my old friend. I tried to cheat fate. I attempted to alter the date of your return. I know well when you returned, yet I tried to send you back earlier. I am no different from you. I tried to change the path of life so you would return before…before so much had passed. But I failed. You shall return, not months, but many years after you left."

"Many…how many?"

"Almost twenty."

"Twenty years…and my kingdom?"

"I have said all I will. Gawain awaits. He shall tell you what he knows, and he shall bring you to me. I shall tell you what I knew, then."

They took one another in a four-arm grip. "What must be, shall be."

Then Amber broke the grip and hugged the old man. "Farewell, old friend."

I found myself staring at Amber. If she really had been the Ambrosius of the past, twenty years would have changed everything he'd fought to achieve. His friends, if not dead already, had aged beyond him.

He could still say, *No, I don't want to go back to start all over again. I'd rather stay here as a woman and share a life with the girls.* I thought I would've. Instead, he hugged Neve and said his farewells.

His blood pulsed with nobility. He didn't try to be a hero. He just did the right thing. I had no noble blood, but I could try to be a hero for Lolly. If Neve was right and I couldn't have her, I hoped she would have a good life without me, even if that left nothing for me.

"I shall not miss you." Amber leaned toward me on the bier. "But for your part in helping the girls, I thank you." I rose as she shook my hand, formally but sincerely. She stepped away.

The old man stepped to me. His smile looked odd, rueful, I thought. Then he did something uncharacteristic. He hugged me, patting my back up and down as he spoke to me.

"I have another vision for you, Alfred. You shall see Arthur's return." He pulled away. "Now, to your place under the tree, and I to mine by the stream. The power is about to peak."

As I turned around, I almost bumped into Neve. She took my hands in hers. "Alfred, there is so much I'd like to tell you, but you don't want to hear it."

I tried to pull away.

"Wait," she said. "I want you to know that you are a better man than you realize." She kissed my cheek and then bent around me and kissed the other one.

My eyes filled with tears, but they didn't spill. I took a deep breath and kissed her forehead. "Thank you," I murmured, and squeezed her hands.

She released me and turned to Merlin. "Where do you want me?"

"Remain here, on the bier. Lolly shall need your physical presence. Your knitting of her mind will follow my work. There shall be a time after Ambrosius leaves before we feel the effect here. An echo in time. You must do your work in that interval. I know not how long it shall last."

I expected the old man to dance around or make hand motions or something, but he just walked toward the stream. I went to my tree, wiping my eyes dry.

The old man sang and my hair prickled. I couldn't understand a word he sang, but Neve took a harmony part. Then Amber joined in. Somehow, now she knew that song.

Merlin had planted his staff beside Amber. As they chanted, the staff lit up and pulsed with the beat of their words.

The song stopped, and Merlin shouted at me. "Sit, you fool."

I barely made it to the ground before the vision came.

CHAPTER

30

"Today is a good day to break the siege."

Merlin speaks to a tall old man with a bushy beard and sandy-brown hair. The sun burns from high in the sky: it's just past midday.

"Why? We have no more men today than yesterday. We are too few to overcome that rabble out there."

"I have good portents."

"Bosh! Does their druid tell them the same?"

"These Franks have no druid. Had they one, he should tell them it was propitious to break the siege and go home."

The brown-haired man scans the countryside. My mouse body scurries along a wooden beam, and I peek out as well. I peer through the wooden battlements of a hill fort. A small stand of apple trees partway down the hill emits sweet fragrance from the blooms. The field below the wall contains green grass and spring flowers. Beyond the distance of a bowshot, tents sit willy-nilly and an unkempt crowd mills about, some drinking, some gaming, and others sleeping in the sun. Even I can distinguish a lack of military order. But if they surround the whole town like this, many hundreds of Franks besiege us.

"Very well, druid. What do you suggest?"

"Send a small mounted sortie out the northwest gate, comte. It is the least defended because that direction provides the least immediate use to us. Your horsemen can cause great damage in a short time. Those barbarians hunger for battle, and many will run to a fight. Tell your men to create havoc until they see the hordes rushing, then retreat to the gate."

"That's it?"

"That is the first feint. Send the main body of your footmen out the east gate as the horsemen return through the northwest. Use the confusion to press your advantage."

"Your plan won't work. We can't defeat their army or even hold open a path with our fifty men. What the enemy lacks in discipline, they overwhelm in numbers."

Merlin looks to the distance.

"I expect help from the east."

The other man follows Merlin's gaze. "I see nothing."

"We must begin."

"You have a reputation for magic victories, druid, but the stories are old. You better have some spells left, or you will lead the next charge. Alone."

The tall man climbs down the ladder to arrange his forces. After a short time, I hear horses galloping out the far gate and men shouting from that direction. The Franks at the bottom of this hill jump to their feet, gathering their weapons, unsure what to do. Some point to the sides of the town, and soon men run, both left and right, to join the fight on the opposite side of the fort.

The comte deployed his men well. Franks run too close to the walls in their haste to get to the action. The fort's archers skewer many, staining the grass red.

The enemy's leaders restrain as much of their force as they can, keeping them at their posts. Almost as many men remain in place outside this wall as the town will be able muster, and now they are alert. They pound spears against their shields.

I hear a great jeering shout from the other side of the fort as the horsemen race back through the gate. As it slams shut, men pour out the gate to my left, racing down the hill, shouting. The enemy run up the hill to meet them, and the two waves of men break into tens of individual fights. The townsmen have the advantage of gravity, letting their downward momentum carry them through the first groups of besiegers. For several minutes they wreak great carnage, but enemy forces race back around the sides of the fort. Again, many succumb to arrows from above.

The comte joins us on the wall. He has taught his men well. They retreat partway up the hill, forming a large triangle so they don't expose their flanks. Archers on the walls continue to pick off Franks who venture near, but they cannot shoot close to the wedge of townsmen.

"We are losing men," said the comte. "And we have none to lose. I must sound the retreat."

"Not yet. They can hold longer."

"Dammit, man. Another few minutes produces another ten dead men. Ten fewer men to hold the walls."

"Do you see my hawk?"

"What? No. I haven't seen it all morning."

"There, on the horizon, flying toward us."

"My men are dying! Sound retreat," he orders the trumpeter beside him. Merlin pulls the horn from the trumpeter's mouth.

"My hawk accompanies the expected assistance. We must hold the enemy eyes in this direction. Not much longer."

The bearded man peers into the distance. I can't see the hawk, but he must have, because he nods to the trumpeter. The boy stands down.

"This is our death if you are wrong."

The lines of the defensive wedge heave and weave with the enemy onslaught. As men fall, the line withdraws toward the gate.

"Now," Merlin says. "Orderly retreat."

At a nod from the comte, the trumpeter blows a clear tone, followed by a second, higher tone. The men in the triangle back up now with purpose, withdrawing twice as fast as they had before but still holding their formation. The whoops of the enemy grow louder.

"Be prepared to sound the attack again."

"Where is your help?"

Merlin points. *Several horsemen appear at full gallop on the road from the east. A short distance behind, there are more, then more.*

Hope lights the comte's face. "How many?"

"About twenty."

"Twenty horsemen?" *He scans the field again, concern back on his face.* "Have you no more magic than that? We are lost."

"These twenty are enough," *Merlin assures him.* "Of that, I am certain."

The horsemen gallop below me. The sudden change of perspective into a hawk soaring high above the ground spins my mind for a moment.

The man riding in the lead waves his arm far to the left and then far to the right. The other riders spread into a wide line on either side, each separated from his neighbors by about eight feet. The horses raise no dust and only muffled beats as they sprint through the wet spring grass.

The leader of these knights wears a red cup on his shield. Another rider, hanging a pace behind him, carries a white symbol on his golden shield. The other riders bear no designs. The men lean into their mounts, and the horses race faster toward the battle. The smell of sweat and blood makes me shriek with delight.

About half the town's defenders have re-entered the gates as their wedge continues to shrink. The Franks smell victory and press their advantage. Those outside the east gate do not see the approaching horsemen. A few still running around the walls spot the advancing line of horses and make wild gestures, calling to warn their compatriots. However, the loud din just feeds their lust for victory.

The new assault strikes the throng from behind. The knights ride in, slashing left and right. The horsemen remain just far enough apart that the riders can swing their swords freely, yet few of the enemy footmen escape sharp steel.

I hear the trumpet play a three note signal, and Merlin nods with approval. I rise enough to watch the town's horsemen gallop out the far gate. They catch the stragglers coming around the wall. First a few, then more of the rabble turn toward the distant woods.

At the east gate, the Franks find themselves caught between the town walls and a fierce band of mounted warriors slashing through their line.

With another blast of the horn, the fort's footmen reverse their retreat and attack. The barbarians had no military discipline when they had the advantage, and with that now lost, most of the mob break ranks and run. One Frankish captain gathers his men and attempts an organized retreat. The knight of the golden shield swings across their path, slowing them. Two riders join him, cutting the group off from the woods long enough for soldiers from the town to encircle them. No quarter is given, because the Franks had offered none for the townsfolk.

The other riders begin the hunt, chasing down panicked men and slaughtering them. The three knights who had cut off the organized retreat now race for men seeking shelter in the woods on the south side of town.

The troop of knights gathers in the field below the hillfort facing the setting sun. Their exhausted horses enter town at a proud walk. The comte arrays his men as an honor guard. I sit in a shadow near the gate, nibbling a chunk of moldy cheese.

"Brave knights. My town thanks you for your assistance, coming just in time. You are most welcome here. I am Garn, Comte of Armorica. Who leads your band, and what are your names? My people will sing of you for all the days."

The man carrying the shield emblazoned with a red cup removes his helm. He looks familiar, but I can't figure out why I know him. He's middle-aged, with a tough, lined face. His hair drips with sweat, and dried blood streaks his neck. Blood has splattered his clothing as well.

"Good comte, my name is Gawain. And with one exception, these are my men."

Gawain. Yes, but a much older man than when I saw him before.

"I thank you, friend Gawain. And your men."

"Do you count yourself a Briton, Garn, Comte of Armorica?"

"That I do. I came across the sea as a young man with many of these people you saved today. We are Britons."

"Then kneel, Garn, Comte of Armorica, and receive your king. For the man who leads me is Arthur Ambrosius Aurelius, High King of the Britons, Lord of Dubonni, Overlord of the Dumnonii, Silures, Catuvellauni and Cornovii, Protector of Armorica, Defender of Powys and Dyfed, Scourge of the Saxons and Scotti."

Garn stares openmouthed throughout the recitation. When Gawain stops, he finds his voice. "Impossible. Arthur Ambrosius died all these years ago."

Gawain puts his hand on the hilt of his sword. "Kneel, or be called to task for your insolence."

Garn makes a quick calculation, recognizing the uncompromising strength of Gawain, still menacing him with a firm grip on his sheathed sword. He drops to his knees. At a sign from Gawain, the rest of the townsfolk kneel as well, and he calls out to them.

"Behold the High King: Arthur returns from the dead at the time of our greatest need. Our king once and forever."

The horsemen part, placing themselves between the townsfolk and the man riding out of their formation. He carries the golden shield with the design of a white dragon. His helmet sits in front of him.

This is the Arthur I had seen before. He hasn't aged at all since the tragedy of the stone. He took time to comb his hair and clean his face, but the blood on his leather armor and breeches makes clear that he had been active in today's battle, even if he didn't lead the vanguard.

An old man cries, "Arthur, king. I fought with you against Euric. You saved my life."

Murmurs pass among the townsfolk. "The cobbler knows him." "He must be Arthur." "King Arthur has returned." "Praise the Lord." "Our great king again." "Arthur." "Arthur."

It becomes a chant as they kneel before their king, returned in their time of great need.

"My liege," a familiar voice calls after the chant dies down. "I had hoped you would return someday. You chose an auspicious time."

"Merlin, you old goat. We must speak. And let these good people prepare a victory feast."

Turning to the comte, he says, "The Franks hunted your woods well these days."

One of the horsemen pulls a laden travois into the square. The hungry people of the town shout with joy. Arthur grants the comte and his people leave to rise, and they rush to empty the travois and prepare food.

Merlin leads Arthur away from the bustle. A young maiden reaches up to place a fresh spring flower in his hair. He kisses her forehead, then joins Merlin right beside where I'm sitting in a shadow. The old coot led him to the mouse on purpose. He means to keep this as a memory he can transmit to others.

Arthur asks, "Have you no questions for me? Or do you already know the answers?"

"You left this world. Beyond that, I do not know."

"I traveled to another place, that is true. You brought me back."

"I did nothing beyond preserving your body for your return."

"You will bring me back."

Even in the dusk, I can see the old man raise an eyebrow. His eyes catch the little light that reaches this corner. They sparkle with humor. "You know my future? Most unusual."

"You jest with me? Have you no curiosity about what happens to you?"

"I am curious about many things, including my fate. But between curiosity and knowing yawns a dangerous gap. Would I then choose a path to hasten that future, thinking it a good end? Or would I choose a path hoping to change it, thinking it bad? I could make a choice that appears to lead to the end but has the effect of diverting me. No, Arthur, knowing the ending affects too much of the path. Tell me nothing of my future."

Arthur laughs, rubbing his beard. "Nonetheless, I have a message for you. Shall I keep that to myself as well?"

"Who sent the message?"

"Why, you did." Arthur suppresses another laugh.

"Either I am myself in the future and should not send a message I would not wish to receive, or I have changed so much that the message shall have no meaning to me. Either way, it should not tell me my future."

After a moment, Arthur asks, "I don't know if that was a yes or a no. Do you want the message?"

"Yes."

"Persevere."

"Persevere?"

"That's the whole message."

"It is not a message I would expect. Therefore, it must be useful. Or meaningless."

Arthur shakes his head, experienced with the old man's illogic. "I have fulfilled my obligation. Now. What news of my kingdom?"

"Your nephew, Mordred, assumed the throne three years after you went to the other place."

"Recent news, man. Gawain has told me such things, but he has been at Aballo these past years."

"The place of your supposed demise is called Avalon here in Armorica."

"The geography lesson can wait. Tell me of my kingdom."

"Did Gawain tell you that your nephew styles himself Arthur Mordred now?"

"He dares to take my title?"

"High King Mordred, Lord of the Britons and Saxons."

"Saxons?"

"The Saxons are again ascendant," Merlin says. "Mordred strikes bargains with them, as was done in the days before you came to power. He cedes what they have taken, thinking they shall stay where they are. Instead, they push onward, establishing themselves in new places, and he cedes to them those places. This he calls peace. This he calls ruling over them."

"I must regain my kingdom. There is only one Arthur, and that is me."

CHAPTER
31

First I hear the lovely birdsong. A few last autumn leaves cling to the surrounding branches. It's no longer spring. I cock my head, jerking my view to two men sitting below the tree. When I inhale, I realize I am the singer.

My focus hops to two other men a short distance away. An armed guard stands alert. His head scans slowly and his eyes jump rapidly to watch all sides. The other man wears a silly grin. He carries no arms. Twigs bearing intense red and orange oak leaves dangle from the edges of his brown coat.

One man below me raises his voice. "We should have dealt with him ourselves when he first got here." He sports a rich velvet cloak with a purple sash.

The other man bows his head. "Brilliant as always, my liege." This man wears a white robe with a fur trim, similar to the one Merlin is wearing now. Later? During the ceremony with Amber.

"Whoever this usurper is," says the lord, "he's got Ambrosius Aurelius's tactical genius. With every victory his following grows."

I hear singing, but it isn't me. It sounds like a female. My head jerks from view to view until I find the source. It's the simpleton in brown whistling a perfect mating call of a female jay.

He's much younger than I thought, a few years from manhood. He gazes at me, and I'm shocked to see that he has my eyes. One greenish, one blueish. It's like staring at myself in the mirror.

"Quiet your fool," the lord says. "Or you'll need a new one."

I look down to see the druid, as I believe him to be, make a hand gesture. The whistling stops.

The lord turns his glare from the fool to the druid. "This usurper. He comes for me."

"Yes, Arthur Mordred. His victory in the east was most decisive."

"My true allies have mustered perhaps a few thousand men here in the south. The others wait to see which way the winds blow after I meet this imposter. We must stall for reinforcements from the north."

Mordred looks to the north, right at me. Shock crosses his face. He shouts to the guard, "Kill that jay bird. It's Merlin's creature."

I take to the air as the guard swings his sword, missing me by feet.

"Kill it next time, Gogyrfan, or your life is forfeit," Mordred says.

I'm in a cave with Merlin and Nimuë, who looks no older than when Bedevere, Gawain and Lancelot left Arthur with her. From the perspective I see them, now I must be in a mouse.

"Would that we had another way," Merlin says. "Riding another person's mind carries hazards."

"Mordred would rather the whole of Britain go to the torch than abide your presence. Arthur expressed certainty that he could control our essence in his mind." Nimuë brushes the hair from Merlin's forehead, her fingers lingering with affection.

His hand comes up and covers hers. He returns a smile. "Persevere."

"Yes, as Arthur did. He came back to us in our hour of need and is more renowned than ever."

The light in the cave comes from Merlin's staff, reflected from the faces of natural crystals exposed on the walls. Nimuë's diaphanous gown shimmers in the soft light. The light also creates highlights on the ermine trim of Merlin's robe.

"It is time. Arthur expects us," he says.

Her gown undulates as she walks toward a room beside me. Merlin sits on one side of a large flat-topped crystal, and the woman takes up a mirror-image position. Their arms entwine, his long, white hair and her long, black hair flow together, covering their faces.

They chant.

Now I'm hot and uncomfortable. My head seems to be about eight feet off the ground, but I'm not flying. I'm bouncing up and down, moving toward three leafless oak trees in the middle of a field of dead grass. In the distance to the right, water splashes in a sound of rapids.

"We are here with you."

Merlin's voice.

Merlin is surprised at being shuffled into a confined space. Arthur recreated Merlin's cave in his head.

I realize he learned from Lolly how to do this. It seems that Merlin doesn't yet know the trick.

His cave appears as a second image overlying the field, like a double exposure. Merlin and Nimuë watch and experience along with Arthur, but I know they have no access to the rest of his mind. The woman has linked her mind to Merlin's and followed his mind into Arthur's.

In the cave, Merlin and Nimuë sit, arms entwined and heads together. On the field, Arthur rides his horse, heading for a meeting by the river Cam for a discussion that Bedevere, now an old advisor, will have with Mordred's man: Who shall be the High King of the Britons?

That is the knowledge of Merlin, coming through the vision. I sense his hopes for peace.

Three horses carrying riders dressed for ceremony walk from the other side of the field. A large army, dressed more for show than for battle, waits in the distance behind them.

"The one in the middle is your nephew Mordred," I hear from my left. Gawain. "His captain of the guard is Gogyrfan. The third is the druid Outigyr. He claims to be a miracle-performing Christian."

Merlin speaks inside Arthur's mind. "I knew him as a druid in train-ing. He is a weasel."

Arthur hears Nimuë also. "In the past year, he has acquired power from somewhere. He is a dangerous man."

Arthur's army stands behind us. Merlin's thoughts tell me that Mor-dred has the advantage of numbers, but his many Britons pressed into ser-vice will not fight well. They will run if the battle turns against them.

Today represents a chance for peace: a parley to avoid battle. Neither leader would choose this field for a battle. The river protects one flank, but the field extends too far in the other direction for either army to pro-tect that side.

Arthur's short and long swords both remain sheathed. Merlin knows that he wears leather armor over a bright white blouse. A helmet sits on his head. The shield with his sigil, the white dragon segreant on a golden back-ground, rests against the saddle.

In the second image, Merlin and Nimuë relax against one another, lounging on comfortable cushions. Merlin teases a few strands of his lover's thick, black hair.

He says, "There is nothing to do until we reach the tree. I know not how Arthur penned us into this mental cave. I did not teach him that."

"I've had recent experience," Arthur says.

Bedevere leans forward. "Pardon, sire?"

Nimuë laughs, and I feel amused, too. Or Arthur? Or is it Merlin who feels amused?

"It's nothing," Arthur assures his old friend.

"The pupil has surprised the teacher," Merlin says, but only to Nimuë. "The man I molded from childhood has grown into the greatest king Brit-ain has ever known. His actions today shall be known forever. I have seen the augury."

Nimuë says, "It's been long since we were your pupils."

"It is good I had completed Ambrosius's education before you came to me with your ambitions. Had you competed for my time, one of the three of us would have been destroyed."

"You were a harsh master, my love."

"And you a demanding pupil," he says, "always wanting more than you were ready to receive."

"More than you were ready to give."

"I give you my all, now."

"Ah, but it is never enough," she says.

Arthur stops just beyond the crown of the tree. He removes his helm. Mordred's party reaches the far tree, and Gogyrfan and Outigyr stop. Mordred and Arthur start for the central tree at the same time.

I feel a tension rising and prepare for battle. No, Merlin prepares for a battle of words. His specter holds his shining staff. Nimuë stands behind him, hands resting on his shoulder blades. Power flows from her into him, and he feeds it to Arthur.

Mordred stops several feet from Arthur, his eyes wide with surprise. He makes the sign of the cross. "Truly, you are Arthur Ambrosius Aurelius. I did not believe. Yet you have not aged. What deviltry is this?"

"I am here and I am flesh. And I am the only Arthur Britain needs, nephew."

Mordred examines the two men behind Arthur, and then scans Arthur's army. "Where is your demon Merlin?"

Arthur laughs. "You fear him so much? You should fear me, for Merlin is here," Arthur pounds his chest, "and here," he rests his hand on the scabbard of his sword. "Merlin is everywhere that I want him to be."

Mordred looks askance at Arthur.

"Push him," Merlin suggests to Arthur.

"We come to terms today. You cannot stall me while you wait for troops from the north."

"The bird! I knew it was his." Mordred spits.

"Today, nephew. Today, you return my kingdom to me."

"Even today my army outnumbers yours. I don't need more troops."

"And yet you ask to talk, while I would fight you man to man. I parley to save the lives of my Britons."

Mordred raises his head, haughty. "I don't know what part of hell you hid in these past years, but the Britons are mine. I protected the realm for many years."

Arthur bristles. "You have retreated, league by league, from our enemies."

He pounds his horse's neck. "I hold the peace."

"You give away the pieces."

"I made allies of the Saxons."

"You made them overlords of your people. You are no king. You are a joke."

Mordred's hand goes to his sword, but a loud hiss from Outigyr stays his motion.

"Your druid shows wisdom," Arthur says. He did not react to Mordred's near-threat.

"Outigyr is no druid. He is a Christian, like me. We are a Christian land now."

"I have no doubt that he is a Christian like you."

Mordred frowns.

"Invite your Christian druid to join our discussion."

Mordred nods. "And you may call your old counselor."

Outigyr and Bedevere urge their horses forward at a slow walk. The kings' horses each back up a few paces, leaving the other two men face to face.

The advisors begin a heated discussion over who should rule which parts of the kingdom. I'm confused by the names and places and details. The discussion drones on for hours.

Outigyr shouts something in outrage while Bedevere waits. When Outigyr finishes his tirade, Bedevere allows a few moments to pass before responding. It's been a favorite trick of his all morning, a way to show the absurdity of the other man's position. Into this span of silence comes the harsh call of a jay. It's the same call I heard from the druid's fool in an earlier memory-vision, but it sounded much prettier when I was a male jay.

I hear a sharp intake of breath from Mordred. "Merlin," he hisses.

Gogyrfan locates the bird first. He lets forth a guttural shout and kicks his horse into motion, drawing his sword. He rushes the jay with the single-minded purpose to kill it.

All hell breaks loose.

Both Mordred and Outigyr shout, "Noooo!"

Bedevere swings his horse sideways, providing a barrier between his king and his enemies.

Gawain goes into motion, drawing his sword as his horse flies toward the central tree.

Mordred's army shouts and starts running and riding toward us in confusion. Based on the din behind me, I know that Arthur's army also rushes headlong onto the field.

Mordred puts his horse to a fast gallop toward his army, with Outigyr's horse at his heels.

Bedevere kicks his horse into motion, grabbing Arthur's reins as he rides by.

Gogyrfan swings at the jay. The jay drops as the sword passes above, and it flies away.

Arthur mutters in disbelief, "Merlin, what have you done?"

"Sire, that was not my bird. It gave the call of a female."

CHAPTER
32

My army lurches forward in disarray, and I know I must stop them, must stop both armies before they clash and all hope for peace ends. I shake off Bedevere's grip on my reins and ride toward my army, my arms spread wide, signaling the men to stop.

No, that isn't me. Those are Arthur's thoughts, Arthur's actions. Merlin feels his anxiety, as earlier he had sensed Arthur's hopes for peace. I think the walls of the mental cave are more permeable than he'd thought, now that action has begun. No, Merlin thinks that. I struggle to sort through Arthur's and Merlin's thoughts without losing my own.

The central part of the army slows, stumbles to a halt as I approach, but the flanks press ahead. Gawain has ridden to join me and points back, making me look across the field. Mordred rides behind his army and goads them forward, seeing an advantage in the confused lines I have created of my own men.

"We must meet them," Gawain shouts, and I know he's right.

"Go to the left. And you, Bedevere, right. Bring order to this chaos."

I turn my horse and raise my sword. The men behind me shout, then roar when I wave my sword. The tumult becomes a rush after I give free rein to my horse, and we race to meet our brethren and enemies on the field of dead grass. The pause gave time for the center, at least, to form into a reasonable battle order. A phalanx of horsemen forms around me, and I lead them on a frantic gallop back toward the trees.

We meet the first of Mordred's army at the closest tree. These are Saxons, eager to avenge the kinsmen we slew during the summer campaign. As usual, Mordred sends others to die for him. My short sword opens the neck of the first Saxon I meet, but then I'm past and I see none of his blood until I swing the sword again, hitting another man just above the eyebrows. I see in his eyes that he had not expected to die today.

Our thundering assault breaks their front line, and when my footmen arrive, we push back to the central tree. Most of the horsemen continue to race through the enemy lines, but I pull back with a few riders to assess the battle. Gawain has stabilized the open left flank and now sends a group of riders to attack bowmen who are firing over the line into our rearguard. The battle remains fluid on that side, the men too spread out. Both sides know how difficult it will be to protect this flank.

Bedevere is having more trouble on the right, so I send a few men to fill a gap between the center and his flank.

The sun disappears behind inrushing clouds. I welcome the cooling breeze but hope no rain comes. It would disadvantage both armies, but I do not want to have to factor in the havoc it would cause.

A rush of Mordred's knights up the center pulls me back into the fight. Three men assault me. One of my knights engages the first one through. I swing my great sword, unbalancing the next horseman. He rides on, flailing in the saddle. The third approaches on my left, probably expecting the short sword to be easier to avoid. At the last, he spurs his horse forward, sword swinging. I block it with my short sword, angling the momentum of his arm downward, then slice across with my long sword onto his exposed arm. He screams as the arm comes off.

The other rider has reseated in his saddle and races toward me while I'm unbalanced from the first assault. Rather than try to parry, I kick my horse to avoid the man. He swings as he passes, but misses me and my horse. My longsword does not miss his broad back, and when I feel the resistance of his backbone I pull it out.

I say a quiet thanks to Merlin for the strength he adds to my stroke, and to Nimuë for its swiftness.

More of my horsemen have come to the gap. Two men sit their horses, trading blow for blow, neither able to get past the other's shield. The horses regard one another and snort, feet planted far apart for stability against the wild movements of their masters.

A spearman and two men with axes hack away at a horse and rider. The horse tumbles forward on a severed leg, and the rider is unable to defend himself.

A man with a bushy, brown mustache staggers across the field. He has a tall helmet that is too small for the top of his head, and it is cocked back too far to protect him. Blood streams down the side of his face. It's unclear which army he's with, and since he's unarmed, he is ignored.

This is chaos, nothing like the clean battles in my computer simulation game.

Two horses gallop from ahead and to my left. I let the first one pass me, since it carries one of my men, then behead the man in pursuit. My fleeing knight continues for several paces before he turns the horse, shakes his head, and rejoins the battle.

The lines form again between the central tree and the one to my left, and between the central tree and the one on my right. Neither side has reserves, because neither side expected a battle today. It will be an endurance contest. I think we will endure.

"Sire, the lightning," I say…that is, Merlin says inside Arthur's head.

To the right, bolts of lightning strike the earth, one after another. The strikes concentrate at the line of battle.

"It is Outigyr," Merlin tells his king. "He pulls power from somewhere to do this. But he is clumsy. Many of the bolts hit Mordred's men."

"Nonetheless, he does damage to my men. We must stop him."

"He has a force about him. An unseen repellant. Approaching him would be dangerous."

A bolt strikes one of my knights. It also kills two footmen, one of mine and one of Mordred's. I do not like these odds. "An answer, Merlin. Now."

"Sire, have your archers target the druid."

"Will the arrows get through?"

"I do not believe so. But I shall, mayhaps, discover where he draws his power."

I ride to a group of bowmen who are in range of the druid and give them the order to shoot all together. At Merlin's suggestion, I tell them to disperse as soon as they shoot. Then I ride away from them.

A dozen arrows fly together. None of them reach the druid, even though many should have—at least—come close. He aims the next few lightning bolts at my archers, but they had run out of his effective range. The bolts strike in random locations.

"It's the fool," Nimuë says. "Outigyr's fool is marked. He is the source. See, he stands apart from Mordred."

Arthur doesn't recognize the boy, but I do. It's the boy with eyes like mine. He sits on a small rise leaning onto his elbows.

"What do you see?" Merlin asks.

Nimuë leans her head against Merlin's. Now he sees the boy's left shoulder glowing almost sun-bright. A stream of brilliance pulses from him, around Mordred and thence to Outigyr. The druid pulls another lightning bolt from the air every time a radiant pulse reaches him. The boy's power also supplies his invisible shield.

Arthur looks over the battlefield, and through Merlin in his head, I see glowing gossamer strands everywhere. Scores emanate from every man on the field.

These must be the famous threads Merlin talks about. It seems like millions of them. Some strong ones connect man to man. Friends, comrades. Others are dim, thin, connecting acquaintances. Some men carry more of the thick strands than most. These appear to be captains. I realize thousands extend from Arthur's body, and Mordred also has too many to count.

Some threads disappear over the horizon, connecting men to wives, children, mothers, fathers, friends.

I see a man gored by a spear. He dies, and the threads fade. Within a few seconds, all but one dissolve. Then that one pops out of existence.

Such a waste. This didn't have to happen. We were supposed to have peace. Was it the butterfly principle? A bird sings, a battle rages, a nation suffers.

"Sire? We have no time to consider butterflies and birds. We must deal with Outigyr and his fool," *Merlin tells Arthur from inside his head.*

Those were modern thoughts. Amber?

I'm getting lost in who's thinking what. Where am I, Alfred? Which are my thoughts, and what thoughts am I experiencing through the vision?

"Very well," *Arthur says.* "It's time we gave Mordred's British allies an excuse to run."

I gather my mounted guard at a small rill, a stream feeding into the Cam. I cannot see the field, but neither can Mordred or his men see me.

I send word to the archers to begin a steady rain of arrows on Outigyr. This is just a diversion, making the druid concentrate on personal defense rather than the battlefield. My next move is to send a knight to the left, with instructions to gather every second or third horseman to ride around the open flank. This, also, is diversion, to stretch the line as Mordred's men shift to meet the flying assault.

With Outigyr occupied and the line left of the trees thinning, I ride out with my phalanx of knights. We thunder through the line, creating as much havoc and confusion as we can, but always moving toward Mordred. The usurper calls his defenders to him.

"Excellent," *I think. The fool has only one guard, but we can't cut toward him too soon or the defenders could shift.*

I've cleared the front line. The scattered remnants of the Saxons rush over, seeing a chance for vengeance at close range. Before they reach their doom, I scan the battlefield. Our attack is achieving its end. Gawain is leading the assault from the left flank. Mordred's men on that side retreat from battle in disarray.

The first Saxon meets my long sword and finds his shield split a moment before the sword cleaves his face. I have no time to bring the sword back up before a second Saxon swings. I parry with the sword, but it flies from my hand. Someone else kills the Saxon.

We are too far from the line for our footmen to help. Our progress slows under a frenzied assault by the Saxons. I'm almost close enough to turn toward the fool, but I must fight through another group. I switch my short sword to my right hand and lift my Pendragon shield.

Mordred holds his guard close, keeping his horsemen in check. Cowardice. A good commander would have sent both horsemen and Saxon footmen at our assault, and he would have won the day. Instead, our horse-mounted height and mobility provide the advantage over our disordered enemy.

I turn my horse toward the boy and kick for speed, leaving my horsemen to finish the last of the Saxons. I do not look to Mordred, but he must realize he's no longer the target, because I hear him order his guard to attack. I close the distance to the boy.

My horse stumbles and drops. As I fly from the saddle, I see an arrow buried in its chest—a lucky shot around the horse's armor. I land in a roll, clear of the horse, but also clear of my short sword. In the two paces I take to pick it up, I see Mordred's guards fighting to get past my men. I have a few moments, not enough time to run to the boy. His lone guard stands to his right, waiting for me.

The boy's tunic has pulled back, revealing a dark mark at the base of his neck above the shoulder blade. I don't need a clear view of his back to know it: an acorn birthmark. No other mark could give a druid access to so much power. He must hear me coming, because he looks at me. The sight reminds me of someone else. Someone my rage threw a sword at in anger.

That was me, I think. Alfred. The boy has both the eyes and the acorn birthmark, like me.

This time, Arthur isn't enraged. He's in battle mode. This time, the short sword flies true, severing the boy's collar bone and continuing a long hand's length into his torso. Blood pulses out of the wound.

"Your turn, Merlin."

Arthur's sword strike cut the flow of energy to Outigyr. A thick thread still connects the boy to his druid, but it dims as I watch. Arthur turns toward Outigyr so Merlin can see his prey. The enemy's druid tries to fling another bolt, but his gesture creates nothing.

In the second image, I see Merlin raise his arms toward the illusion of a cavern roof. Nimuë stands behind him, hands still on his shoulders. He holds his arms high for a long instant, then slashes them down. In the field, a lightning bolt larger than any Outigyr had called flashes onto his hill. The druid burns in the flash.

The thick thread recedes back to the boy who has my eyes. Other threads that had converged on the boy fade as well, except for a thin one stretching into the Aether. The boy lives, but just. The sword sticking from his collar rises and falls with the rapid beat of the boy's breathing.

"Arthur!"

The distant shout from Bedevere warns the king before the boy's guard strikes him from behind. The blow glances off Arthur's leather.

"I've done all I can for you," Merlin says. "Even with Nimuë's help, blocking that sword was my last effort."

Arthur's battle instincts take over. The attacker is off balance since he expected the sword to meet resistance inside Arthur's body. Arthur slams both fists into the man, and then knees him in the face. The sword drops. Arthur picks it up and the man meets the point of his own sword.

Arthur takes a moment to appraise the battlefield. Over the wider field, the battle line has broken in his favor, and his men run to the aid of their leader. Nearby, his horsemen conduct a pitched battle for their lives against Mordred's guard and a few Saxons. At this moment, the battle around the kings could be won by either group.

Mordred slips through Arthur's knights and runs toward his uncle and foe. Although unhorsed, he retains his sword and shield.

"You are spawn of the devil, and I'll send you back to your master," he shouts, brandishing his sword.

"Your army is defeated," Arthur says. "The battle is over. Lay down your weapon and your only punishment shall be banishment."

"This has been my land longer than it was yours. Take your deal to the demon who brought you back from hell."

The two men spar. Even with an inferior blade, Arthur commands the clash, weaving and blocking Mordred's attacks, while forcing the ersatz king to keep his distance from Arthur's purloined sword.

"All I need do is avoid your thrusts, nephew. Soon we shall be sur-rounded by my men. Yield now, or I will let them kill you."

With Merlin's eyes, I see gossamer threads severing from Mordred. I don't know how many of them are men dying and how many are men removing their allegiance by running away, but it doesn't matter. Arthur speaks truth.

As Arthur and Mordred continue to dance on the hillock, I see Merlin in his cave. He sits beside the large flat crystal, legs crossed, bent over, head almost touching his knees.

I'm not sure if this is in his real cave, or in the cave inside Arthur's mind. I can't keep track.

Nimuë dances and sways behind him, making signs in the air. It looks like she's weaving a spell or something to restore Merlin's strength. When Merlin sits up, I think it has succeeded.

"Do what you must, Nimuë. You think your time has come. I know my time is past."

Nimuë's dance picks up speed. I can no longer follow the movement of her hands.

"I beg of you," he says, *"leave me awareness long enough to see the end of Arthur's battle."*

With a shock of knowledge from Merlin, I realize Nimuë is casting a spell on him. She steals his power and knowledge as she condemns him to death. And somehow, Merlin knew she would do it and weaves his own spell into hers. He drifts toward a sleep that will last until he finds Ambrosius. He doesn't know it will last one and a half millennia.

The woman's dance slows again. She leans forward and kisses the old man's white hair. *"You shall see the end."* She spins away, her dress rising and flowing around her thighs.

Mordred circles me, trying to find a way to get close enough to strike. When he rushes, I strike him with the flat of my blade, laughing. But when I try to face Mordred, I find my foot is caught. The boy fool's guard has hold of my boot and clings with the last of his strength.

Mordred leaps to take advantage. I kick, trying to free my foot, but I am unable to dodge. I parry the first thrust, but cannot regain my balance in time to parry the second.

Mordred buries his sword in my gut. The pain is sharp. I cannot survive this.

My nephew smirks with triumph. He's already looking around, calculating how to retain the throne, even with my men in command of the battlefield. The victorious gleam in his eyes becomes one of pain and shock. I press my sword farther into Mordred's chest from below his leathern armor. I feel a thrill as I push it deeper, forcing the tip into the usurper's heart.

Mordred falls, gripping his sword in one hand and the hilt of mine in the other. I slide down on top of him, my shoulders resting on my shield.

"Oh, Merlin. Why did I have to return, just for this?"

Merlin doesn't answer. I try to call up the image of him and Nimuë in the cave, but I am too weak to sustain both images in my mind.

I can't move from atop Mordred. I have no strength even to lift my head. My last view is the dying boy. He had tried to crawl toward us, me and Mordred, but he also has collapsed. If I could raise my arm, I could grasp the sword that rises and falls just a bit, oozing blood with each of the boy's heartbeats. I stare at his eyes, mismatched green and blue.

Through Merlin's failing vision, I see the boy's lone Aethereal thread approach its breaking point.

His blue and green eyes beseech the dying king, asking, Why? What about my life?

"Is this what it feels like to die?" I wonder. "Merlin, end this vision, please. I don't want to see the rest."

Maybe I'm feeling Arthur's life bleeding out. The pain has become a numbness. The smell of blood overwhelms. Is it mine, or the boy's? I no longer hear sounds of fighting. My whole experience reduces to gasping for breath, mine and the boy's. My eyes are fogged, but Merlin still sees a brightness as the Aethereal end of the last thread snaps back toward the boy. I blink.

The face in front of me no longer looks like the boy. I see a middle-aged man with long black hair stringing from his helmet. I want to shake my head to clear the vision. Now all I see is a vague shape hunched over a white dragon with talons raised to strike.

Is the whoosh-swoosh sound my blood flowing, or his? The beat slows.

Merlin, end this vision. The sound is dying.

The beat is slowing down.

The beat…

Goodbye, Lolly.

EPILOGUE

A LOUD POPPING sound woke the young red-tailed hawk. His head jerked up. He thought his master might be calling, but he didn't hear the calm and commanding voice in his head. He still felt the connection, but his master had not used it this night.

All his feathers ruffled and his body shuddered. The hawk sensed a shift and wondered what it was. Something had happened.

He looked around but saw no difference in the woods. The change was within. He felt lighter. He had lost a sense of dread that had been with him since the day before. Then he realized that the connection the mean man had forced on him had been erased. His master had broken it, but the bird had still felt its presence. Now, with the certainty of instinct, he knew that man would never bother him again. The sad, angry man was gone.

He left his aerie near the top of the tallest pine and flew up, higher and higher, into the rising sunlight. Flying in the clear, cool air became a pleasure again. The forest below burst from predawn shadows into green pines, with oaks rising amidst the brambles.

Soaring high aloft, feathering his wings to circle, the bird looked for his master. He felt near, the bird knew that, but since he felt no call, he couldn't trace it to the man.

The young hawk hesitated before flying to the clearing. That's where the mean man had caught him and hurt him. Despite the pain he had endured, the hawk felt pity for the mean man. He had been so sad and lonely, and now he was gone.

The bird veered toward his master's favorite spot and glided down. The edge of day crept above the trees as he neared the place, and he saw a brilliant white gown reflecting the first light. He felt a flush of warmth.

His master.

The hawk still had much to learn about the ability to read prey, but even he could see his master's exhaustion. The man's shoulders hunched over, and his chin rested on his chest. His arms sagged down from his grip on the tall staff planted in the ground.

Had the hawk seen similar behavior in a rodent or other small animal, it would have meant an easy meal. Although he had been bound to his master for only a few days, the bird knew him as a commanding presence, not this empty husk.

It heartened him to see the man's face lift, to see the bushy eyebrows rise in a sign of recognition, and to see the broad smile. The old man would be all right.

Lighting on a branch at the edge of the clearing, the bird scanned below. Two women sat on his master's bier next to a dying campfire. The older woman had one arm over the shoulders of the other, massaging her back.

The younger woman's body heaved with a large sigh. She raised one hand, moving her hair back from her face as she looked up. The bird could see a glint of tears on her cheek. "I did'n know it would hurt so much ta be alone. I miss them, already."

The older woman made cooing sounds and continued rubbing.

"It's so quiet inside. How will I ever stand it?"

The bird heard her words but didn't comprehend. He looked into the twisted shadows of the huge oak tree beside the clearing. That had been the sad, lonely man's place. The bird could taste his essence in the air, but it seemed like the smell of an eaten mouse on another bird's breath. A thing that had been but is no more.

The old man stretched. Grasping his staff in one hand, he raised his other arm. The bird recognized that as a signal to come. He leapt into the air and flew.

Dear Reader,

I hope you enjoyed *Merlin's Knot*. Merlin, Neve and Lolly are taking a short break before appearing in the sequel, *Merlin's Weft*.

It means a lot to me as an author to hear your honest opinion of this book. Please take a moment to post your comments on the site where you bought it. Don't forget to post on Goodreads.com also.

Thank you so much for reading *Merlin's Knot*!

Sincerely,
Mark Andersen

At the beginning of this book, Merlin appeared in Houston drained and unkempt. How did he get there, and why was he so weak? In *Merlin's Shuttle*, a short story prequel to *Merlin's Knot*, we find him standing against a hurricane in the Gulf of Mexico.

Get your free copy of this story by signing up at my website at www.MarkAndersenTales.com/signup/.

ACKNOWLEDGMENTS

Merlin's Knot has been a long time in the making. It began as a writing exercise in a critique group in 2001. The meeting discussion centered on strong openings, and after the group leader finished her comments, we each took a blank piece of paper to write a compelling opening.

An image came to me of Merlin approaching a seemingly random person in Houston. He announces an urgent need for help to find King Arthur. The first line of the very first draft of the story follows: *The wrinkled old man with a scraggly white beard stepped into my path, held up his right hand, and slurred, "I'm Merlin. I need your help."*

That sentence introduced a slew of questions. Why was Merlin in twenty-first century Houston? Why was Arthur here? And why did Merlin approach this particular man for help? I had no idea about the answers then, but I found the process of forming the questions and seeking the answers fascinating. I pondered many of those plot points while commuting daily ten miles home from my job in Sugar Land, Texas. I specifically remember making the decision to go into the heart of darkness and let Rage have her vengeance.

By the middle of 2004, I had written a novel then called *Another Time*. I continued to edit it sporadically throughout 2005, and at some point that year changed the title to *Merlin's Knot*. However, my day job—executive editor of a technology journal and later technology guru for a laboratory—took all my creative energy. The book sat on my hard drive, transferred every few years to each successive computer's hard drive, until I retired in 2015. I did another editing pass and quickly wrote the sequel, *Merlin's Weft*, which I had first outlined in 2007.

Between the time I drafted this novel and now, the publishing industry changed dramatically, and that change is spelled e-b-o-o-k. When I picked up my fiction writing again, I assumed I would seek an agent and a traditional publisher. Then I heard Pamela Fagan Hutchins at *Indiepalooza*, a conference sponsored by the Houston Writer's Guild devoted to independent publishing. I have since read and watched webcasts full of advice for indie publishers, and as you see before you, decided to follow that path.

As a writer and editor of science articles for eleven years, I learned to appreciate the skills of a good editor. Of course, I sought professional assistance to edit my book. I was fortunate to find Catherine Jones Payne and her colleagues at Quill Pen Editorial Services. Catherine not only brought expertise in editing modern fantasy, but also her own love for tales Arthurian. The story is tighter and moves better, but probably of greatest importance: her observations helped me to see how to make Alfred a better character. I also received valuable comments from my friends and beta readers, Joann Hazard and Denis Klemin.

A good book deserves a professional cover. I worked with Blue Harvest Creative to design both the cover and the print layout of the book. Not only did they develop a wonderful cover, but they were extremely helpful in guiding me in publishing this novel.

My greatest supporter is my wife, Holly Gilliland. Even before I retired, she started planning my writer's office. I have a view out the window of sun shining on trees, pictures on the wall to remind me of all the places we've traveled together, and a comfortable chair and desk with my Mac sitting on it. She even bought me a new mousepad with a wonderful writer's logo: *I Make Stuff Up*.

Mom is still active at 90, and I'll be most pleased when I hand her a copy of this to show to her friends in Amarillo.

The most important thing for any writer is the reader. I hope you enjoyed the book, because I enjoyed writing it, and because I want to keep making things up.

ABOUT THE AUTHOR

Mark Andersen began writing professionally in 1999. He has written both fiction and nonfiction.

His first novel, *Merlin's Knot*, was published in 2016. A sequel, *Merlin's Weft*, is expected out later in 2016. He is writing a historical drama set against the backdrop of the Three Musketeers. He also is working on a collection of short fairy tales.

He served as executive editor of the technology journal *Oilfield Review* (www.slb.com/oilfieldreview) for nine years and was a journal editor for two years before that. Each year he wrote several 8,000-word technical articles. He spent three to four months researching each topic and talking with experts, and then he wrote the article. In addition, each journal staff member edited the work of all others. As executive editor, Mark managed the business of the journal, overseeing all aspects of its editorial plan, production and distribution as well as the staff of editors.

He published *Petroleum Research in North Sea Chalk* in 1995 through Rogaland Research in Stavanger, Norway. The book is an acquired taste, best consumed after a few glasses of champagne from the chalk cellars of Rheims, France.

Mark earned a PhD in Physics at the Johns Hopkins University in Baltimore, Maryland. He started working in 1981 as a research scientist for Amoco Production Company in Tulsa, Oklahoma, and later worked in Stavanger, Norway, and Houston, Texas. He joined Schlumberger at the *Oilfield Review* in 2000 and in 2011 began the role of a core physics domain expert for the company. He retired in 2015.

Mark lives in Houston with his wife Holly. His son lives in Colorado.

MERLIN'S ADVENTURE CONTINUES
IN THE EXCITING SEQUEL,

MERLIN'S
WEFT

BOOK 2 OF MERLIN'S THREAD

A SHATTERED SOUL...A PAINFUL PAST...
A FIGHT FOR SURVIVAL

When evil threatens Lolly and her friends, she must fight to unify the fragments of her soul, forcing Merlin and Neve to tap into unforeseen powers to defeat their enemies while protecting their home...and their world.

COMING LATE 2016